Daahn Rising

Xxan War #1

Brenna Lyons

Fireborn Publishing Copyright Statement

Daahn Rising
Close Enough to Human © 2009/2013/2017
Mating Season © 2010/2013/2017
by Brenna Lyons
Print ISBN: 978-1-946004-78-9
Print Publication: March 2017

Cover Artist: Brenna Lyons
Photo Credit: 123rf
Editor: Kathryn Lively
Logo copyright © 2014 by Fireborn Publishing and
Allison Cassatta
Licensed material is being used for illustrative
purposes only. Any person depicted in the
licensed material is a model.

sales@firebornpublishing.com or via the author's
personal email.

This book is written in US English.

PUBLISHER

Glossary

Dominant- Xxanian males with Dominant personalities and larger bodies

elder- the head of a Xxanian nest—this is always a Dominant male, usually the oldest and wisest Dominant male in a nest, even if younger males are stronger ("The elders" can also refer to all the older members of a nest as a group.)

first- the first lover a Xxanian female experiences; this male is usually chosen by her *seir* when the quickening strikes or is decided by fate when a female unexpectedly hits her quickening in close proximity to Xxanian males (Xxanian Dominants will fight for the right to sate a quickening—to the death, if necessary—and the one left standing will be her first.)

gran-Hauaa- grandmother

gran-seir- grandfather

gran-vvaash- granddaughter)

gran-vvaashee- grandson

gran-vvaasheen- grandchildren

Grea Elders- ruling class of the Xxan, comprised exclusively of the strongest elders

grippers- lightweight shoes that allow engineering division military to grip to wet decks and oily machinery

Hauaa- mother (Unlike other family relationships, *Hauaa* is always capitalized, no matter whether the person is speaking about or directly addressing the *Hauaa*.)

High Xxan- one of the seven forms of Xxanian martial arts; considered the most advanced form, this form is usually only taught to Dominants and is only practiced regularly by *Grea* Elders

IAC- Inter Agency Command, a panel of the heads of all military and government offices concerned with alien affairs

Interstellar War Pact- an interstellar Geneva Convention, covering war and treatment of prisoners (For the record, the Xxan do not practice or recognize it.)

nest- home of a Xxanian family; typically an armored underground bunker populated with gardens and pools of water

pregnancy block- a drug to prevent pregnancy, given to both men and women

quickening- a Xxanian female's sexual maturation, as experienced in a mating frenzy with her first

ripen- the process of making a female fertile by way of mating (An unripened female is usually unable to conceive a child, which ensures no offspring for Xxanian females until they are bonded to their mates.)

Saahaal- a clove-like spice that grows on the Xxanian home world, a sacred part of their religion (They use clove instead on Earth.)

scaly/scalies- an offensive term for Xxanians

scaly-lovers- an offensive term for those sympathetic to Xxanians

seir- father

Seir-God- the Xxanian deity

sister-moon- *Xxania Hethhh*; the Xxanian home world is actually a moon in the Xxanian solar system, and *Xxania Hethhh* is the twin moon to the home world, sharing an orbit with the home world.)

s'saahhta- a sickle-shaped weapon carried by Xxanian warriors

s'sanuea- preparation room; akin to a locker room (Inhabitants of and guests of the nest change clothing in the *s'sanuea* before entering the nest proper.)

S'suuhhea- female Xxanian clothing

S'suumea- male Xxanian clothing- comes in formal and informal styles

STD block- a drug to prevent STD transmission from person to person; can be administered to both males and females

Subdominants- Xxan males with beta personalities and smaller bodies; Xxanians identify Dominants and Subdominants by scent

swamp skin- an offensive term for the Xxan

tongue-scent- using the tongue to collect more scent information than the nose gives; the Xxan have slightly-roughened tongues with a way array of scent receptors

Xxan- the collective Xxanian people; also, their language is called Xxan

Xxan-Dree- one of the seven Xxanian martial arts

Xxania Hethhh- the Xxanian sister-moon; a twin moon to the Xxanian home world

Xxania Uuaahth- the Xxanian home world

Xxanian- adj referring to the Xxan

Zhigaaah- female sex hormone

Zhigaaal- male sex hormone

zuahhhbeahhh- a spiked weapon used by Xxanian Dominants

z'haahn- the spiced meat the Xxan and crossbred Xxan eat daily

Section 1:

Zondra

Mating Season

Dedication

*To Tamer and the Putzboy Crew of Sunshine Court
and Topaz Lane.*

Chapter One

Zondra Daahn sashayed toward the base club, dressed for man-hunting. The quickening was her only reason for being here; it was rising in her, driving her mad. She needed a cock to ease the passage.

She winced. *What a lousy pun that was.*

I don't have to do this. That thought stopped Zondra dead in her tracks halfway to the door. She hesitated, considering it.

Raashh's nest wasn't far from the base. Zhaahvan's wasn't much farther. Though she didn't dare show up at the door to one of the nests in her state unannounced, one call to Aleeks and preparations could be made to have an unmated young Dominant prepared to serve her needs.

And all the others dismissed. If she showed up in a nest with more than one unmated Dominant in residence, every unmated male would fight for her, possibly even the Subdominants. They'd likely kill for her.

That truth sent a shudder of revulsion down her body. Terror made her take a step back. *What if there are Dominants inside the club?* If there were, she could start a massacre.

Common sense intruded. The Xxan were unlikely to go to human clubs. The smells and sounds were intolerable. The human food was inedible, and some drunken humans enjoyed picking fights they couldn't possibly win. After nearly half a century on Earth and working as allies, many humans still saw all Xxan as alike—invaders, foes.

I don't want a Dominant for my first. She would likely mate with a Xxan-human crossbreed like herself. She was unlikely to take long-term human lovers, no matter how appealing she found them. Prejudices ran hot in too many humans for that. *This is probably the only chance I'll have to fuck a human.* Zondra didn't intend to waste it.

If there was any place she was likely to find an alpha type, the human equivalent of a Xxanian Dominant, this would be it. Human military men were often alphas, and they certainly weren't adverse to the idea of screwing something appealing with few questions asked. Her *Zhigaaah* would make her very appealing, perhaps appealing enough for a single human man to last as long as she'd need a male tonight. If she found a human alpha that appealed to her, she was going to indulge her many fantasies about humans while she sated the quickening.

Her stomach cramped and complained, and her body heated another degree. *If I don't find a suitable alpha quickly, I will have to call Aleeks and have him prepare a nest for my arrival.*

With that a given, she sauntered into the club.

She hadn't even crossed the distance to the bar when the first male approached her. "Interested, doll?"

Zondra stopped and turned her head to size up the male who'd addressed her. She inhaled deeply through her mouth, evaluating his scent. Her determination was sealed that quickly. *Subdominant. Wannabe. Unsuitable.* "For the right man," she returned coolly, making it clear he wasn't that man.

Unfazed, the Subdominant moved toward her. "Oh, I *am* the right man," he drawled.

"Impossible. Now if you'll excuse me—"

Her attempt to round him was cut short when the Subdominant grasped her arm and dragged Zondra to his chest, burying his face in her hair.

"Little tease," he accused.

Zondra jerked away from his body, then pulled her fist back to strike, but another man's hand encircled her wrist.

"Now don't do that," the new arrival chided her gently. "That would be destruction of government property."

She turned her head, meeting the newcomer's ice blue eyes. Zondra licked her upper lip, tongue-scenting him. *Dominant.* She moved closer to him, making her choice clear.

The Dominant smiled widely. "Let me." He punched the Subdominant hard, sending the lesser man sprawling.

Both hands released her. Before Zondra could press herself to the Dominant, he stepped between her and the sap levering himself off the floor. The Dominant was protective of her; he was turning out to be just what she needed so far.

The Subdominant staggered to his feet, glaring at them both. Before Zondra or her protector could react, shore patrol ambled over, two rather unhappy-looking sorts.

The one with the chief's rating patch looked from one combatant to the other, then shook his head in seeming exasperation. "I might have known. Duncan and Reynolds. Do I have to have *another* discussion with your captain?"

The Dominant made an irreverent show of his hands being tied, and Zondra swallowed a laugh.

The chief bit back a smile of his own. "This just might be why you've gone to chief's board four times and been turned down, Duncan."

"Yeah. Life sucks." But his tone didn't make it sound like it did. The Dominant's amusement was impossible to miss.

The Subdominant—Reynolds—wiped a stream of blood off his chin. "There's nothing amusing about the charges I intend to file. Assault mean anything to you?"

Duncan laughed harshly. "Sexual assault, simple assault, and sexual harassment mean anything to you? You never manhandle a lady that way. As I heard it, she said you weren't her type. Was rather blunt about it, too. Even a blockhead like you couldn't have misunderstood it."

"Little cock-tease," Reynolds grumbled.

Duncan tensed, and the chief stepped between them. Zondra didn't doubt he did so at the risk of his own skin.

"That true?" the chief asked Zondra.

"Which part?" she quipped. "The part about Reynolds grabbing me and insisting my search was over? Yes. The rest? I'm no one's cock-tease. I've been in this bar for all of five minutes. I've had no time to tease him up."

"Want to press charges?"

She considered that. As much as she'd like to see Reynolds pay for presuming to touch her, pressing charges would have three very negative results.

She'd have to show her military ID, which would land her in the cell next to Reynolds. Although she hadn't ordered a drink and had no intentions of doing so, she was still a minor by human laws, her Xxanian genetics disregarded.

And shore patrol will disregard them.

Once the officers knew her age, they would contact her *seir*, which would lead to the final unfortunate result to this fiasco: her *seir*, *granseir*, and brother would lock her up until she was an elder.

Even if she managed to escape all those outcomes, she'd spend the next two hours giving a report while the quickening drove her mad.

"Miss?"

Zondra feigned indifference. "If he leaves and forgets the charges he was planning to file against Duncan, I'll drop mine." She smiled sweetly. "And that saves you a lot of paperwork, Chief."

All four men gaped at her, Duncan giving his adversary his back to accomplish the move.

"Your call, Reynolds," the chief intoned. "Night in the cell and being called to the carpet, or walking away now with nothing but a loose tooth or two as punishment."

The Subdominant scowled at her, then stalked away. Zondra watched Reynolds leave. If there was one thing a Xxanian child learned, it was to never give an enemy your back.

"Guess that's that," the chief decided. "Have a nice night, miss. Duncan..." He sighed. "Stay out of trouble."

Duncan didn't answer that, smart-assed or otherwise. She could see him glaring at her in her peripheral vision, his arms crossed over his broad chest.

When the shore patrol was gone, he unclenched his jaw long enough to speak. "You shouldn't have done that."

"You'd rather—"

"I'd rather see Reynolds in the brig than see him get off scot-free to do this to someone else."

"Even if you were in the cell next to him?"

"I wouldn't be there for as long as he would."

Even a marginal win was a win to a Dominant with a cause. Zondra turned to him. "Maybe I had other plans."

"For instance?" he challenged.

She chanced stroking a hand along the line of his shoulder, well aware that he might rebuff her. "Reynolds isn't my type, but you are. There are much better things we could be doing than spending a few hours at the shore patrol office, answering questions and staring at iron bars."

A glimmer of interest lit his eyes. "And what *might* we be doing?"

Zondra leaned toward him, whispering her answer. "Climbing into your lap and fucking your brains out isn't out of the question."

He lowered his arms and encircled her body with them. His face dipped to her throat, and she smiled. Right now he was getting a lungful of *Zhigaaah*. If the *Zhigaaal* worked on humans, it stood to reason that the *Zhigaaah* did as well.

"I like to be in charge," he warned her. "You climb nowhere unless I want you there."

"I'm counting on it." She was. A woman in the throes of quickening needed a man to fuck her, not one that pussyfooted around the subject.

He turned Zondra and walked her two steps farther into the room, pressing her back to the bar, one large hand cupping her ass under that cover. "I'm hungry tonight."

"So am I." *Ravenous.*

He nipped at her throat, and Zondra hissed in pleasure. He was taking the *Zhigaaah* in. Once it hit his bloodstream, he was hers for the duration.

"Now," he breathed. "Come with me."

Duncan turned so abruptly, it made Zondra's head spin. He took her hand, leading her toward the exit, his shoulders and arms tensed for a fight and his eyes scanning for any threat.

She smiled at that, his movements clear to her, even if they weren't to him. Duncan was challenging the other males to try for her. He was prepared to fight someone for her, as Xxanian Dominants often fought for a quickening female. If Reynolds—or any other male—approached her now, Duncan's response would be swift and painful.

He has *fought someone for me...and won the right to sate my quickening.* That fact sent a shudder of pleasure down her spine.

The quickening advanced, sending flaming shards through her abdomen. Zondra forced slow, deep breaths. She just had to make it a little longer, and Duncan would ease the fire in her blood.

He led her to a truck situated in the far reaches of the darkened lot, coded the door open, and helped Zondra up. Then he slid behind the wheel and closed them in.

Her glasses transitioned to clear plastic, and a shaft of fear settled in her gut. With them clear, he could see her eyes and call a halt, making her start from scratch again.

Or call Aleeks.

It's too dark for him to see. And the dark glasses hadn't caught his attention so far.

Her gut searing, the need for sex reached a fever pitch that stole her ability to reason or stall. Wherever he planned to take her, it was too far. Zondra nestled to his side, stroking her hand up and down his cock through his jeans.

Duncan paused, the key halfway into the ignition. "We're in a parking lot," he reminded her.

"I don't care. Do you?" Some back corner of her mind insisted she would care when this was all over and the quickening wasn't driving her. The rush of pheromones crushed that line of thinking along with all the others.

"What's your name, darlin'?" he drawled.

"Zondra." Her voice sounded strange in her own ears.

"Zondra..." He drew in a ragged breath, dipping his face toward her throat, his eyes slipping halfway shut and his cock going rock hard beneath her fingers. "If you don't take your hands away, the first time is going to be a rough fuck." His eyes narrowed and his jaw tightened, indicating a challenge he wanted her to take him up on.

Her heart raced. "Mmmm. Sounds good," she taunted him. Surely a taunt would push him to something extreme. *He's already talking about more than once.*

Duncan dragged her into his lap, capturing her mouth in a kiss that proved "toe-curling" wasn't a euphemism.

I need more. With that thought in mind, Zondra played her fingers inside the waistband of his jeans.

* * * *

Evan's head spun, and his heart did a mating dance between his scorching lungs. If he didn't know better, he'd suspect she'd drugged him, but they hadn't even had a drink together.

Realization that they weren't going to make it to the house he and three other E-Divvers shared off base floored him. It was the truck or the lodge twenty meters away. His cock opined that the truck was acceptable. His mind countered that Chief Marris arresting them would mean an unwelcome interruption to what he intended, and Evan intended a lot more than a kiss with her hot little fingers down his jeans.

Growling, he pulled away and shoved the door open before she could unbutton his jeans and end the debate of where he was going to make her pay for teasing him.

His keys slipped from the ignition and jingled their way to a heap on the floorboards. He ignored them, lifting Zondra out of the truck and slamming the door. The keys would be safe in the truck until he coded in to get them later.

Her legs encircled him, and she got the first two buttons on his jeans open. Evan ignored his body's demand that he press Zondra to the door and ravage her mouth. If he did that, he'd be inside her, screwing her outside the truck instead of inside it. Overall, that wouldn't be an improvement.

Instead he carried her from the bar parking lot, through the lodge lot, and to the automated desk kiosk, their mouths meshing and parting. Evan buried his face in her throat, groaning. Whatever her perfume was, he could spend the rest of his life drunk on it. It was something musk-heavy and smelling of clove, and her long, dark hair was like silk against his cheek.

Fumbling out his military ID, Evan slipped it into the kiosk and gasped out a request for a king. The computer voice informed him they had room twelve, and he pushed off the wall and headed for the stairs, his mind evaluating every surface for a possible place to deliver the first thrust of his now uncovered cock.

Fortunately, enough of his mind was still functioning to nix that idea. As appealing as the stairs were—or the banister or the carpeted floor— he intended to avoid arrest on a public decency charge and a premature end to the night.

His ID opened the lodge door, and Evan pitched the bit of plastic ahead of him. He kicked the door shut as Zondra pushed his jeans away and the lights came up automatically. They came aground on a bureau that was a comfortable height, and Evan thrust inside her body. He fisted his left hand in her hair and positioned her hip with the other. She screamed in delight, her head falling back, giving him access to that clove-and-musk perfume.

As promised, it was a rough fuck. Evan pistoned his hips, his body slapping hard against hers. He nipped and suckled at her throat, moaning at the spice in his mouth. His tongue tingled as if she had actually used clove as a perfume.

Her body climaxed around his, and her scream echoed off the walls. Evan went into overdrive, pounding hard, his cum jetting into her in a long, steady stream.

Her scent surrounded him, enticing him. Evan didn't question it. He went to work on his shirt, and Zondra stared up at him, licking her lips.

She was still dressed, and that was unacceptable. His mind processed that she was naked beneath the skirt, but it wasn't enough. He wanted to see her delectable body; Evan *had* to see it.

He dragged his shirt off and dropped it to the floor, easing out of her body. "Get undressed," he ordered.

His move to dispose of his jeans ended on the sobering sight of her blood on his cock. A glance at her slit confirmed it. *Virginal. By the stars!* They hadn't discussed anything. They hadn't even discussed...

"I'm on STD block," he blurted out. But not pregnancy block. He didn't like what the drug did to him, the lessening of his aggressive work ethic.

"Good." She didn't pause in her disrobing. Zondra slipped the cropped sweater over her head and tossed it away.

Evan's mouth went dry at the sight of her erect nipples, and he had to force his unresponsive brain to string thoughts together. Her breasts were larger than his hands—but not by much—soft, responsive, and tight to her body. "But you're not—"

"I can't, Duncan." Her short skirt disappeared, leaving her clad only in the come-fuck-me heels and dark sunglasses.

"Can't—"

Zondra wrapped herself around Evan, nipping at his chest, scattering the last of his thinking mind. "Can't have a child. It's...medical." She stroked up and down, surrounding him in her scent.

Ordinarily he would have suspected she was a fuck machine looking for the benefits carrying a military man's child would get her. Something told him that wasn't the case. She was telling the truth. Zondra really couldn't carry a child.

He wondered when she'd learned she was sterile. The certainty that it had been a recent discovery and this was her rebellion shot a rare shaft of guilt through him.

Why do I care? He suspected his overactive protective instincts were kicking in again, but they'd never kicked in for something like *this* before. Usually they pushed him to protect a woman from physical harm, as he had with Reynolds in the bar.

I've never been in this situation before. How can I know how I—

The pain in his shoulder roused him from dark thoughts and fired his anger. She'd bitten him. What the hell was she—

He stared at the wraparound dark glasses, the clues clicking into place. She didn't fight him when he removed them, though she squeezed her eyes shut to the light.

"Twenty percent light," she ordered the room.

The lights dimmed, and she opened her eyes. It was hard to tell the color, but the vertical slits were impossible to miss.

She's a Xxanian crossbreed. Facts and stories about the Xxan filtered through his mind. They were a sexual bunch, screwing like rabbits, and their females only submitted to Dominant men.

That explains why Reynolds wasn't her type. He was a bad-ass wannabe at best.

Evan had never considered sleeping with a Xxanian female before. Then again, the opportunity had never arisen before. It was new, enticing, and a challenge.

Damn, this is going to be good. If she wants a Dominant, I can show her what a Dominant is.

* * * *

There was an air of violence about Duncan that put her teeth on edge. Zondra prepared to fight him off.

Then what will I do? With the quickening worsening, if he refused her, it could be catastrophic. The twisting in her gut seconded that. Fire flicked at her belly, and sweat coated her skin.

His cock was still hard, which was a good sign, but he could be erect because of her *Zhigaaah* and nothing else. If he wasn't willing, his arousal might make him angry and more aggressive.

He pitched her glasses across the room. His mouth slanted over hers in a fierce kiss, and Zondra opened for him. He explored, tracing her hunting teeth with a groan.

Duncan pulled away, dragged her off the bureau, and turned her to face it. His cock was inside her before her head stopped spinning from the abrupt move. "You are mine. Every"—he thrust deep and held there, grinding against her—"centimeter of your luscious body. Isn't it?"

"Yes. Every millimeter."

He covered her hands with his, threaded his fingers with hers, and pinned her hands to the bureau. His hips lifted slightly, taking her to her toes to accommodate him. "Anything I want. Anywhere I want. As many *times* as I want."

Seir-God, it is a dream come true.

"Zondra," he warned.

"Yes. All night. Please, Duncan."

"Evan. And you will be screaming that. Won't you?"

So self-assured. "Yes, Evan."

As if rewarding the answer, he started riding her hard. Their sounds rose and crested, and the wave of his cum inside her punctuated it.

He traced his lips over the newly blue mating stripe across her shoulder blades, picking up more of her *Zhigaaah.* "You didn't scream my name," he teased, "but you will."

Zondra nodded. Oh yes. There was little question that she would before the night was over. She smiled. Perhaps refusing him that as long as she could would be just the challenge he needed.

Chapter Two

Evan performed his early morning stretch, wincing at the slice of pain in his left shoulder. He searched out the facts in his muddled mind, smiling at the memories of Zondra.

That quickly, his cock was hard and aching again. Evan turned to her, tracing a hand along the line from her waist to her knee.

Zondra's eyes opened, then squeezed shut against the light. She turned toward him, burrowing her face into Evan's chest. His emotions rioted—tender, protective instincts mingled with fierce pride that she'd turned to him.

Evan didn't understand himself. Usually, protecting a woman was a duty to him. If someone had protected his mother, the scumbag who had beaten her to death wouldn't have gotten in more than the first punch, and Evan wouldn't have been orphaned at fifteen and tossed into the foster system.

When he'd protected Zondra at the club, it had been half duty and half the enjoyment of putting Reynolds in his place. But this... Evan had no name for what he wanted from Zondra or what he felt when he was protecting her.

He reached across her body, making a blind sweep for her glasses. The heavy light-reactive plastic in hand, Evan eased Zondra away from him and settled them on her nose.

Her eyes opened slowly, revealing the heart-stopping green and gold that mesmerized him. She stared at him, hesitating, seemingly unsure, as the lenses darkened for her comfort.

Evan dipped his head, sealing his mouth to hers. The kiss wasn't as forceful as the ones they'd shared the night before. It was slow, deep, dizzying.

"You know what I want to do?" he whispered against her lips.

She shook her head.

"Take you to the shower and bathe you from head to toe again."

Zondra's breathing hitched. "And then?"

"I'm going to bury my tongue between your legs. You bury yours between mine... Aside from eating—food, I mean—I suggest we spend my entire day off right here." The insane need to play with Zondra as long as she'd allow was impossible to shake.

The scent rising from her said she wasn't ready to kick him to the curb and go find one of her own kind yet.

Evan captured her mouth with a grumbled curse. The shower could wait. Food could wait. Everything but the woman in his arms could wait.

Sounds played at the edges of his consciousness, a door opening somewhere in the distance. Evan dismissed it and pulled Zondra flush to his body. He trailed his fingers over that luscious blue stripe on her back that drove her crazy for his cock, intent on spending his entire day off inside her.

The hands dragging her away came without warning. Evan launched up, swinging, growling out promises of killing whoever had dared touch her. Two bodies hit him at once, driving Evan to the mattress.

Voices rose from somewhere across the room, Zondra and another man. Evan tried to fight his way up, to throw off the two men holding him down, but their grip was nearly unbreakable. All the time, the third man was arguing with Zondra, driving Evan to the edges of madness.

Evan wrenched one arm free and laid a punch that unseated the attacker on his right. The answering punch came from the left, and prisms of startling color exploded before his eyes. The one he'd ousted landed hard, winding Evan in the process.

"Aleeks, no," Zondra ordered.

"You might want to get her out of here," the one on the right suggested.

"I'm not going down quietly," Evan warned.

"As if you ever do," the one on the left growled.

Evan's fist shot out, but the smart-ass was faster than he'd counted on, and he missed. The one on the right got a bone-crushing hold on Evan's wrist, and he faltered, which allowed the one on the left to do the same. That simply, Evan was pinned.

Across the room, the third was pulling a now dressed but deliciously mussed Zondra toward the door.

"You have no right to do this," Evan shouted. "Zondra—"

"Is my little sister," the one on the left snapped. "And she's leaving with our *seir*, whether you like it or not."

Something in his tone gave Evan pause. "How little?" he asked weakly. Zondra looked and acted adult, and he'd picked her up in a bar. He hadn't asked her age. He'd just assumed she was over twenty-one.

I didn't ask anything until after the first time. Not even if she was protected from pregnancy and disease.

How badly have I screwed up? He remembered something about the Xxan aging faster than humans did. How young were they when they appeared adult?

"You're not going down for statutory," the one on the right assured him.

Evan breathed a sigh of relief that was sadly short-lived.

"Sixteen," the brother answered.

Evan grimaced. The slamming door echoed his mental vision of career and life.

"Better," the one on the right breathed. "Now I highly suggest you get a shower to clear your head, Duncan. After that we're going to have a long talk about my goddaughter, who is nearly *seventeen*, by the way."

He nodded, and both men eased off the bed, clearing the way to the bathroom. On his way to his feet, Evan got his first unencumbered look at them.

The taller was a Xxanian mix like Zondra, based on his dark glasses and his claim of being her brother. He appeared to be about Evan's age, with dark hair and a jaw that was locked tight in anger.

Who could blame him?

19

Evan moved his gaze to the other. He was older by at least thirty-five or forty years, based on his graying blond hair. His very human and piercing blue eyes, as well as his calm demeanor, attested that he would either be the safer of the two or a formidable enemy.

Evan paused, staring at him, a fractured memory niggling at the far recesses of his mind. He knew this man from somewhere, in some context that he couldn't place a finger on.

As if he'd spoken the thought aloud, the old man offered his hand. "Matthew MacNair."

"*Admiral* MacNair?" Evan qualified.

A slight nod of his head was his only reply.

Realization left Evan cold. He'd not only slept with the fleet admiral's sixteen-year-old goddaughter, Evan had given the officer in question one hell of a shiner. Ignoring the offered hand, he turned for the shower.

"I am completely screwed," Evan muttered to himself.

"That goes without saying," the younger man quipped.

Evan turned to glare at him, then disappeared into the shower.

* * * *

"Do you have any concept of what you've done?" her *seir* asked. He made the turn out of the base gate and toward home.

"You won't be pressing charges against him," Zondra ordered. "I won't forgive it."

20

"Of course not." He had the good sense to sound offended at the suggestion that he might do it.

"And I won't stand for anyone battering him again, either."

"They were defending themselves!"

"Evan was defending *me*." Just the thought of that heated her blood, as it had when he'd defended her from Reynolds the night before.

Of course, nearly anything would arouse her right now. There was a reason the Xxanian *seir* removed the female from her first lover in the aftermath of the quickening. She wasn't thinking clearly right now, and neither was Evan.

There was a moment of silence. "Do you think you'll choose to bind to him?"

Zondra's body exploded in pleasure at the thought of it.

She'd heard females wanted to choose a mate after the quickening. The idea of actively seeking out an overbearing Dominant had always mystified her. But now that Zondra had enjoyed the quickening with Evan—*enjoyed is the understatement of the millennium!*—all she wanted was to mate with him.

Females rarely chose their first as mate. Then again, the male to sate the quickening was often a matter of chance or the choice of a female's *seir*. Maybe Zondra only wanted Evan because she'd chosen him personally.

Maybe she wanted him because she'd always been drawn to human men.

Or maybe it was the aftermath of the quickening speaking out of turn. The female was always separated from her first after the quickening and confined to her nest for three nights. Until his *Zhigaaal* was filtered out of her system, and her *Zhigaaah* cleared his, the decision to mate could be attributed to the pheromones swaying the choice.

Evan has no Zhigaaal. And still she wanted him this morning. A smile pulled at her lips.

She sobered, noting her *seir* scenting the air. *Scenting the change in me.* Whether or not she ultimately chose Evan was none of his business.

"Does one typically ask that question the morning after the quickening has been sated?" she asked pointedly. Zondra hurried on, not giving him a chance to answer. "He doesn't have *Zhigaaal.* How could we—"

"You knew we intended to get you a crossbred Dominant for your first. You should have told us you were—"

"It came on suddenly," she snapped. "And I don't regret that Evan was my first."

"He may," her *seir* muttered.

Her temper flared. "What? How dare you say such a—"

"He's human, and your *Zhigaaah* may well have begun the binding. Your pheromone is most potent at the quickening and mating. Why do you *think* we'd intended to call in one of our own males to sate you?"

Her heart stuttered. "It's only been one night, not three days. The pheromone will work its way out of his system."

Her *seir* shot her a hard look.

"Won't it?" It came out a squeak she wished she could take back.

"We don't know. When we learned a single infusion of *Zhigaaal* could bind a human woman—thanks to my own oversight—we made certain to call in crossbred Xxan for the quickening."

Zondra worried at her lower lip. She hadn't known that. Why hadn't they told her? What if his hold on her waned, and he was bound and driven crazy? What would she do?

Her *seir* sighed. "If he is irrevocably changed, I pray you feel the same for him in three days as you feel now."

I will. What caused the certainty was a mystery to her, but it brought a smile to her face.

Her *seir* growled.

But I will be confined to the nest for at least three days. Her renewed smile faded that quickly.

* * * *

Evan strode from the bathroom and went still at the sight of Admiral MacNair and Zondra's brother. "I get it. You're warning me off, and I'll stay away."

If he didn't promise that much, he'd find himself in the brig. Now that he knew Zondra was sixteen, she was hands-off. He didn't have the excuse of ignorance anymore.

The brother snorted, curling his lip in seeming disgust. Bracketing his eyeteeth, his serrated hunting teeth were clearly visible. Evan didn't doubt it was a warning.

"Enough, Aleeks," MacNair ordered.

"Yes, sir." But it was delivered in barely leashed fury. Aleeks looked much like one of the feral race he was descended from.

The admiral panned his gaze up Evan's body, passing by bare legs and towel-wrapped midriff. His eyes stopped at shoulder height, and Evan's muscles tightened in preparation for a fight. There was no question what MacNair had taken exception to.

Yeah, old man. Not only did I fuck her, we played hard. Have a problem with that? Before he could open his mouth and flush his career, the old man started talking.

"How deep are they? Superficial, I hope."

Evan shrugged. "They'll heal. I've taken worse shaft riding."

Of course, he'd only worked on an unsecured driveshaft once, and it had been an emergency. Though the band holding the hundred-and-fifty-feet-long, twenty-feet-in-circumference shaft motionless had slipped minutely, and the shaft had managed less than a quarter turn, Evan had been bucked off the top and dragged between the shaft and the tunnel wall. He'd come away with fifteen stitches in his leg, and it remained the single most terrifying moment of his life.

It was better than what *could* have happened, and Evan knew it, but he wasn't about to admit that to MacNair. Let the admiral think he was reckless, if that's what the old man wanted to think. The captain of Evan's first ship hadn't dared record the second incident, when Evan had refused the unlawful order to shaft ride again, so the only thing MacNair would find if he looked was the notation of the time Evan had been injured in the attempt.

If the illegal and highly dangerous activity shocked MacNair, he didn't show signs of it.

"She didn't have a choice, you know," Aleeks stated.

"Enough, Aleeks. One more time and you can wait in the car."

A slice of pain hit solidly in the center of Evan's chest, somewhere in the vicinity of his heart. Evan attempted to hide it. "So this was...what? Some kind of alien mating season? She'd have taken any stiff cock?"

"Climbing into your lap and fucking you senseless isn't out of the question," Zondra's voice purred in his memories.

And why would he care if it was? There hadn't been any promises between them. It was supposed to be the one night, and it had been one *hell* of a night. He pushed away the errant thought that it had been the single best night of his life.

"Yes and no." MacNair interrupted the sex tape running again in Evan's mind. "Yes, it was the quickening, Zondra's sexual maturity. No, she wouldn't have taken any cock offered. You know as well as I do that she turned away at least one man before you. Zondra needed someone strong enough to dominate her. You were."

He nodded, trying to force his cock to subside. Just the reminder of how he'd pinned her hands down and—

Stop thinking about it, or you'll never go down, asshole.

As if reading his thoughts, MacNair answered. "Ah, yeah. And there's that."

"I'll stay away," Evan repeated, abruptly aware that he was growling much as Aleeks was.

"You're not going to want to."

No shit! Was it my boner that tipped you off? Evan kept his mouth shut tight, well aware that it wasn't too late for MacNair to destroy him. Why the admiral hadn't so far was a mystery to him.

"Her *Zhigaaah*—Zondra's sex pheromone—is going to keep you somewhat...aroused for several days. Maybe two. Maybe three."

"Bonus plan all the way around," Evan muttered.

"Fuck off, Duncan," Aleeks shot at him.

Evan returned fire. "I guess I'll be doing a lot of *that* in the next few days, huh?"

Even if he wanted to pick up a few one-night stands—the idea made him ill—the last thing Evan needed was to pick up another teenager and complicate this further.

MacNair stepped between them, glaring at Aleeks. The younger man nodded his grudging agreement.

The admiral turned back to Evan. "I can arrange for time off, Duncan." He let the offer hang between them.

"Don't do me any favors." Maybe work would keep him sane. At least it would give him something else to think about.

"If you change your mind—"

Evan locked eyes with him, warning MacNair off. "Any other cheery news?" he asked.

"Maybe."

"Might as well kick me while I'm down." Something told him Aleeks would, given the chance.

Aleeks didn't comment.

MacNair smiled a tight little smile. "If the attraction lasts past three days... If she feels the same way, Zondra is legally an adult and allowed to make her own choices."

"Meaning?" Evan tried not to focus on the comment about Zondra being legally an adult. That was a road his mind didn't need to travel in his present state. If it did, his body would be breaking promises made twice in the last half hour.

"Once both of you have your heads on straight again, no one will stop you from" —he raised an eyebrow—"from doing whatever you want to do."

That succeeded in bringing Evan fully erect. His mind turned the offer over. "Can we—" He shifted his attention to Aleeks and back to MacNair. He'd heard that it took a Xxanian male to make a female fertile, that they were sterile without that step.

"I can't, Duncan. Can't have a child. It's... medical."

"Is she able to...reproduce...with me?"

MacNair's smile faded. "I don't know. The doctors believe—"

"Then she won't want me. A woman like Zondra...she'll want children." He didn't question it. "She deserves them." If that meant she'd have them with someone else, he'd live with it. The wish for more was her damned pheromone talking.

"Duncan," MacNair began.

"Get lost...sir. You won't be seeing me again."
The rest seemed to stick in his throat, and he
looked away from Aleeks's surprise. "I guarantee
it."

Evan stomped to the bureau and scooped up
his clothes, his head reeling at the pungent scent
of Zondra and sex. He pulled on his shirt, trying to
hide his response from the two men exiting the
room.

"You won't see me again," Evan whispered, a
stern reminder to himself that it had to go that
way. Her family wanted him gone anyway. It was
better that he stay gone.

Chapter Three

Zondra lay curled on her bed, wishing she could shed tears as her friends did. Anna told her a good cry solved everything, and Sandy said it was better than chocolate, but Zondra couldn't cry. Her parents had told her it was a blessing that she couldn't cry, that the pain of tears on her sensitive Xxanian skin wasn't worth the emotional release shedding them provided.

"And even if I *could* cry, it wouldn't solve anything."

"Sure it would," Aleeks stated. "I'd go beat some sense into him."

She laughed, though her heart was breaking. "What's the point? He doesn't want me." Her throat bobbed in overwhelming emotion. "And what are you doing in my room?" She stopped short of saying she'd tell *Gran-seir* on him. That would make her sound like a pouting child.

"I'm worried about you, little sister." There was a moment of comfortable silence. "And I wouldn't bet on it."

"Bet on..." Was he insane? "It's been a week, Aleeks. In case you haven't noticed, Evan hasn't come back." Zondra buried her face in the plush Angora pillow, wishing she could soak it with tears—pain or no pain.

"And he's not *going* to come back," he added.

She shook in silent dry sobs at that pronouncement. It was time to move on, and Zondra knew it, but she didn't have the heart for it.

"He doesn't think he can be what you need in a mate."

"He's a Dominant," she protested. Evan was much more the Dominant than she'd thought a human alpha could be.

"He doesn't think you can have children together."

Her heart stuttered, and she turned to look at him. She picked out Aleeks easily, even in the darkened room. "How do you know that?"

"Because he said it that morning. He said that you deserved children. He wants you to have them, without him, if that's the only way."

Aleeks raised one knee, planting his foot on the dresser before him. He must not have been home long; he was still dressed in trousers and not the *S'suumea*. Like all males in Daahn's nest, Aleeks was barefoot and bare-chested. *Gran-seir* tolerated trousers on the others for short periods of time, as Zondra could wear human clothes in and to her room but had to don the *S'suuhhea* before she ventured into the center nest and lounging areas.

Her brother continued, a smile pulling up at the corners of his lips. "How...protective of you he is."

"But I don't believe that," she managed shakily.

"You think Dominants always fight? You think he can't make a harder choice for you than that? If he reasons it's the right choice?" He was lecturing her, chiding her as if she was a child.

And he had the wrong idea about what she'd meant. "No. I meant that I don't believe he can't ripen me. I think— Oh, Aleeks! I still ache for him. I still carry a bit of his scent. I'm telling you, he's strong enough. If we'd had three days instead of the night, I know he would have bound me."

His smile widened. "Even if you're wrong about him being able to ripen you, you can be ripened."

"By another male?" she shot back. Her stomach twisted uncomfortably at the thought of it. "No. I want Evan. I won't take another male just to secure children."

Aleeks laughed heartily. "He'd kill me if I suggested it. And I won't." One brow went up. "I've been talking to MacNair's buddies...Steven Rayn and the other scientists up at SLAL. They've done a lot of research in the last three generations, examining Xxanian and crossbred physiology."

Her breathing hitched. "And?"

"*Zhigaaal* is no more than highly-concentrated musk, heavy in sex pheromone."

Zondra nodded, her hands fisted in the blanket, praying her brother was going where she thought he was.

"They can concentrate Evan's own musk if he's willing—"

"I have to see him."

"I have a plan for that...if you want to hear it."

"Anything." She meant it. If Evan was willing, there was no question that she wanted him to take her as his mate. *And a Xxannian female will go to any lengths to secure the mate that calls to her.*

* * * *

She was over him, surrounding him in her heat. Evan bit back a moan, arching his back. He could smell her...taste her. He ached to finish, ached to thrust into her as he had the first time.

The knocking shattered the illusion; Evan snapped awake, coated in sweat, gasping for breath, rock hard. To his knowledge, he hadn't been fully flaccid in over a week. That was all it took to set his temper on a rolling boil.

"Yeah?" he demanded, tensing to give someone a verbal trouncing.

They'd been told not to wake Evan for less than an emergency. With the way he'd been working himself to death—sleeping only when he literally staggered into berthing and collapsed into his rack—an emergency was unlikely.

"Captain wants to see you, Duncan." Reynolds's voice was gleeful.

"What time is it?" he grumbled. He'd wager he'd only slept an hour or two, which would make it nearly dinnertime.

"Eighteen hundred."

Evan pulled the curtain back, dropping to the deck plates from his top rack, dressed in a pair of dungaree pants. "What's *he* still doing here?" he wondered aloud, coding himself into his coffin locker.

"Looking for you, I'd say." Reynolds leaned against the upright between the columns of racks. "So... Duncan, what did you do this time?"

Evan didn't look at him. If he looked at Reynolds, memories of the asshole touching

Zondra would lose Reynolds some teeth. "Message delivered. Get lost." *Permanently.*

I should be so lucky.

Reynolds strolled away, no doubt smirking at the idea that Evan was in trouble.

And he probably was. When Captain Pira wanted a status report, he asked for it when Evan was awake. Moreover, there were no major repairs going on that would require updates. Excellent repair record or not, it was unlikely Pira was rolling Evan out to recognize his efforts.

That in mind, he dragged on a clean T-shirt, dungaree shirt, and his grippers, steel-toed climbing shoes that would hold to wet decks and oily equipment. Evan didn't procrastinate; he'd always been the type to take problems head on and not hide from them.

Yeah, right. And that's why I won't admit I still need Zondra. That's why I'm hiding from her.

He hadn't even gone home since the third morning, because she could come to him there, and he wouldn't turn her away. Aboard ship, there was no chance of that.

But it was more than that. Confining himself to the ship had been a necessity. Three days in a row, he'd found himself heading for the base club, the command building where MacNair had an office, or the Xxanian consulate building. Evan had even looked up MacNair's home address.

What he'd say when he showed up on MacNair's doorstep aside, they both knew why Evan shouldn't do that. It was better for Zondra if he didn't. Evan couldn't ask about her—even to assure himself that she was okay—or he'd want to see that she was for himself. He'd feel he had a *right* to see it for himself.

But locking himself away in the massive starship hadn't stopped the dreams. They varied from slow, sweet shared candlelit baths to hot sex where he claimed her as his own by pinning her down and taking what she'd offered the night they'd spent together. Though he didn't want to examine them too closely, there had even been dreams of her carrying his child, a child that could never be. Just thinking of her carrying someone else's baby made Evan want to put his fist through the fictional other man's face.

I'd settle for a wall.

Fuck that! It was an illusion. It was a mating cycle.

But Evan's memories of that night called Aleeks a liar. There had been more between them than a biological imperative. He knew it. Biology didn't explain the tender feelings he had for Zondra.

Maybe there is more. MacNair said her pheromone would only last a few days. Maybe I should go see him, just to ask if feeling the attraction this long is a problem.

If there's more, it's more that can't go further, and going to see MacNair is just an excuse to get close to Zondra again.

Evan shook away the thought that he was nothing but a spineless coward, looking for reasons to see Zondra again. He had reasons for staying away from her. It was for her own good.

He strode down the corridors, heading aft and up until he reached the captain's office. The chief yeoman at the desk buzzed Evan in, then jerked a thumb at the door. The lack of announcing his presence to Pira confused him, but Evan headed through the door without questioning it.

Face it. Just get it over with.

His greeting short-circuited halfway up his throat. Pira wasn't the only officer sitting behind the desk. A second chair contained the most unlikely of apparitions—Admiral Matthew MacNair. Evan swallowed hard, his jaw aching from the healing bruise Aleeks's punch had left. His gaze locked on the yellow-green of the bruise on MacNair's cheek.

I am screwed. He wasn't sure why MacNair had changed his mind, but that fact was a given. Whether the charge was statutory rape, drunk and disorderly, assaulting a superior officer, or all of the above, there was little question that MacNair would have his balls on a platter.

"At ease, Petty Officer Duncan," Pira called out, his mouth quirking up in amusement.

Evan forced his shoulders to relax, waiting for the hammer to come down.

The haunting scent of Zondra surrounded him, and Evan let his eyes slide shut, taking a deep breath reflexively.

I'm dreaming again. I must be dreaming.

If it wasn't a dream, he didn't want to know it. If he knew it was real, he'd have to do the right thing and put an end to it.

Her hand settled at the small of his back, and her heat soaked into his starved body.

The words to dismiss her stuck in his throat. He didn't *want* to dismiss her. Not when she was so close, smelling so good.

Then she was moving, circling his body like a cat, her hand cupping his already erect cock between their bodies.

Evan licked his lips, his mouth watering to taste her again.

Common sense slapped him upside the head. "You need to stop now, Zondra."

"You don't want me?" she whispered into his chin. Her stroking hand challenged any negative response he might have made.

Hell yes, I want you! His hands twitched with the need to touch her, to hold her.

No. This can't happen.

Oh but I want it to. Evan didn't question that she wanted it as well.

As if in reply, she squeezed his cock lightly and started to massage.

She was taunting him. The need clawed at him. His reasons ceased to matter. All that existed was Zondra and himself. She wasn't going to get away with teasing him.

Evan grasped her by the back of the head, meeting her parted lips, trading need for need and heat for heat. His senses reeling, Evan forced her backward, seeking out a surface other than the floor, locked in a soul-searing kiss.

I'll take the floor. I'll take any available—

They landed hard against something. Evan thrust his right hand out to steady them, to keep their momentum from crushing her beneath him. His hand settled on paper-covered wood, and visions of the bureau in the lodge room danced behind his eyelids.

As if in agreement, Zondra hoisted herself to the edge. Evan fisted his left hand in her hair, cupped the right around her thigh, and pushed at her short skirt. He broke off the kiss, trailing his mouth down to her throat. He inhaled the scent that was uniquely Zondra.

"You *never* tease me," he growled at her.

"I'm convinced," Pira stated calmly.

Evan forced his eyes open and his head back, fighting the turmoil inside him, his libido at war with what little remained of his rational mind. His heart rate and breathing were erratic.

He met Zondra's gaze, noting the narrowed slits that announced how aroused she was through her dark lenses. He wanted to see the green-gold again, to watch her eye slits widen at climax.

She was deliciously mussed, her dark hair fisted in his hand, her lips kiss-swollen, and her skimpy clothing rumpled. He stroked her hair between his fingers but didn't release it. His heart ached. What was he doing? How could he walk away from this?

"My desk, Duncan," Pira hinted.

Evan cleared his throat, trying to force thoughts that were anything but coherent into words that were. MacNair's voice brought his gaze to the two officers.

"I *told* you this is beyond his control, Captain. That's why he's working himself to death, and he literally *will* work himself to death, given enough time to do it."

"And letting the mating take its course will give him back his control?" Pira asked.

Evan slid his hand to the inside of Zondra's thigh, tracing the edge of her panties with his thumb. "These are new," he managed to whisper.

MacNair's voice sounded far away. "Humans seem to get their heads on straight after mating, the same as the Xxan do. He shouldn't be any different."

Mating... He liked the sound of that. He liked her wet, inviting heat even more.

"And a two-week transfer to SLAL is all you need from me?"

The space stations in geostationary orbit over the North and South Poles: SLAL...*Scientific Liaison to Alien Life.* Evan stared at him, anger cutting through the misty confusion clouding his mind. "I'm no one's experiment," he protested.

MacNair met his gaze. "You said your only concern was whether or not Zondra could have children for you."

The spike of pleasure at that idea was as unusual for him as it was undeniable. *I can't be what she needs.* Evan nodded, his heart sinking...but not his cock. The reasons for his refusal of her stole his peace...but not his arousal. That was as potent as always.

MacNair kept talking. "Two weeks at SLAL. Maybe three, and Zondra will be bonded to you, as she would to a Xxanian male."

"Bonded?" Evan's voice was thick, his mind still struggling. Zondra's stroking hand wasn't helping. He pinned her hand to the desk, staring her down in warning.

MacNair's answer took a moment to sink in. "Her scent—Zondra's biosignature—will be permanently altered. She'll carry your scent, be tied to you, crave you...for the rest of her life. And you will crave her as well."

He nodded, digesting that. He'd heard the Xxan mated for life. *It's not like I don't crave her now. Would life with Zondra be that bad?*

"She'd also be ripened; she'd be fertile...for you."

His muscles tensed, and he glared at MacNair. "By who?" If they thought he'd stand by and let some Xxanian male fuck her to finish Zondra's sexual maturation—

"You, Duncan. *You* would ripen her."

Evan faltered, abruptly confused by that pronouncement. "We're that compatible? I thought—"

"Not quite. If you were, I'd rent you a honeymoon suite and be done with this insanity. But I can promise you that Zondra will be ripened by you. Not a Xxanian Dominant. You."

His heart pounded in excitement. *There went my last reason for refusing her. Maybe.* "You're sure we can—"

"It works in reverse," MacNair reminded him. "There's no reason it shouldn't work for you and Zondra, and these guys have had three generations of trial and error to get it right. If I thought for a second they were dabbling, I wouldn't make promises to you."

Evan focused on Zondra. "And you want this?" he asked her. "You're sure? Bound to me forever?"

"Oh yes."

"I take it this means I can have my desk back?" Pira asked.

Evan lifted Zondra into his arms, sealing his mouth to hers. Her legs wrapped around his waist.

* * * *

The trip to the shuttle bay was a feast of sensation. Evan's mouth meshed with hers, trailed to her throat, nuzzled her breasts, and returned to her mouth again.

The corridors sped past without making an impression on her senses. With his musk so close at hand, she didn't even smell the recycled air and oil that usually bothered her aboard ship.

She heard someone make a sound of appreciation, and Pap Mac snapped an order that no doubt sent the sailor hauling backside away. Normally Zondra would have cared about making such a spectacle of herself, but this wasn't a normal day. Evan was with her, and he'd agreed to be her mate.

Zondra gasped at the feeling of Evan's weight over her on the cushioned couch in the shuttle's passenger cabin. Before the outer door was secured, his hand was under her skirt again. This time, he found the tie at the waist of the panties and pulled it loose. Then the other. He eased the fabric away, leaving her nude beneath the skirt.

"I'll just secure this door," Pap Mac stated, heading into the control pod of the shuttle.

Evan ignored him. He worked his pants open and shoved them away from his cock. Both doors slid shut, and he was inside her, heedless of who might have seen them.

Zondra didn't care either. All that mattered was his cock, working her hard.

And I thought he didn't want me? By all indications, he'd been nearly mad for her. *Thank the* Seir-*God.*

"You never tease me," he repeated.

Answering that was difficult. Her breathing was ragged, and her head was spinning in pleasure.

"Say it."

"Never," she gasped. "N-never tease y-you."

Evan withdrew and leaned over her, issuing a challenge. She whispered his name, at a loss to understand the challenge to answer it properly.

Two fingers speared inside her, and Evan started working her with them. Zondra reached for him.

"Hands on the edge of the lounge," he ordered.

She complied, and he smiled. Her legs trembled with the need to move, but she was sure that was part of this game.

"Very good. I want a better view of you. Bend your knees and hang on to those come-fuck-me heels of yours."

The position pushed her skirt to the tops of her thighs, giving him an unobstructed view of her body beneath.

"Mmmm... Very nice. And all mine. Isn't it?"

Zondra nodded.

"Say it."

"Yes, I'm all yours."

His eyes demanded more. His fingers slowed, denying her the climax rising in her body.

"After mating, I will never want another man."

"Do you now?" That was falsely calm if she'd ever heard the tone.

And I have. "No."

"That's why you did this, isn't it? Because you still want me too."

"Too."

Oh Seir-*God.* Hearing it was enough to make her come.

As if he knew what she was thinking, Evan withdrew his fingers and started stroking her clit in lazy circles. "An answer, Zondra." He wasn't asking. He was ordering her to answer.

Her body reacted fiercely to the aphrodisiac of him dominating her this simply. "Yes. I couldn't bear to think of another male—"

He moved like the proverbial snake humans compared lunges to. She squeaked at the suction against her clit. His tongue teased a trail down to her slit and thrust inside. Evan sucked at her musk, tested her responses, driving her mad for what he'd started.

He groaned into her body, nearly bringing her off the couch. "I missed your smell and taste so much," he breathed.

Zondra fought for a steady breath.

"And now you're here." He rose up over her again, the challenge still in his eyes. "And you're going to do everything I want you to do. Aren't you, Zondra?"

Yes. He was everything she'd ever wanted and more. How could she refuse him?

"Everything I want," he demanded.

Oh yes. She nodded, then managed to stammer out the answer.

* * * *

That was all Evan needed to know. He stripped off his dungaree shirt and dropped it to the floor. His T-shirt came off next.

"Lighting twenty percent," he barked. When the computer complied, he pulled off her glasses and tossed them away.

Her green-gold eyes went right through him, making his cock bob excitedly for its...

Mate.

He turned her on the couch, situating her delectable bottom off the edge, and bound her wrists with the T-shirt. Zondra moaned and pressed her buttocks toward him.

"You like that," he teased.

"Yes." It was more a gasp than a word.

Evan thrust deep inside her. *Where I should have been for the last week.* "You're mine."

Zondra met him, thrust for thrust, rocking her hips into the cradle of his. Her cries rose and went harsh.

"Mine," he insisted. He wanted to hear her say it almost as much as he wanted to take his next breath.

"Yes!"

"They took you away too soon last time. I wasn't nearly done with you."

"M-mating..." She gasped, then screamed in pleasure, her inner muscles fluttering around his length.

Evan pushed harder, spurred on by the thought of it. "What about it, Zondra?"

"Lasts thr—" A gasp. "Three d-days."

"Nova eclipsing!" Three days? They hadn't told him that.

Zondra climaxed around his length, milking him with her tight little body.

The combination of that and the thought of three days lodged inside her shot him over with her.

"Fuck!" he exploded. It felt like he was expending a week's worth of cum at once. *And I'm still ravenous for more of her.*

Visions of their first night together dragged a groan from him. "I want what you promised. Now."

"Promised?" Her voice was a wisp of sound.

"Climb on my cock and fuck me senseless. You never have followed through, you know."

Her arms jerked to a stop against the T-shirt in her hurry to comply. Evan reached out to untie it, but Zondra wrenched her wrists apart, popping the knot open.

The Xxan are stronger than humans of the same size. He would have to remember that.

The thought faded into the background at her move up and off his cock. Evan sank to the floor, his head spinning. Zondra turned, straddled his bent legs, and lowered herself to sheath him again.

He clasped his hands on her hips, and Zondra raised an eyebrow at the move.

"What is it?" he asked.

"I believe you ordered me to fuck you senseless," she hinted.

"I see." Evan started to move his hands to the lounge, then hesitated. "One more thing." He grasped her crop-length peasant shirt in both hands and ripped it open, popping buttons off the lightweight material.

She seemed stunned by the move but not upset that he'd destroyed the confection hiding her breasts from him. After a moment of stillness, Zondra eased the shirt off and let it fall.

He planted his hands on the edge of the lounge, lowered his head, and sucked one deep pink nipple into his mouth. Zondra's body trembled in response, causing a massage effect against his cock.

Her hands closed on his shoulders, and she started circling her hips slowly. "Evan, I can't fuck you properly if I can't move freely."

He released her, mourning the loss already. "For now, but soon I'm going to spend a long, leisurely time sucking those pretty titties." This time she was going to take his cock down to the root, just as she'd promised.

Her thigh muscles tightened against his, and she levered herself up to nearly the tip. Her descent was brutally quick and efficient, to the base and a little wiggle there before she rose again. Demonstrating perfect control of her muscles, she repeated the move...faster and faster, until his breathing was ragged and harsh.

It took a few moments to relax into the sensation. Evan kept expecting her to move too far up and lose his cock, coming back down on the edge. That would be extremely painful for both of them. But Zondra wasn't human, and yet another bonus plan to mating with a Xxanian crossbreed was her athletic prowess. There was a reason why the Xxan were only allowed to compete against other Xxan in sports.

Her sounds were sharp and excited, and his rose to meet them. Evan let his eyes slip shut, embracing the sensations. Though he loved being in charge, there was something addictive about Zondra committing herself to making him come this way.

He held back for her, wondering at how long it was taking her to come.

"Please, Evan," she begged.

His mind moved sluggishly toward an explanation for her plea. "You want me to come first?" He was so accustomed to making her come before him that he hadn't even considered coming without her.

Zondra voiced a faint sound of agreement.

Evan captured her lips, meeting her thrusts, letting himself go. Her scream of delight started at the first jet of his cum into her body, and her contractions started a few heartbeats later. It was a glorious feeling, forcing him to extend his normal release. The effect was mind-altering; his vision blurred, and his body tensed and jerked in response.

She leaned into his chest, her inner muscles slowing their frantic clenching. "Oh *Seir*-God. We will have to do that again."

Part of him wanted to tell her she'd be doing exactly what he wanted to do. Another wanted a repeat too badly to consider arguing. "Definitely. But I have other things in mind first."

A hum of satisfaction rumbled from her lips, vibrating her body. The sensation coursed up his still-buried length, spurring him toward whatever his muddled mind decided was next on the list of sensual delights.

Candles. Living out the dreams of long, slow seductions in a tub for two or more was definitely on that list.

The overhead speaker crackled to life, and MacNair's voice filled the space around their sweat-soaked bodies. "Ten minutes to dock, Duncan. I'd really like you both to be dressed and ready to meet the team when we arrive."

Evan let loose a string of curses that their reunion had ended so soon.

The admiral laughed heartily at his response.

"Something funny?" he snapped in return.

"Nope. Not a thing. It just brings back memories of old times with Daahn. Just remember...the sooner we get past the preliminaries, the sooner you get to bond Zondra to you."

"Yeah. Got it."

The speaker went silent.

"It's an intercom system," Zondra offered. "When the speaker is off, the mic is, too."

So MacNair had granted them privacy. Evan nodded.

Zondra reached for the lacy underwear, and Evan swept them into his hand. She stared up at him, her eye slits widened as a result of her climax.

"I believe I'll keep these." He slid them into his front pocket. "You can sit there and inspire me for a few minutes while I dress." But there was no question that looking at her lithe body was going to keep him aroused.

Who am I kidding? Her scent on my skin will do that. Memories of her scent and touch will do it and have for more than a week.

If the order to sit naked while he dressed surprised or offended her, Zondra showed no sign of it.

Evan pulled his half-opened dungaree shirt on and tucked it in. He fastened his pants over it and decided to leave it open. SLAL knew why they were here. What sense did playing at social graces with them make?

None. But that didn't mean he was going to expose Zondra to them.

With exaggerated care, Evan smoothed her miniskirt down her thighs. Zondra rose against his hand, seemingly begging for another quick round before they docked.

"Soon," he promised her. "As soon as they're done with us, you'll take me in every possible position there is." He didn't question it.

Zondra moaned at the command.

Evan stuffed her ripped shirt in his back pocket and retrieved the knotted T-shirt she'd slipped out of. He untied it and shook it out, then pulled it over her head. It was vastly oversized, covering her chest and extending past her skirt. To someone that didn't know better, it would appear to be all she was wearing, especially with her scrumptious nipples tenting the fabric. Just seeing her in his clothes made him hard.

Again, Zondra tipped her hips in silent offer.

Silent plea.

Evan was on the cusp of talking himself into another quickie when MacNair tapped a warning that he intended to enter through the control pod door.

Evan stood, disgusted with himself that he'd wasted their chance deliberating. He lifted Zondra to her feet, then called out a terse, "Come on in," to her godfather.

MacNair slipped into the main cabin and focused his gaze in their general direction. A moment of stillness passed.

Evan stiffened in response. "Problem, MacNair?" he challenged.

"No problem. You're more fully dressed than most soon-to-be-mated men are, I suppose."

"Would having my dick hanging out be more appropriate?" he growled in response.

"No!" Zondra and MacNair's exclamations came in unison.

Their reaction forced a smile to his face.

Zondra huffed in seeming exasperation. "Are we going to—"

"Absolutely." He waved MacNair toward the outer door.

Halfway there, MacNair stopped, lifted something small from the table's surface, and stuffed it into his shirt pocket.

"Pap?" Zondra asked.

"Just a button." He peered at her as he worked the door controls. "I imagine I'll find more of them."

"I imagine you will," Evan agreed pleasantly. He scooped the discarded glasses from the floor and offered them back to Zondra.

"You won't need those," MacNair informed them. "When there is a Xxanian aboard, all areas of the lab he or she will visit are set to a Xxanian's comfort level."

"Good. Seeing her eyes really fires my cock for more."

The admiral shot him a dirty look, then turned his back. The door opened with a hiss of equalizing pressure, letting in a blast of warm, moist air.

Chapter Four

If Zondra could blush, she imagined her cheeks would be a fiery red. It seemed Evan and Pap Mac liked needling each other.

At my expense. It was a Dominant show to them, she was sure. *Dominants must establish a line of ascension.*

Pap Mac went down the ramp first. Evan took her hand and preceded Zondra down in Mac's wake.

The lighting wasn't the only thing set to her comfort level. The air was made to simulate a nest environment. It was humid and comfortably warm, smelling of green, growing plants and a faint hint of musk and clove.

Not enough to seem ostentatious to the Xxan but enough to hint at home. Zondra wondered if the intent was to put mating Xxan at ease with the environment.

There was a group of six scientists waiting for them at the far side of the landing bay. One stepped forward and extended his hand to them, and Evan released Zondra's hand to take it and observe the niceties.

"Welcome aboard SLAL One, Petty Officer Duncan."

He nodded and released the scientist's hand. "Duncan will be fine."

"I'm Doctor Rayn, head of Xxanian studies." He motioned to one after another, firing off names and job descriptions.

The one he'd identified as Doctor Tamsen reached for Zondra, and she recoiled behind Evan. Before she could reason herself out of the instinctual response, Evan had planted himself firmly between them.

Pap Mac slid a glance over them and took a step closer, blocking any attempt Tamsen might make to reach around Evan. "Your men don't know better than this, Steve?"

Dr. Rayn scowled at Tamsen, and the latter darkened in a flush.

"We hadn't anticipated such a powerful bond between them, considering how long they've been separated." He tipped his head to Evan. "Our apologies. I assume you'll want to be present for Zondra's testing."

"Expect it." His muscles were strung tight, and the Dominant show made his scent even more enticing.

Zondra wrapped herself around him, burying her face in his throat, moaning at the heavy musk she'd soon carry. She looked up and met Rayn's startled gaze.

The head scientist cleared his throat. "You couldn't stop them?"

"Did you really think I could?" Pap Mac countered. "Duncan was still affected when we got to him. We're lucky he didn't launch into a killing rage."

"And he stayed away how long?" Tamsen gushed out.

"Can we get this over with?" Evan barked in return. "I don't intend to wait forever to finish getting acquainted with my mate."

The scientists shot wary glances at one another.

"What is *that* look for?" he demanded.

Rayn cleared his throat. "We need you to abstain for a while."

"How...long?"

Zondra inhaled his increased scent. *By the* Seir-*God!* As hard as it was going to be on Evan, it was going to be just as hard on her. And there was no way Evan would allow them to be separated while they waited. She repeated his question.

"That depends on the two of you."

* * * *

"You need to do what?" Evan asked in disbelief.

Dr. Rayn's assistant peeked around nervously. "We need to get a mold of your erect length to make the collection bags from."

"And you'll do this...how, precisely?"

"You need to be erect for ten minutes. And still. You definitely need to stand still for it."

Words deserted him. Out of the corner of his eye, Evan saw Zondra smirking. He scowled at her. "You think this is funny."

"Well...yes. I guess. But I don't see the problem. I can keep you erect for that long, easily."

"Yeah. Erect but without any chance of sating myself." He wanted to grumble curses at the scientists for their decreed moratorium on sex.

The assistant looked to the far corner of the room, probably issuing a silent plea for someone else to tell Evan he wasn't getting any. He nodded. "One time, after the mold is completed," he agreed. "But then—"

"Nothing until the collection begins," Evan parroted.

"The good news is—"

"There is some? Stars be praised." He was being sarcastic and more than a little juvenile, but the lack—with Zondra around to stimulate his senses—was unbearable.

The assistant darkened to crimson. He cleared his throat. "The good news is that, once the mold is made, we can have the first of the collection bags made in about two hours. After that, it will be whatever you want until we've collected enough of your various fluids. As long as you use the collection bags every time, that is."

That was enough to make him hard. "You better clear out the minute that mold comes off my cock, because I'm not waiting for anything." And he certainly wasn't going to stand for someone watching him have sex with Zondra. He'd regained that much control over himself.

"Got it. Anytime you're ready, Duncan."

Zondra turned toward him, her hands going to work on his trousers.

Evan lowered his head and inhaled her pungent *Zhigaaah*. It seemed sex with him had strengthened it again. It wasn't enough to smell it. He sucked at her throat, leaving love bites in his wake while he feasted on the musk.

The door behind him closed, most probably some of the scientists clearing out. The assistant remained.

She stroked him, moaning against his temple. His trousers retreated, baring his ass to whichever scientists remained across the room.

The assistant opened a metal lid at the edge of the table.

Evan glared at the semisolid mass in the receptacle beneath. "I see you were prepared for this," he grumbled. *And does it have to be pink?*

Zondra nibbled at his earlobe and thrust her hips against his.

"Oh yeah. That was the visualization I needed." Evan lifted her by the waist and settled Zondra on the table, her legs spread around the pot of pink goo. There were appealing pink places that he could use to make him forget where he was really placing his cock.

She wrapped her legs around him and dragged Evan toward her body. Forcing himself to angle his cock down into the waiting mold material took all his newly recovered self-control.

"All the way in," the assistant reminded him. "Balls, too."

"Fuck off," Evan grumbled.

Zondra urged him closer to her, and Evan grimaced at the warm ooze sucking at the base of his balls. The urge to pull out and tell them to get bent rode him hard.

"That's right," the intruder complimented him. "Now just hold it there for ten minutes."

"You want to eat this shit?" Evan snapped.

The offensive little man retreated, and Evan focused on Zondra.

She dipped her head and laid kisses on his chest. Her nimble little fingers undid the few buttons he'd fastened on his shirt. When they were all open, she straightened and pressed her lips to his chin, inviting his face down.

Their kisses were deep and slow. Zondra wrapped her hands around his waist. At every shift of his weight, Zondra dug in her nails or tightened her legs to remind him not to move.

Evan growled in frustration.

"Do you want to do this twice?" she asked.

"And wait longer than two hours? Not a chance."

Zondra stretched up and nibbled at his lips. "Then we should get on with this, I think."

"Five more minutes," Rayn's assistant murmured.

Just five minutes. Already half done.

It was endless.

Waiting the two hours will be worse. By far.

Just kiss her. Surely he could spend five minutes kissing Zondra.

It was easier thought than done. By the time the assistant announced four minutes left, his muscles were strung tight in restraint. Another minute and sweat rolled down his bare chest. Another...

Stars burn, a second attempt doesn't sound that bad, if I can have her now.

"Okay. Let me get you out of that." The young man moved closer and reached between them.

Evan tensed, then calmed in the realization that he was reaching for the hardening goo. "I thought you said ten minutes," he complained.

"I lied. I knew it would take a minute or two to get you out of this. If I told you eight and took two more—"

"I'd've kicked your ass," Evan assured him.

The assistant chuckled darkly. "Good thing I lied to you then."

Against his better judgment, Evan smiled. "You're okay, kid."

"Tim. Tim Carew."

The solidified mass pulled away from Evan's body with an odd tingling sensation. Tim waved him back, and his cock slid free.

"Great. Now if you don't mind—"

Carew pulled the receptacle out of the table. "I get it. There's a bed through there." He jerked his thumb toward the door opposite the corridor. "If you can wait that long."

With that, he was gone through the corridor door. It closed behind him.

Zondra started working her skirt up. Evan took one look at the view, scooped her up, and headed for the promised bed.

* * * *

There was no denying that Evan was at the edges of control. Zondra wasn't certain what he'd do when they reached the bed, but it would be an adventure. She was sure that the next two hours would drive them both nearly mad.

His grumbled curse brought her head around. Zondra didn't have to question what had him so pissed off.

The mirror took up the top half and two-thirds of the length of the wall to the left of the king-size bed. There was little question it was a two-way mirror with an observation room on the opposite side.

"I am covering that fucking thing," he promised.

The speaker in the wall next to the mirror squawked. "Not this time, Duncan."

Rayn. Zondra considered shooting a rude Xxanian gesture at the mirrors.

The head doctor continued. "And not in the bathroom either. Not now."

"I said I wasn't going to put up with anyone watching us," Evan warned him.

Zondra silently offered her agreement. If there was one thing a Xxanian woman learned, it was to stay out of a battle between Dominants, and she didn't doubt that Rayn was a human alpha, though she hadn't tongue-scented the human to be sure.

As if proving that point, Rayn pushed back. "Are you saying you can promise you won't break the rules set for you?" the scientist asked with exaggerated calm.

Evan's muscles tightened down, and he seemed about to tell Rayn where he could shove his rules.

"It's simple, Duncan. Either I can sedate you for the next two hours, or I can make sure you follow orders."

Evan opened his mouth to retort.

"Not to mention, if you keep wasting semen and musk we could be collecting, we'll have to use the collection bags longer." Rayn paused a moment. "Maybe a few days longer. Maybe a week. Typically I wouldn't allow you to have sex again at all until we were collecting."

Allow? Zondra bristled at that and knew it was seriously pissing Evan off.

Is it intended to? She was sure Rayn wasn't oblivious to the instincts of a mating male. That meant he had to be doing this on purpose. *Doesn't it?*

Evan's mouth snapped shut with a clack of teeth against teeth.

"So, Duncan. What's it going to be?"

"Fuck!"

"I'm sure that's your choice as well," Rayn taunted.

"When this is over, I'll feed you those words...along with my fucking fist."

"So every Xxanian male I've dealt with in the last thirty years has threatened, more or less. Until then, you need me, and you will follow my rules, Duncan."

He's challenging Evan to make his musk more potent. It was brilliant but suicidal. Rayn had a serious set of balls to do this to a male involved in mating.

"And when this is over, and I *don't* need you?" Evan countered.

Rayn's chuckle was dark and somewhat mean. "I manage to stay out of a Dominant's path until mating settles him."

Zondra bit back a smile at that.

"Awfully sure of that. Aren't you?"

"As sure as I am that you're about to choose to have sex with your mate and find some way to keep me from seeing her body."

Evan hesitated long enough to make Zondra wriggle nervously in his arms.

"You're damned right I am," he growled.

"See? You only wasted five minutes arguing with me, coming to that decision."

Before Evan could reply, the speaker clicked off.

"Fucking asshole."

Telling him Rayn had good reason to taunt him and torture him would be counterproductive, so Zondra kept her mouth shut. The more potent the musk, the less time they'd need to collect it, most likely.

Maybe I'll tell him once we're mated. A completely outrageous thought made her smile. *Maybe that's how Rayn has survived this long.*

Her smile faded at the sight of Evan glaring at the mirror.

Let him. The more time he wastes, the less time we have to wait later.

He didn't waste much time at all. Evan settled her in the middle of the mattress, her back to the mirror. Zondra started to peel his T-shirt off, but a sharp hiss from Evan brought her up short with the cotton blend material gathered beneath her breasts. He motioned downward with his eyes, and she smoothed the fabric to her waist.

That settled, Evan dragged the button-down shirt over his shoulders and dropped it to the mattress. Zondra stared up at him, her mouth-watering at the sight of all that luscious man.

And he's mine.

In the next breath, he was between her knees, his mouth parting hers. The kiss was hard and deep and tasted of a challenge.

Most likely a challenge to Rayn.

Zondra followed Evan's lead, though she ached to be skin to skin with him.

One hand kneaded a breast. The other traced the line of her hip from front to back, pausing at her spine. Then he slid it down and cupped her ass through the layer of skirt. Her breathing went ragged that simply.

His voice was slightly muffled against her chin and throat. "I made you a promise, and I always keep my promises."

He did? Zondra would fully admit that her nearly photographic memory had deserted her. She couldn't remember what he'd promised her, though she was sure it was sexual in nature.

As if in answer, Evan lifted her and sucked her breast into the heat of his mouth.

"I'm going to spend a long, leisurely time sucking those pretty titties."

That was the promise he'd made. The decree. Zondra reached up and tunneled her fingers in his light brown hair.

There was nothing leisurely about what Evan was doing to her. The suction was bruising in its intensity.

Marks. She understood perfectly why he wanted to leave marks of ownership on her. While human men often disregarded scent, marking was a sign they wouldn't miss. *Especially the human doctors that have only done the most preliminary testing on me so far.*

His sucking became harder and more avid, first one breast and then the other, back and forth, until she felt she would come from that alone. Zondra looked between their bodies, a mew of pleasure escaping at the sight of her swollen nipples, clearly visible through the sodden material.

She allowed her head to drop back and arched into his sucking mouth.

Evan placed one hand at her shoulders and forced her upright again. She stared at him, at a loss to explain the move. Zondra looked over her shoulder at the jerk of his head toward her left, noting the mirror out of the corner of her eye.

"They are not getting that clear a look at you," he vowed. His eyes were narrowed, lending a dangerous edge to his appearance.

That was enough to make her wet for him again. She'd thought overbearing males were a nuisance until she met Evan. Now it seemed she couldn't get enough of him telling her what to do. She met his gaze solidly. "Yes." *Tell me what you want.*

Evan offered a curt nod. He didn't tell her what he wanted. He took it. Evan went back to his avid suckling, one hand still planted at her shoulders in a reminder not to drop to her back where Rayn could see her.

He trailed his lips up her cotton-covered chest to her throat, then to her lips. When he pulled back, Evan picked up his dungaree shirt and shook it out.

She watched, confused. "What are you doing?"

His smile was lopsided and accompanied by one raised eyebrow. He didn't answer aloud, but she started to get a clearer picture when he urged her arms into it and left it open around her body. He resumed his sucking, tugging at her nipples lightly, until musk was running freely down her thighs.

"Damn this. I can't wait." His complaint was muffled in one well-loved breast.

Evan lifted her, settling Zondra onto the head of his cock. His shirt tickled at the skin just above the back of her knees.

Blocking Rayn's view entirely. It was brilliant.

He smiled in triumph, and Zondra laughed at his competitive streak. Of course, being an alpha, that was to be expected.

Her laughter died off as he eased her down his cock. A shuddering breath escaped her clenched teeth.

"Good?" he teased.

"Mmmm..." It was the most coherent sound she could make.

Evan moved smoothly, in and out, each stroke burning a trail over her lately underused tissues. Zondra held tight to his arms, her talons dimpling his flesh, her sounds harsh.

Seir-*God, but he is better than I ever thought a male could be the first time we had sex, and it gets better every time he touches me.*

The slow approach didn't last long; the week apart had taken its toll on both of them. In moments, he was pounding into her, his fingers clenching against her hips as if she might disappear from his arms.

At least Zondra assumed that was his fear, since it was hers. If someone tried to separate them now, she'd rip the bastard's throat out with her hunting teeth for the trouble.

If Evan doesn't get to him first. The fact that he would kill for her sent pleasant shivers down her spine.

As if he felt them, Evan's pace increased by half again, and he grumbled something incoherent. That was all the impetus she needed to shatter around him, her vision graying around the edges and her lungs sluggishly moving heated gasses that seemed to sit too long before the next contraction spurred her to breathe.

The end was kinetic. His heat sent memories of her quickening through her. Their shouts overlapped and reverberated against her skin, the currents of air caressing her. The effect aroused her all over again.

Kinetic...and over far too soon. She wrapped her arms around his shoulders and buried her face in Evan's shoulder. *How are we going to survive two more hours without touching each other?*

As if in answer, Rayn cleared his throat for attention.

The speaker and mic didn't just turn on. How long had he been listening to them?

As if Evan was asking the same question, he tensed.

"Now that we've taken care of that, please report back to the lab. Tim will lead you to the medical bay. You can spend the rest of the two hours getting the baseline testing out of the way."

The electronics shut down just as Evan expelled his response toward them.

Chapter Five

"Oh, hell yes," Evan gasped out.

Zondra's tongue trailed along the curve of his balls, stealing a hint of his musk before she'd bag him. He arched up, inviting her to suck, though he knew she couldn't yet.

"Last time," he grumbled.

After five days of collection, interrupted often for medical tests and what seemed to be spurious annoyances the scientists had invented for them, Rayn had informed them that the first batch of *Zhigaaal* was in production, and they would have only four more collections to use for future reproduction of the Xxanian musk. They'd done the first three in a thankfully-uninterrupted glut of sex. This was the last. After this, Evan fully intended to get back to everything the damned collection bags made impossible.

The bath. He'd had the candles hidden away since Tim had provided them.

The slick sheath covered him from tip to the ridge behind his sac, designed to soak up not only his cum but also his musk, his pheromones...every biochemical that identified him as the Dominant he was. It would be intolerable if it wasn't for Zondra's body gripping him through the barrier, the length of her body draped over him, the smell and taste of her *Zhigaaah.*

Evan let his mixed emotions drive him into her. His frustration with the five days of collection warred with the near-endless arousal he was sating.

Zondra moved over him, meeting his body, her sweet pussy engulfing him. Her sounds were low and primal, wordless begging for all he had to give...and more that the scientists were taking to satisfy the physiological gap between human and Xxan.

In eight more days, she'd be his. Zondra was well on her way to it, riding him hard.

In five more days, the mating will begin.

That thought in mind, it took only moments for Evan to bag what he hoped was his final deposit. Zondra worked the sheath off, careful not to lose a drop, lest they order more collections. She sealed the bag tight and shifted off him.

Before she could leave the bed, he cupped the back of her neck, drawing Zondra's throat down to his mouth. Her *Zhigaaah* was tangy, not as powerful as it had been the first night or their first day back together, but close enough to prepare him for more. His renewed erection was fierce and uncompromising.

She gasped his name out, her nipples going hard against his chest.

He released her. "Pass that off and come back quickly. They've got theirs. Now you'll have mine."

She nodded and hurried away. From the next room he could hear Zondra open and close the specimen door. She sounded the buzzer to make sure the scientists got the freshest possible sample to start with.

It didn't take long for Zondra to return. She stopped in the doorway, her gaze panning up his body and locking on his cock.

"Take a taste," he invited.

Zondra glided to him, placing one knee on the mattress. Her tongue peeked from between her lips, seeking out his scent. Then she was on her knees, her mouth surrounding him, working his length in and out.

Evan fisted his hand in her hair, watching her fellate him. He'd eaten her out several times in the last few days, but coming anywhere but in the collection sleeves had been nixed.

She moaned around his length, sending a tremor of pleasure through him. He'd learned quickly what fired her sex drive, and swallowing a load ranked up there. Watching her suck him, when he knew her hunting teeth could leave him dickless, fired his.

"Drink it," he ordered. "The next one goes in that hungry pussy."

The answering groan nearly sent him over.

"You're going to drink my *Zhigaaal*," he reminded her, enjoying the trilling of the alien word off his tongue.

He enjoyed what would happen to her when she *did* drink it even more. According to the SLAL doctors, Zondra would be mindless for sex once she had.

Zondra took him to the root, her breath teasing his pubic curls.

Evan held back, denying her. "Four or five more days, and the mating begins. Until then, I intend to be inside you every minute Rayn isn't annoying us."

Zondra's sucking became more insistent. Her head bobbed, and her breast brushed against his thigh. Her tongue flicked in a wicked little pattern. The novelty was cruelly pleasurable. Evan hadn't known a tongue could be that flexible.

He wanted to hold off, to make it last longer, but there was no holding back. Evan came harder than he had since the shuttle. His shout echoed off the stark walls, muted from the direction of the covered mirror.

Thank goodness.

Her tongue performed a little swivel against the veins on the underside of his cock, sending him into aftershocks.

In the next heartbeat, Zondra was over him, his still-hard cock buried inside her. Evan sucked a line of little love bites up her throat, feeding himself on *Zhigaaah.* Then he flipped her beneath him, taking what was his.

* * * *

"So it was really an accident?" The flickering candles highlighted the lines of Evan's relaxed face. Once the frenzy of rediscovery had passed, he'd started experimenting with slow touching that had put Zondra in a stupor of pleasure.

And now the candlelit bathing. It was so very Xxanian, and yet Evan seemed to know little about her culture.

He shot her a questioning look.

Question. He'd asked a question. Zondra nodded. "My *seir* had no idea his *Zhigaaal* on her skin would affect my mother that way. It doesn't affect Xxanian females the same way."

"But he loves her?" Evan stroked the cloth along the lines of her breasts, spreading the clove bath gel over already peaked nipples.

"Definitely. It's not that the Xxan don't love their mates. That's a lie the prejudiced like to spread to cause discontent. Mating is just one more step in that bond. My *seir* felt my mother was too young to choose to mate with, but he loved her and would have waited for her had he not...well, messed up and started the bonding accidentally."

The cloth moved to the other breast, and Evan watched her body's reactions to it avidly, seemingly cataloging each one. His question drew her out of the near mesmerized state he was putting her in with his handling.

"Younger than you?"

"Older than me by more than three years, but I'm a crossbreed, and my mother is human. Human females aren't adult at sixteen or seventeen years old."

"Will your parents be upset that you mated so young?"

Zondra smiled, sure that she knew what he was heading for. "Mating is an adult female's choice. When I mate and to whom is none of my *seir's* business. Or *Gran-seir's*."

Evan was silent for a long moment. "Tim told me the Xxanian male typically sends a gift of spice to his mate's family. A sort of dowry."

"Usually."

Evan wasn't worried about that, was he? She opened her mouth to ask.

"I had him send some. I want to show respect for your culture. Your family."

Zondra leaned toward him and pressed a kiss to Evan's chest. Now that his mercurial temper had calmed somewhat, she was getting to know the considerate side of the domineering alpha.

"Do you love me, Zondra?"

The question came out of nowhere, stealing her breath for a moment. "Of course I do." How could he question it?

"When did you start loving me? When did it become more than biology?"

"Can anyone answer that for sure? Even the initial rush of human love starts with the outpouring of neurochemicals and pheromones, the olfactory matching of genetic immunities and—"

"When did you realize it?"

She considered that. It wasn't as early as the morning after. She wasn't sure then, much as she'd argued she was. The answer wasn't hard to come to. "When I realized that every sleepless moment in my bed at home, I was listening for some sign that you were at the door looking for me. Every minute was a torture. I wanted to cry. I wanted to find you. I wanted to curse you...and couldn't."

"I'm sorry."

Her heart stuttered. "Why?" Was he sorry that Zondra truly loved him? Was Evan saying he wasn't sure he loved her? That it was no more than biology between them?

"I'm sorry I made you go through that. If it's any consolation, I wasn't doing much better without you."

It wasn't a proclamation of love, but it seemed to be honest remorse. "You had good reason to." She dismissed his concerns.

His eyes narrowed. "MacNair had no right to tell you that."

"He had every right to tell me what was keeping you away, but he didn't. Aleeks did."

Evan snorted. "Aleeks? You're joking."

"Yes. Aleeks. Why would that surprise you?"

His cheeks darkened, and Evan kept his gaze focused on the meandering rag.

"Evan?"

"I thought Aleeks hated me. He certainly wanted to feed me my teeth back at the lodge."

Zondra couldn't help laughing. "Xxanian males are protective of females in general. If the female is part of his nest, his family, he's doubly so.

"Would Aleeks have fed you your teeth? If you'd made one move that might have injured me, or if you'd tried to claim me as your own before the three days of separation were up...or if I hadn't agreed to be your mate, yes. He would have."

Evan met her gaze. "What changed?"

"A week later, I still wanted you."

"That simple?"

"Mating is a serious thing for the Xxan. Females choose their mates. If you separate a female from her mate after they are bound, you are sentencing her to death."

The next question came slower. "Xxanian parents never disapprove of the man a woman chooses? Before they're bound and unable to be separated?" His tone left no doubt that he didn't believe it.

"My *seir* could *try* to disapprove, but the female's determination is rumored to be formidable. My *seir* made it clear he didn't intend to disapprove.

"Aleeks just hated seeing me unhappy. He would have done nearly anything to help me be happy again. He even talked to Doctor Rayn and told me why you were upset."

A smile flirted with his lips. "And *are* you happy?"

"Yes. I am. Very happy." But something told her the discussion was only half-finished. "Are you? You seem very concerned about what my family will think of you."

"I am happy, and...shouldn't I be concerned about your family?"

"*Should* you be? Typically the only concern in mating is whether the male's family will—" His pained look stopped her cold. "They won't approve of me. Will they?" Why had she never asked it before? Had she stupidly believed humans didn't concern themselves with what their parents thought of their mates? Or had she—equally stupidly—assumed his family would love her because of the alliance with Daahn such a mating would bring?

"There's no one to approve or disapprove of you." It was offered in a gruff voice, a blunt statement of fact.

"You have no family?"

He didn't answer.

Zondra cupped his chin in her hand and drew his face up so she could see his eyes in the semidarkness. "You have no family?" she asked gently.

"None that wants anything to do with me," he corrected.

"But...why?" He was a strong, able man. Why would his family not revel in him?

"Ask my father. He left when I was less than two. I don't even remember him. Apparently he had other things he wanted to do with his life."

"And your mother?"

"She died when I was fifteen."

The words to soothe him wouldn't come. Losing a mother was shattering to anyone, child or not, and Evan had still been a child. Whoever had cared for him after her death seemingly hadn't stayed in his life.

"She was murdered. Beaten to death by some drunk she'd cut off at the bar." His lip curled in disgust. "Guess she cut him off a few drinks too late."

He must have seen the urge to cry in her expression. Evan made a soothing sound and smoothed her hair.

"I don't know much about this whole family thing anymore. It's been a while for me. But I want to learn."

The question she had to ask stuck in her throat. Zondra cleared it and forced it out. "Do you love me?"

It's the wrong time to ask. But when would be the right time? After they'd bound themselves irrevocably? *If we haven't already done that.* Evan had been breathing in her musk for well over a week. If he was still affected after a week separated, did that mean he'd already been bound to her?

Evan hesitated for a moment. "I can't say that I've ever been in love before, but I went through all the same things you did. If that's love, yes."

That could just be my Zhigaaah. Zondra forced a smile that felt strained to her face.

He didn't seem to notice it. "I can't explain the way I feel about you. It's powerful. It's so powerful, it's downright scary sometimes. I want to hurt people that hurt you. I want to hurt people that take you away from me. I want to protect you. I want to make you happy, and I don't know why I want to do any of it. I'm not *un*happy doing it. In fact, it feels really...good. How do people know they're in love?"

Finding her voice was abruptly difficult. "I think you're off to a good start. Most men never manage to say what you just did."

He ground his teeth and offered a terse nod.

"It's the most beautiful thing I've ever heard," she admitted.

Evan started rinsing the bath gel off her body, his gaze locked on what he was doing. "I think I'm in love, because nothing anyone has said to me in my life has ever made me feel like that one compliment does."

* * * *

"Zondra," he called softly.

She stirred, stretching beneath the sheets. Her nostrils flared, and she hummed a happy note. "Breakfast." A yawn followed, showing her hunting teeth. Her brow furrowed, and she finished her catlike stretch. "And something sweet."

Evan settled on the bed and set the platter of food between them. "Birthday cake. I asked Tim because I knew it was coming up soon. Almost missed it." He'd come way too close to missing the event.

Zondra scrambled to her knees, deliciously naked, the sheet pooling around her waist. "Birthday cake?"

"Well, white chocolate cake with coconut icing. I sent a comm to MacNair and asked him what your favorite is. If he's wrong, I'm beating him senseless later." A smile pulled up at his lips, but his stomach clenched in something that felt suspiciously like fear. What did it matter if it was her favorite?

It does!

"You asked Pap Mac?"

He offered one decisive nod of his head.

"Why?"

There was no easy answer to that. Evan shrugged. "It's your favorite. Isn't it?" *Please, tell me it is.*

She dipped a finger in the icing and brought it to her mouth, a mischievous little smile on her lips. "Ummm...yes. Enough to make me consider not eating the meat and gorging myself on the cake instead." She sucked the icing away with a moan of pleasure.

"And what would that do to your...*sensitive* constitution?" He pulled out his best impersonation of Tamsen.

Zondra sighed, and a forlorn expression settled on her face. "I wouldn't feel very well for at least a few days. That much is sure."

Evan lifted a cube of meat and brought it to her lips. "Then I suggest you eat the meat first and then the cake."

Her eyes went wide, then narrowed. Her rising scent said he'd done something to arouse her.

"What is it?"

"Nothing."

"Zondra," he warned.

"Xxanian males feed their mates. It's silly. It's—"

"Tell me how." Chances were it was important in their mating. Even if it wasn't, if it made Zondra happy, he was willing to at least try it for her. *It is her birthday, after all.*

"The male puts the meat in his mouth and chews it for her. Then they pass it, mouth to mouth."

Evan stared at the meat in his hand.

"It's okay if you—"

"It's no worse than eating meat rare." *If you let it go warm on the plate instead of hot. Who hasn't while eating rare meat?*

She moved her mouth as if to speak, but nothing emerged for a moment. "You're saying you want to?"

Evan popped the cube of meat in his own mouth instead of hers. It was marinated in spices that complimented the natural flavor. It wasn't nearly as unpleasant as it might have been if the meat had been bland.

Zondra watched him, her breathing low and choppy. Her nipples came to enticing little points.

He leaned toward her and parted her lips. The kiss that followed was hard and hot, and the meat spread between both of their mouths. Evan backed away, his head reeling. If this was what a Xxanian couple got out of sharing a meal, he could understand why she was so aroused by the idea. He popped another cube in his mouth, anticipating passing it to her.

Zondra moved closer, her fingers tunneling through the curls on his chest. Evan grasped the back of her head and brought her mouth to his. Passing the second cube was even more involved than the first had been.

The third followed. Then the fourth. The loudest sound in the room was their rasping breaths. Zondra sank to the bed beneath him, Evan stretched out over her, and the feeding went on.

It became a pleasant blur of touching and tasting. The kisses went on longer, and the time between bites of meat extended. Evan sank over her and fit his body to hers, his skin sensitized to every slide of her flesh against his.

Evan couldn't mark the moment when it became more. One moment, he was passing meat into her mouth. The next, he was sliding into her heated body, his hands fisted in the sheets, his muscles bunching with each thrust.

Zondra's sounds were sharp, and her talons against his skin were sharper, urging him deep into her body. Her hips rose and fell, and her inner muscles tightened and loosened, milking him toward release.

It was over in heartbeats, leaving them both gasping for breath, her *Zhigaaah* tantalizing his senses.

Evan recovered first. "Happy birthday, Zondra."

She pressed to his chest, holding tight to him. "It is now." There was a moment of silence. "What do you think of Xxanian feeding?"

"I still get to eat the occasional hamburger?" he teased.

She laid a smack across his bare ass. "If you insist."

"It's the most incredible meal I've ever had," Evan admitted. "I'd be glad to do that anytime."

"Family meals in the nest with *Gran-seir* are only once a week, unless there's a celebration. Anytime we choose to visit, it will likely be something of a mini celebration."

He scowled. "We are not doing that in front of your *gran-seir*."

"Of course not." She smiled. "Want to feed me cake now?"

"Mouth feed?" That didn't sound as appetizing as passing shredded meat.

Zondra shook her head. "Not a Xxanian's way."

Evan reached for the fork. "Hmmm... Of course, there are interesting ways to use the cake."

Her expression said she was more than open to experimentation.

Chapter Six

"This is what happens next," Dr. Rayn announced, settling on the edge of his antique desk. "We have to do some final tests on the two of you and some minor preparations, and then we can let you get on with mating."

Evan wrapped an arm around Zondra and drew her to his side, much more relaxed after four days without the collection bags, interrupted for Rayn's seemingly endless testing. They'd talked, fed each other, bathed each other, slept in each others' arms, and had indulged in a feast of sex that had both their pheromone levels higher than the doctors had ever seen.

Tim had suggested that bagging Evan now would give them much more potent stock to work with. Evan's answer wasn't fit for many military men to hear, let alone women and children.

"I've heard it's a three-day stretch," he responded to the head scientist.

"Yes, it is." Rayn waved them closer and turned a screen to face them. "There's a typical way this is accomplished."

Evan narrowed his gaze on Zondra, and she wriggled at the attention.

"Is there now?" he drawled. "Maybe Zondra would like to enlighten me."

She cleared her throat, her mouth going dry at the thought of telling Evan what he had to do to finalize their mating.

"Zondra?" he pressed.

"You will anoint me with your *Zhigaaal*. The usual erogenous zones...my breasts, inner thighs, pulse points, the musk wells at my throat...my mating stripe eventually."

"And how do I do that?"

She looked up at Rayn. "I have no idea. The male uses his secondary."

"I've heard Xxanian men have two cocks."

Rayn nodded. "Since we don't know how much of Xxanian mating depends on that difference, we will be creating one for you. To answer your other question, we will create a *Zhigaaal* bladder for you that will be strapped to the secondary."

He nodded in response, seemingly assimilating all the new information. Then Evan focused on Zondra again.

She recognized the demand in that. "First, the female typically sucks the secondary and gets a mouthful of the *Zhigaaal*. While the anointing will arouse her, that step will render her momentarily drugged and unable to move. But that is short-lived. When she comes out of that, she's in a frenzy and fights the male if she can." Zondra trailed the fingertips of one hand over the injury she'd given him. "He often has to subdue her."

His smile was all male satisfaction and interest. His cock rose, most likely at the idea of being asked to dominate her.

Or it's the memories of our first night together.

"I think I can handle that," Evan offered smoothly.

"He uses the secondary inside her..." She glanced up at Evan, at a loss for a moment to continue in front of Rayn.

"Pussy?" Evan suggested.

Zondra nodded. "Yes. Like when she sucks him, it will drug her for a moment only. With each infusion, at this stage, it will make her more frantic."

"Go on."

"The next step is using the secondary...uh..."

"In the ass?" he guessed.

She winced at his crass description. Humans often found that a perversion, she'd heard. Would Evan be repulsed by it or aroused? "Yes. Often they accomplish the final step while they perform that one."

"Which would be?" he asked.

Rayn started to talk, and Evan shot him a quelling look.

"Zondra will fill in the blanks, if you don't mind."

"Of course, Duncan." He waved a hand to Zondra.

She nodded. "The *Zhigaaal* makes the female crazy. It sets off a burn not unlike the quickening."

"The mating urge I sated, you mean."

"Yes. Your cum will cool that burn and soothe the ache, much as it did that night."

"I see." He seemed to consider that closely and carefully. Just when Zondra would have questioned him, Evan started speaking again. "I'll use the secondary for some of the times I double penetrate her. But I'm not claiming Zondra with a strap-on, when we could both be enjoying what we're doing."

"Are you sure?" Dr. Rayn asked.

Zondra's heart skipped at the press of Evan's fingers, trailing up the center line of her buttocks as if in consideration.

"Absolutely," he rumbled.

"And you concur?"

She nodded.

"Okay then. I'll have them make the secondary on the mold we already have. In the meantime, we'll fit the *Zhigaaal* bladder to your own cock. If you decide to use it on the secondary for some reason, you'll be able to move it from one to the other without resetting the straps. In the meantime, we need to run more tests. And there are a few other differences between what has to happen and what Xxanian males usually do during mating. We'll go over them."

Evan smiled a big old shit-eating grin. "While we take care of that, I have a few requests. Things I'll need before we start...mating."

Zondra stared at him, at a loss to explain what he meant by that. His expression said she wouldn't be finding out until he damn well wanted her to.

Chapter Seven

Evan panned his gaze over his preparations, smiling at what was to come. He'd given Zondra orders, and he didn't doubt that she was following them to the letter.

Just the thought of it had him hard, and he considered putting the bladder on.

No. That is something Zondra is going to do for me...for us.

Still, he reran his orders in his mind, allowing himself to visualize her preparations. Precum beaded at the head of his cock in excitement.

Zondra would have used the enema first, preparing herself for the one pleasure he hadn't indulged in yet.

The bath would have been next on her agenda. He'd ordered her to be thorough...and attentive. She would return to him tasting of climax and not until she did.

As if in answer to the thought, she sauntered into the room. Her gaze locked on the restraints on the bed, and she came to a halt, seemingly stunned.

Evan closed on her position and wrapped his arms around her. "You're going to look so beautiful. Tied down and open to everything I do to you." He paused at the scent of her rising *Zhigaaah.* "It won't last long. Once you're in the full frenzy, you'll do anything I say. Won't you?"

"I will now."

"Now," he conceded. "And then. But when you're mindless, you're going to try to fight me. I will not allow that."

She seemed skittish at the prospect of being tied down.

He stroked a fingertip along her lower lip. "You are my mate, and I love you, but you will be bound." He smiled. "Considering what I have planned for you in those restraints, you will beg me to use them again."

Her raised eyebrows and pursed lips said she wasn't so sure he could count on that.

"Did you follow my orders?" he asked.

"I told you I *would.*" It was as close to mutiny as she'd come since Pira's office.

Evan thrust his hand between her thighs and started finger fucking her with his index and middle fingers. Zondra's eye slits narrowed, and she moaned. He rewarded her with a massage of her clit with the rough pad of his thumb.

"Tell me what you want, Zondra."

Her knees trembled against his. "Mating."

"More specific."

"Your *Zhigaaal*—"

"More specific."

"Your cock...everywhere."

Evan eased his hand out of her. "Then you can start by getting on your knees and sucking me."

Zondra took a step back, stopping at the sight of his bare cock. Her head tipped to one side in consideration. Or perhaps she was asking a silent question.

86

"You get to do the honors, after you suck me. But don't make me come. I want all my cum for your ripening."

She sank to her knees, her lips parting. Her mouth was hot and wet. Evan swore he could feel her salivating against the head of his cock. Her moan worked its way up his cock, and she started moving back and forth along his length.

There was something of an adrenaline rush in knowing a woman could shred your cock with a mouthful of serrated hunting teeth but chose to suck you instead. Evan allowed that thought to push him toward climax.

No. There are more important things to do. "Stand up."

Zondra released his length, laid a lick over the head, and stood.

He picked up the greased leather cock ring and slid it on, hissing out a breath at the pressure it was putting at the base of his cock. *Deal with it. It will let me get Zondra into the full frenzy without counteracting what I'm doing to her.*

She stared at the device, clearly at a loss to understand what he was doing. Evan didn't offer an explanation. Instead he handed her the pump that would be strapped on to his cock. Zondra didn't hesitate. In moments, the unit was in place.

She looked up at him, seemingly confused at what to do next. Evan took her by the hand and led her to the bed. Again she stopped and stared at the restraints. Her breathing went ragged, but her scent said she wasn't too frightened or unnerved to find the scene arousing.

He lifted Zondra and settled her in the middle of the bed. Her attention wandered to the covered mirror, and Evan cupped her chin and guided her gaze back to him.

"You know the drill," he reminded her. "The speaker and mic will be open, but the mirrors will be covered." Even that much rankled, but Rayn had insisted that the chance of a human male reacting to the mating frenzy badly was too high to ignore. Someone would listen to everything they did and intervene if it seemed either of them was in distress.

Let them whack off to what they hear. It would serve them right to suffer days of blue balls for being voyeurs.

She nodded, and Evan released her chin.

There was no question what he had to get accomplished to bind her to him and little more question about the general order it had to happen in. But this wasn't going to be a clinical experience for either of them. Not if he had anything to say about it.

Evan eased Zondra to the bed with him and captured her lips for a brief but heated kiss. Her *Zhigaaah* beckoned, and Evan rubbed his fingertips along the ducts that secreted the heady pheromone. The stimulation forced her production into overdrive, and he feasted on it.

Zondra tipped her head back, opening her throat to his suckling mouth. The move also pushed her breasts to his chest.

The invitation was too enticing to ignore. Evan supported himself on one hand and used the other to perform a rough massage of her breasts.

Sharp little sounds escaped her throat, and she wiggled away from him. Evan responded by pinning her shoulders to the mattress, and she screamed in delight. He nipped at her throat, prompting a second one.

Her retreat thwarted and her arousal approaching a sharp peak he'd seen on countless occasions in their short time together, Zondra settled beneath him. Evan stroked his hand down her body, circling lightly at her hairless mound and then her clit.

"*Seir*-God, yes!" Her shout echoed off the walls.

Hope the voyeurs' ears ring for a week. That brought a smile to Evan's face.

He moved his fingers from her body to the pump attached to his and pressed the smaller of the two buttons on it. His condensed *Zhigaaal* oozed out the end of the tube and slid a fiery trail down his cock.

The effect was less noticeable against his calloused fingertips than it was against the more sensitive skin of his cock. At the first circle over one pebbled nipple, Zondra arched beneath him with what was most likely a curse in Xxan. Before she had a chance to react, he'd refreshed the slick of *Zhigaaal* on his fingers and anointed the other.

That wrenched a shout that sounded like shock from her. Evan forced his weight down, preparing for a fight that never came. He rolled her nipples between his fingers, his cock complaining at her whispered pleas.

Her head rocked back on her neck, and Evan seized the opportunity to collect more *Zhigaaal* and anoint the ducts at her throat. Her breathing went choppy, and she shuddered hard beneath him.

"Did you come?" he teased.

"Yes." Her voice was slurred already, and he'd barely begun.

"You know what I'm going to do next."

Zondra shook her head, but whether she was begging him not to continue yet or was telling him she was too muddled to remember was uncertain.

"Oh yes, Zondra. I am." He pressed the small button again, renewing the coating of *Zhigaaal* on his cock.

At the first glide of the head down her clit and slit, she shouted something in Xxan.

I have got to learn her language. Her exclamations were lost on him, though the fact that she couldn't seem to remember to speak English was a compliment in itself.

Zondra pitched up from the mattress, and Evan muscled her down, pinning her wrists to the bed.

"Don't make me restrain you yet," he warned. "I'd hoped you'd manage a little longer."

She glanced at the restraints waiting for her and shook her head. "Not yet," she agreed.

Slowly, purposefully, Evan stroked the length of his cock between her thighs, leaving a coat of *Zhigaaal* over her intimate flesh.

Her muscles tightened and relaxed, and her eye slits dilated until only a hint of the green-gold remained around the black ellipses.

"You like that," he grumbled. "Now that the *Zhigaaal* is soaking in."

"It burns." But it was said without conviction.

"A good burn. You like it."

"Oh yes," she moaned. Her hips tipped back and forth, aiding him.

Evan backed away, using the *Zhigaaal* on the underside of his cock to paint her inner thighs. He knelt up between her ankles, renewing the musk for the next step in the mating dance.

Zondra pulled her legs up and pressed her thighs together, gasping out pleas for him to finish what he'd started.

"There's no turning back, Zondra." It was only fair to warn her. "The minute you take my cock in your mouth, you're choosing to be my mate."

"Yes. Now."

He nodded, and she came to her knees, facing him. Her mouth brushed against his, then trailed down his body, leaving heat in its wake. She paused at the head of his cock, and he jerked in response to the taunt. Just when he would have demanded she continue, Zondra sucked in his cock.

"Fuck, yes. Oh...fuck!" He fisted his hand in her dark hair and guided Zondra up and down his length.

Words stuck at the back of his throat and came out rough and breathless. "Swallow the *Zhigaaal*. Swallow now."

The move forced a ragged cry from him. *Now. She's ready now.* And the sooner he sent her into a frenzy, the sooner he could come and end this torture.

Evan forced his cock to the back of her throat, groaning at the compression on the head. They'd told him the musk would relax her muscles, but he hadn't been sure it would relax them enough to suppress her gag reflex.

It was time for the larger button. Evan held her head in place and pushed it.

Zondra swallowed reflexively, and Evan released her. She rose to her knees, already in a daze, looked at him with unfocused eyes, and crumpled into his waiting arms.

It won't last long. He closed one padded shackle on her right wrist, then the other on her left. Laying her on the bed, Evan reached for the first of the matching ankle shackles.

It was too late. Zondra pulled her legs back in a clumsy attempt at fighting him. The fact that she was still disoriented allowed him to grasp her by the thighs and thrust inside her welcoming body.

Her climax was sweet torture on his leashed cock. Evan used her preoccupation with the sensation to press the larger button again, prompting the jet of *Zhigaaal* into her contracting body.

She screamed, her muscles tightening until she bowed up from the bed. Zondra collapsed to the mattress again.

Evan didn't hesitate. Before her glassy eyes focused again, she was spread-eagle on the mattress, all four limbs chained down.

Zondra pulled weakly at the shackles, and Evan smiled. Knowing how strong the Xxan were, he'd chosen metal chains and shackles instead of web or cloth she might have been able to tear or snap. Then he'd had Tim arrange to have the links and welds reinforced. The sex toys—while still padded for her comfort and safety—would hold a *Grea* Elder now.

* * * *

"Time to play."

Evan's voice cleared some of the cotton batting out of her head, and Zondra tried to make sense of what he was saying. That was a lost cause. Her mind was disjointed and prone to wander, thanks to his *Zhigaaal* coursing through her system and changing her.

Motions of his hands drew her attention, and she dimly noted that he was changing out the *Zhigaaal* cartridge. She tried to make sense of that. He'd expended the first one already? The calculations shouldn't have taxed her, but Zondra conceded defeat.

The burning in her gut eclipsed all else. Her mouth was parched, but Evan's taste echoed pleasantly. She licked her lips, trying to wet them, but the remaining *Zhigaaal* seared them instead.

She pulled at the chains, causing the metal to clack and clank. Evan looked up at the sounds, his eyes going hot in arousal, the edges crinkling in amusement.

"So beautiful," he whispered. "I knew you would be."

In the next heartbeat, he was inside her, his hands positioning her and dampening the impact of his wild thrusting on her bound limbs. It was too much.

Not enough.

Too much! Climax crested and rushed along her extremities. Zondra's *Zhigaaal*-coated throat protested her scorching screams.

Evan released the *Zhigaaal*, sending the acid wave through her relaxed *os* and into her womb. Her body tightened until the padded shackles bit into her wrists and ankles. Then she went limp in the restraints, boneless in the numbness of a really good endorphin rush.

"I can't wait much longer," Evan growled.

She tried to make sense of the manic look in his eyes, but her mind refused the simplest commands.

Her body recovered faster. The searing she'd only vaguely recognized moments before got stronger and stronger. Her attempts to close her thighs ended with the frustrating yank of the chains.

Half-crazed for his cum, Zondra wiggled to the extent the chains allowed. His still-hard cock stirred the musk against her engorged tissues, massaging it into the porous layer of mucous membrane.

Evan lifted slightly at her shoulders, urging her gaze up to his face. Once he had her gaze locked with his, he pushed deep inside her and released the *Zhigaaal*.

It was so abrupt and unexpected, Zondra's lungs seized. She stared up at him, marveling at how ruthless the move had been. They'd ordered Evan to plant his *Zhigaaal* in her womb at least three times before moving on, and he had done it in the most efficient way possible.

Her loosening muscles allowed her trapped air to escape in a rush. Her scream gave vent to the torture of the musk rebuilding her womb, ripening her for him. She lay on the mattress, panting her way through the confusing patchwork of sensations assaulting her system.

Evan rose up over her, his expression intense. His cock moved over her anus, spreading the *Zhigaaal*. Zondra arched up, and he planted a hand on her hip and forced her down onto the head again.

One of his fingers worked through the ring of muscle, using the musk to ease the way and relax the muscles he touched. One finger became two, and she moaned at the gentle pressure of him spreading her open. The soft head touched the open iris. Before she could try to retreat again, he sent the jet of *Zhigaaal* through the gap.

Zondra thrashed for the moment until the *Zhigaaal* incapacitated her. Evan didn't waste the time. In a blur of motion, he'd changed out the cartridge.

He worked at his engorged cock, then held something up for her to see. Her muddled mind arrived at the bit of leather he'd put on before she strapped on the pump. She had no more clue what it was now that she had when he'd put it on, but the fact that he pitched it across the room clearly meant he had no more use for it.

Sensations returned with excruciating slowness. As if he'd timed it perfectly, one of the first wisps that registered in her aching, needing body was his cock pushing into her *Zhigaaal*-filled ass.

His stomach muscles tensed and flexed, faster and faster. His sounds were harsh and guttural.

Her clearing head ordered the chaos into the stark reality of Evan pounding his cock into her ass. Every stroke sent shock waves through the scant barrier of flesh and tantalized her *Zhigaaal*-soaked vaginal tissues.

The waves of cum soothed the burn in her ass but did nothing for the need clawing at her, due to the other orifices burning for more.

And I thought the quickening was maddening. Mating was a hundred times worse. A thousand times better.

"You want me to come in your pretty little pussy." Evan didn't question it.

"I need it," she admitted. "I'm incinerating."

"We'll use the bath soon."

Her move to question what he intended next ended when he left her body. The ankle shackles snapped open. It happened too fast to be a key, which meant he'd had a quick-release button all the time.

Releasing her now was dangerous. She could hurt him.

No. Zondra acknowledged that she wouldn't do that. *I can't do it.*

As if he knew it, Evan took his time, turning her over. He positioned Zondra on her knees, her hands stretched toward the headboard of the bed. The shackles were centimeters apart, thanks to the chains that crossed over each other when he flipped her body.

Evan paused, his cock lightly breaching her outer lips.

"Please. I need you." Zondra trembled. The fire licking at her innards stole her strength and left her feeling weak as a kitten.

"You're mine, Zondra."

"Only yours. Evan, pl—"

She gasped as his cock slipped up her channel to the hilt.

"The next move is yours," he informed her. "Give yourself to me."

Zondra didn't question that. He wanted her to complete the step that would finish her ripening. She started moving, working his cock in and out, drinking in his sounds and scents.

He is mine. Evan will always be mine.

The rest was a blur of frantic motion, hers and his alike. The cum neutralized the acid burn to a heat that invited more without the gut-wrenching madness shackling her mind as easily as Evan had shackled her body.

Zondra sank to the bed, exhausted already, though logically she knew they'd just begun. In everything she'd heard about mating, this weakness and fatigue didn't factor in.

We spent nearly two weeks in bed in preparation. Other mating couples don't do that. Zondra let her eyes slip shut, certain that was the reason.

The infusion of *Zhigaaal* from the pump wrenched a weak cry from her, half in longing and half in protest.

"Not nearly done," Evan muttered.

Tired or not, Zondra wanted him again.

Chapter Eight

Evan drifted toward consciousness, every muscle lax and warm. Zondra was sheltered in the curve of his body, her back to his chest. One of his arms anchored her against him. The other acted as a pillow for her head.

He smiled, swallowing down a chortle of laughter he couldn't account for.

Zondra stretched, and Evan rolled her toward him, levering himself over her on the mattress, the sheets and blankets cocooning them in. He wrapped his arms around her and nuzzled her lips.

The kiss was slow and deep. Their hands roamed. Sparks of arousal rekindled the fires of mating, and Evan spread Zondra's thighs.

The speaker crackled, and Evan left her lips long enough to toss a "Fuck off, Rayn" at the covered mirror.

"Sorry, Duncan." That was Tim. "We need to get some tests."

"They can wait until we're done." He tangled his fingers in her hair and slid deep inside her.

Zondra rose against him with a moan, her fingernail-like talons biting the flesh of his back.

"Come on, Duncan. We need to get some figures to make sure Zondra's blood chemistry is stabilizing. And that yours is. Even if you don't care about your own, let us check her."

He powered his hips back and forth, his sensitized cock rocketing toward another explosive release. "Won't take long," he informed the assistant.

As if in agreement, Zondra shouted out her release, her talons drawing blood. Evan followed her, savoring the sweet pleasure and pain sensations coursing through him.

A hum of satisfaction escaped his chest, then laughter.

"Now, Duncan?" Tim prodded him.

"Give us a few minutes."

"Five."

He bristled at the attitude, but it seemed impossible to stay angry this morning. "Maybe," he offered flippantly.

Tim grumbled something that was probably a curse, and the speaker and mic unit turned off.

Zondra sighed. "Lab rat time."

"Not for long," he promised. "How many tests could they possibly have left to run on us?"

One arched brow was his only answer.

* * * *

"I've never seen blood chemistry fluctuate like this," Tamsen complained.

Evan glared at him from a second table set ten meters away, his anger spiking at the sight of Zondra looking so close to tears she couldn't shed. Three days after the mating cycle had ended, they were no closer to answers about why her blood chemistry wasn't settling. His had settled well, according to Tim, but Zondra's system was still in an uproar.

"Did the mating take or not?" he snapped back. "Is she ripened?" If they went through all of this, and he still couldn't be what she needed, it would likely kill them both...literally.

Not to mention there were other unanswered questions, like Zondra's need to sleep for longer than normal periods during the mating and her need to eat during it. All the way around, their mating hadn't borne much resemblance to what he'd been told to expect.

Not that he was complaining. He had never spent three more decadent days in his life.

"Oh, it worked, but something else is going on here. Something I'm just not seeing, but damned if I know what and why."

"Is it dangerous?"

He hesitated for a long moment. "I shouldn't think so." Tamsen focused on Zondra. "You said your fertile cycle took an extended period to settle? After your stripe turned blue, I mean?"

She nodded. "More than a month. My *gran-seir* was very upset by it."

Tim looked up at Tamsen. "That's more than double the norm. Maybe her system is resistant to change. With the mix of human and Xxanian genes, stranger things have happened."

Tamsen grunted his agreement. "Maybe. I still want to run more tests."

Evan's patience snapped with a pop that resounded in his ears. It was probably the tension in his jaw causing the sensation, but the timing was the perfect spur to action. "Take them, and then we're leaving," he announced. That decided, he started dismantling the scan plate and sensors on his own body.

Tim looked like he was about to argue, but Evan cut him off at the pass.

"He said it's not dangerous. You said it's likely just her system taking its time to change. Take the tests, and we're going back to our lives. I have a wedding to arrange and paperwork to fill out...clothing to move into our new quarters... Call us back on my days off every week if necessary, but let us the blazes out of here." Just the thought of rooms with no mics and mirrors heated his blood.

The assistant's expression pleaded with him. "What if we take the tests and something comes back that explains it? Something that needs medical intervention?"

"Then MacNair will have us back here in less than an hour."

Tim and Tamsen shared a look of calculation.

The speaker grid on the far wall came to life. "Let them," Rayn ordered. "For all we know, it's the stress of being here causing this."

Evan couldn't agree more. The sooner they were away from SLAL, the better for all of them.

Chapter Nine

"Aft ten, number six," Pap Mac reminded her, as if Zondra didn't have a nearly photographic memory. "I'll be right down."

Zondra offered an irreverent salute and scurried down the steep staircase, all but giggling in happiness. She stared at the rings Evan had placed on her finger just that morning. She was officially Zondra Duncan, witnessed by two of the officers at SLAL and filed onto Evan's Page Two.

Officially his wife. Officially his mate. Unofficially assigned to the carrier, with the duty of teaching a group of officers the Xxan language.

It was amazing that no one had thought to hire the Xxanian crossbreeds to teach the classes before. What they knew of the language, they'd learned from Pap Mac and passed person to person to create a handful of translators. But translators weren't of much use in the field, when a common language might prove beneficial.

Pap Mac had arranged the job with Captain Pira. Pira had been willing to do nearly anything to avoid losing Evan. If keeping him meant arranging a reason for Zondra to be aboard the vessel and giving them a junior officer's stateroom to live in, it was a small price to pay. Not to mention his troops would be premiere. Translators were in short supply, and cross-training was a favorite tactic used by commanding officers.

Even the scientists' caution as they'd left SLAL couldn't drag her spirits down. They'd run a full battery of tests and fretted that her blood chemistry had changed in ways they hadn't expected it to and not settled completely after mating. They hadn't wanted Evan and Zondra to leave the space station, but Evan had put his foot down and insisted the scientists had worn out their welcome in the bedroom.

Depending on the results of those tests, she and Evan might have to return to the complex. The thought that something might be wrong left a buzzing apprehension she couldn't shake.

Zondra glanced up, making the next-to-final turn to the staterooms from memory. A long-ago tour of this class of warship provided the mental map she needed to navigate.

"Well, well, well..."

The snide voice sent unpleasant tremors along her nerves. Zondra denied the identity her mind supplied, even as she conceded she was correct.

She turned, facing Reynolds. A wave of revulsion threatened to bring her lunch up. For a race that didn't typically vomit, that was quite the accomplishment. The Subdominant stepped toward her, and she backed off a pace.

"Now is that nice?" he chided, his expression intense.

Zondra kept backing away, calculating that the stateroom she sought was no more than twenty meters and one turn behind her. Reynolds followed. It was time to remind him that he had limits.

"This time I will press charges, Petty Officer Reynolds," she warned.

"For?" he inquired coolly. "I'm just walking down a corridor on my ship."

"Walk somewhere else." Unless he'd been summoned here to repair something, Reynolds had no business on this deck. "Enlisted berthing is halfway across the ship, and engineering is three decks away."

He seemed surprised that she knew the layout of the ship so well. "And what are you doing here, little cock-tease?"

Evan's scent enveloped her a moment before his arm encircled her body. A breath-stealing moment later, her mate was between them, Zondra fit snug under his arm.

"My wife's daily routine is none of your business, Reynolds." There was a bite of something unforgiving in that warning.

"Wife? What the hell are you—"

Zondra pressed her left hand to Evan's ribs, and Reynolds stopped speaking, gaping at the rings she now wore.

"Is there a problem, Evan?" Pap Mac asked.

Evan didn't reply.

"Zondra?"

"I believe Petty Officer Reynolds was just leaving, Pap," she managed in a steady voice.

"Yes, he is, Admiral," Evan agreed.

Reynolds offered a tense word of agreement and laid tracks in the opposite direction. Once Pap Mac was between the two adversaries, Evan turned Zondra and guided her to the open doorway of their stateroom.

"Is Reynolds a problem?" Pap Mac asked.

Evan addressed his answer to Zondra. "Next time I tell you to press charges, I expect you to *do* it."

She winced. "The quickening—"

"Zondra, the right answer is 'Absolutely. I will.'"

"If I had, I would have been stuck with someone other than you, you realize," she snapped at him.

Evan's hands fisted and then eased open. "Stuck with?" he challenged.

At a loss for words, Zondra pressed to his chest and raised her face for a kiss. "Not stuck with for you," she breathed. "Only if it was someone else."

* * * *

Like Reynolds. The idea was intolerable. Evan dragged her into a heated kiss. His body reacted fiercely, and he considered kicking MacNair out to finish what he'd started.

Two deep breaths that did nothing to calm his lust later, he turned to find MacNair leaning against the now closed corridor door, a smirk on his face. That just added fuel to the fire.

"I thought you said mating would end this," he grumbled.

MacNair chuckled. "Jealousy is forever, son. Just don't kill anyone. But..." He jerked a thumb toward the corridor. "Charges? I'll assume Reynolds was the dumb-ass from the bar that you pounded down, but...charges? Is there a problem I should know about?"

"Only if he wants to die," Evan offered dryly.

"Not killing anyone does extend to Reynolds. If there's a problem, I can arrange a transfer." He let the offer hang between them.

He thinks I can't handle my own problems? A knock at the door cut Evan off with only a syllable of his protest voiced. "What?" he barked instead.

"You and your wife are requested at Med Call, Duncan."

"On our way," MacNair answered for him.

Evan glared at him. "I am through being someone's lab rat. And so is Zondra." The admiral's preoccupation stopped him there, and the hair at the back of Evan's neck rose in warning. "What is it?"

"I don't know. But, believe me, Med Call was not expecting to run their own tests on you. SLAL is the only division that should be working with you...unless..."

He didn't finish the thought, but he didn't need to. The only reason for Med Call to summon them was if there were problems with the tests SLAL had taken.

Zondra looked up at them, seemingly at a loss for words.

Evan offered his hand. "Whatever it is, you have me."

MacNair wisely kept his mouth shut. Though it went without saying that he was there for Zondra, the thought of him saying it went up Evan's back like sandpaper.

She took his hand and snuggled against Evan's chest. His nerves jumping, Evan guided her to Med Call, MacNair in their wake.

The two doctors on call looked up at their approach. The younger of the two hurried over and reached for Zondra.

Evan shoved him back before he could connect, and an oppressive silence grew.

"Don't kill them," MacNair muttered.

He nodded, though the need to crack heads was riding him hard. "What do you think you're doing?"

The one he'd shoved away motioned to the exam bed. "SLAL asked us to confirm one of the blood tests they ran last night with a scan."

Zondra started toward the bed, and Evan restrained her.

"Which test?" he asked. "No one touches my wife without me knowing why and approving it."

The doctor glanced over Evan's shoulder, seeking out MacNair.

The latter didn't wait for a question to emerge. "Son, you are talking to a bonded Dominant male as deadly as any Xxanian warrior in existence. You do not ask *me* what to do about his mate."

"Yes, sir." He met Evan's gaze solidly, but there was a tremor in his hand that said he'd rather deal with the admiral. "One of the tests had an...unexpected result. They think it's a false—"

"Which?" Evan grumbled.

"They...um...they said telling you would be—"

"Which. Test?" Every muscle in his body tightened down.

"Tell him," MacNair ordered. "You do not taunt a Dominant with a problem with his mate this way. It's a good way to get a scan plate inserted anally."

The senior doctor answered from the far side of the exam bed. "Pregnancy, but it must be a false—" He stopped talking when Evan moved.

The closer doctor fled to the far side of the bed with his boss. The older one backed toward the code pad and the emergency call button for the Marine guards.

"You won't need that," Evan informed him. He lifted Zondra onto the bed gently. "Do the test."

She reached for his hand, and Evan took it. Words failed him. This was life altering, exhilarating...and terrifying. He stared at her, trying his best to avoid obsessing over the plate hovering over her lower abdomen.

The doctors chattered on in the background.

"They were so sure this would be negative, they left it for last."

"I heard they nearly missed it."

"Those guys? SLAL never screws up that badly."

"Oh, like you have firsthand knowledge of them."

Evan snapped. "Answers. Now."

Silence fell.

"Oh, man," the younger one breathed. "There he is."

"He?" Zondra asked.

The other made a vague sound of agreement. "How old do you figure he is?"

"He," Evan repeated. *I have a son. I have to learn how to be a father.*

Zondra smiled and squeezed his hand.

"Ask SLAL. Xenobiology is not my field. I don't know how these sca—"

The senior doctor elbowed him hard enough to knock the air out of his rude young counterpart. He hurried into an explanation before Evan could launch across the table and throttle the bigoted asshole.

"Xxanian fetuses develop faster than human, but I can't say how quickly because this one isn't pure Xxan. If the baby was human, I'd say conception took place between three weeks and a month ago."

"A week," Evan informed him. "We mated and ripened her womb a week ago."

The two doctors stared at each other. The tension rising in the room made Evan's skin crawl.

"What? Damn it, tell me."

"Even by Xxanian standards, I'd expect the baby to be...say double that or a little less. I mean, the—"

"Impossible."

"The Xxan carry for about half a normal human—"

"She wasn't ripened! Are you fucking dense?"

MacNair moved to one side, his glare a message to calm himself.

"Maybe she's human enough that she didn't need ripening," the younger one suggested.

Zondra bit her lower lip, shaking her head in what was surely a sign that she couldn't answer that, one way or the other.

Evan reined in his frustration. "You're telling me it could have been our first night together. Or while we were traveling to SLAL. Or when we mated. In short, you're clueless."

The older doctor cleared this throat. "How long did you gestate, Mrs. Duncan?"

"Six months."

"But her brother gestated for five," MacNair added. "Her *seir* did as well."

"Strong Xxanian genes then," he mused.

"So you're saying there's no way to tell?" Evan asked.

"We might be able to get a closer idea by charting the baby's growth every week over several months. Or you could return to SLAL and let them run more tests."

"No. We are through being lab rats," Evan decided. "We'll wing it."

"No," Zondra agreed. "Evan and I both have work to attend to."

He smiled widely and kissed her cheek.

The senior doctor didn't hide his disappointment well. "We'll see you back in a month for her routine check then."

"No," MacNair inserted. "SLAL will."

That time, the doctor scowled.

Too bad, old man. No scaly baby for your amusement.

Chapter Ten

The snickering at the back of the classroom warned Zondra that the jokers of the group were preparing their first prank. She'd hoped for half a day of peace before it started, but that wasn't in the battle plans.

Oh, well. Set the pace now instead of later.

She turned to them. "My name is Zondra Duncan. I am a second generation Xxan-human crossbreed, and I will be teaching you the Xxan language. Before we begin, are there any questions?" It was bait for whatever trap they thought to spring.

Two hands signaled for her attention. One was insistent and the other tentative. She nodded to the hesitant one.

"I know this class is intended for troops in battle and interrogation teams, but I was wondering if we could cover medical aid as well."

That surprised her. "In what way?"

The young corpsman darkened. "How would a Xxanian warrior ask for medical aid?"

"He would not. Your average Xxanian warrior will die before he asks for aid. It will be up to you to sedate or restrain your prisoner to test and treat him. Make sure to use restraints appropriate to a Dominant, even if you aren't certain of his status."

He opened his mouth to respond, and Zondra continued.

"By Xxanian beliefs, a warrior who asks for aid or begs for mercy is a coward...a pathetic weakling. Forcing care on him will actually save his honor, as well as his life. Assume all captured Xxanian warriors are injured until testing proves otherwise.

"In the same way, you will be treated better by the Xxan if you do not ask for their aid. It would be best if I didn't teach you how to ask at all."

The corpsman hesitated, then nodded. "I think I understand."

"However, knowing you are a human medic will work to your favor when captured. The Xxan would prefer to allow humans to tend to their own rather than waste Xxanian resources on enemies.

"To tell them, you will say zhahhh zee etthhh ahh."

Before the corpsman could repeat it, the other man who'd motioned for her attention asked the impertinent question she'd suspected was coming from him.

"How do I tell him I'm going to peel his scaly skin from his corpse?" His eyes were cold and his smile more of a warning than a sign of humor.

Zondra pretended to consider it. "You want to compliment your enemy?"

His eyes narrowed, and his smile went brittle. "How is that a compliment?"

"Having scales means he's a Xxanian warrior and not a human soldier. And someone bold enough to make such a threat is either a stupid Subdominant or a formidable Dominant." She searched out his rank and found him a lieutenant. "Since most men of your rank and rate are...passably Dominant, he will assume the latter is true."

The man gaped at her, seemingly stunned by her assessment.

"That means your death will honor him. After a threat like that, he will kill you or die trying to. And if he does fell you, he will take your threat to you, perhaps while you are still breathing. If you scream, he will make it last longer."

Several of the soldiers went pasty, and a few swallowed down what was probably the urge to vomit. Humans were so easy to disgust.

Zondra sauntered between the rows of desks toward her prey. "If you wish to intimidate a Xxanian Dominant, it cannot be accomplished. If you wish to insult him..." She placed her hands on his desk and leaned forward. "Zhoe zhathhh s'huuu zayahh ta."

A bark of laughter from behind her drew Zondra's gaze. She turned her back on the stunned lieutenant and headed for Aleeks with a smile of welcome.

"That will get him killed for certain," her brother opined. "Only a Subdominant would be careless enough to lose after that."

"His attitude will get him killed," Zondra dismissed the concern.

Aleeks's jaw tightened, and he assessed the soldier as a threat to her.

"What does it mean?" the man in question asked, oblivious to the scrutiny.

Yes, his attitude will get him killed. Probably before he learns better tactics and situational awareness.

Aleeks answered before she could. "'You are impotent and should be clothed as a woman.'"

"Zoey zath shoe say ah ta?" he asked, grasping at the sounds he remembered.

Zondra shot him a bland look. As she'd expected, he'd ignored the warning Aleeks offered about how a Xxanian warrior would react to it. "You think telling him you prefer fucking his brother rather than his sister will make him fall down laughing and allow you an easy kill? I don't think that is wise. Neither do I think it will work."

Aleeks didn't bother to stifle his snort of laughter. His eyes glittered in amusement.

Of course, he knew that wasn't what the lieutenant had said, but gibberish wasn't acceptable. By the time the men learned enough Xxan to know she'd lied, they would have forgotten what he'd said.

"How *do* you say it?" he grumbled.

She smiled. "There are sixty-two base sounds in Xxan. Once you can make them all, you can learn to speak the language." Zondra glanced at Aleeks. "Don't you have somewhere else to be?"

Her brother shook his head. "And miss this? I don't think so."

But his sideward glance toward the lieutenant said he was staying to protect her.

* * * *

"You know, I heard something very interesting, Jobel," Reynolds taunted.

"Oh yeah? What's that?"

By his tone, Evan could tell Jobel was less than interested. Since almost none of what Reynolds said was worthy of attention, Evan was personally trying to tune it out as well. Sometimes it was better to let Reynolds talk and feign interest. At least that way, the work got done without something Reynolds was working on breaking.

"I heard Duncan has been offering little school girls candy lately."

Evan froze with the wrench in hand. His heart was pounding, and the ventilation fans were the loudest sounds in the compartment. Evan didn't doubt that everyone was staring at him, waiting to see what his reaction to the accusation would be. He went back to work, tightening the bolt and fussing unnecessarily with other things to avoid looking at them. Reynolds could hang himself how he would.

The jackass in question moved closer, and Evan tightened his grip on the wrench, picturing teeth shattering to his swing.

"What is she, Duncan? A high school junior? Sophomore, maybe? How old is your child bride?"

"Zondra has bachelors in archeology and xenoliguistics." It was true and one of the many things he'd learned about her after the mating frenzy passed.

"Yeah. I've heard most of them go through school quickly."

Evan didn't reply to that. There was no need to. It was a fact. Instead he triple-checked the bolts for a tight fit.

Reynolds squatted down next to him, trying to catch Evan's eye. From anyone else, it might have been a challenge, but Reynolds wasn't man enough to make a challenge believable.

"So how old was she the first time you fucked her, Duncan?"

Reining in the urge to bust him in the mouth for that comment alone was difficult. Sarcasm was the lesser of two evils; it wouldn't land him in the brig. "Want a vicarious thrill, Reynolds? Can't get any of your own, so you want other people's adventures?"

"For the sake of argument, let's say I do."

A peek around showed everyone in engineering waiting for an answer. Evan made a show of securing the panel and turned his back to it.

That gave him time to consider his options. If he refused to answer, they'd make up their own stories, and those stories would likely be damning hyperbole. If he played it up, he could make Reynolds green with envy and ensure all that was passed was something resembling the truth.

"All right then. Since you're so hard up, I'll tell you. She was sixteen luscious years of virgin." His cock came up at the memory of their first night together. He'd decided in the last few days that their son had likely been conceived in the excesses of that night.

Reynolds gaped at him. Evan pretended to be oblivious to the response.

"Sixteen?" Jobel parroted, his eyes wide. "You are seriously shitting me."

"I didn't know it yet," he admitted. "Zondra is very mature for her age, being Xxanian. I thought she was drinking legal, at least."

"A virgin," Deacon groaned.

"Ohhhh, yeah." He drew that out, savoring the fact.

"How'd you find out?" Jobel asked.

"That she was a virgin?" Evan replied. "In the usual way."

"No. That she was sixteen?"

Evan laughed harshly. "Her family found us in bed together."

"Her family?" Reynolds had finally found his tongue and ripped it out of the cat's mouth.

"Well...her older brother, father, and godfather." He imagined facing her grandfather— or *gran-seir*, as Zondra called him—would have been very different and pretty bloody. Then again, he wasn't sure how a Xxanian *Grea* Elder would have interpreted the scene. He did know the elder of a nest ruled with an iron fist.

Jobel muttered something unintelligible. "Shit. That must have been ugly."

"All things considered, not too bad. I did give the admiral one hell of a shiner before we got it straightened out."

Deacon shifted closer. "Admiral? What admiral?"

"Guess I forgot to mention that." Evan hadn't forgotten it. He'd been saving it for the right moment.

"Spill," Jobel urged him. "How did an admiral get into the mix?"

"Zondra's godfather is Admiral MacNair. Course, I didn't know I was laying a punch on the fleet admiral when I did it."

There was a moment of stunned silence.

"Let me get this straight," Deacon stated. "You fucked Admiral MacNair's teenaged goddaughter."

Evan hooked his hands behind his neck and leaned his head back. "Yes, I most certainly did."

"He *caught* you in bed with her."

"At the lodge. Still going at it when they came through the door. Almost all night long and still going."

Jobel grumbled a series of curses.

Deacon continued. "You punched the old man in the face."

"He did have his own bruises," Reynolds griped.

"Bruise. Singular, and I was outnumbered," Evan reminded him. "But I held my own."

"And the admiral didn't crush you," Deacon marveled.

"On the contrary, he told us to decide what we wanted and helped us get married."

Reynolds snorted. "It was probably a shotgun wedding. A choice between military prison and marriage maybe. She pregnant, Duncan?"

He smiled. "We didn't know *that* when we got married, but...yes, she is pregnant." He shot a warning look at Reynolds. "To me. And no. It was not a choice of military prison or any other punishment and marriage. It was a choice of go our own ways or get married."

"You knocked up the fleet admiral's sixteen-year-old goddaughter?" Jobel exploded.

Evan smirked. "Oh yeah."

Deacon chuckled. "Man, you are either screwed for life or set for life."

Chapter Eleven

Zondra opened her eyes to the darkness, shivering at the empty space next to her, at the lack of Evan's warmth. She pushed from the mattress and donned a *S'suuhhea*, feeling exposed though she couldn't state why she would.

There was something too still, even for late on an evening when everyone who wasn't on duty would be ashore. Holiday weeks were like that. Those that could take leave took it and didn't look back. Those that couldn't celebrated however they could, legally or not.

Aside from the usual sounds of ventilation and machinery, there was nothing of note. A sudden wish for the sounds of the center nest assaulted her. Zondra closed her eyes, visualizing the whisper of the tabletop fountain as the rushing water of her gran-*seir's* water wall, the splash of water in the family pool, the rustling of plants—

It lasted only until the click of the lock.

She looked at the clock, her mind doing the calculation that it was too early for a meal break. If there had been an incident, the response would have woken her.

The door started to slide, and Zondra searched for a scent, recoiling from the sour smell of Reynolds. As if his scent wasn't unpalatable enough alone, he was unwashed and stank of cheap liquor, sweat, and grease.

Zondra folded herself into the clothing cabinet, working on stilling her air as she settled on the cold deckplates. She shut the door carefully. There was no way to know how sensitive Reynolds's hearing was. If he heard her, hiding would gain her nothing.

Reynolds crossed the room toward the bed, making a poor showing of stealth. A string of foul language left his lips. "Where the fuck is she?" The mattress rattled on the metal frame as he tore the sheets and blankets off the bed with a roar of frustration. The whisper of them landing on the floor caressed her abused ears.

Zondra listened for signs of running feet on the deck plates and shouts of alarm. Holiday or not, someone had to have heard him. There was no reaction. That was bad. It meant there was no one close enough to hear it if Reynolds attacked her.

His muttering was getting louder, a rambling nonsense. "Can't sleep. Don't dream of anything but you. Can't fuck anyone else. Little cock-tease bitch!"

She bit her lower lip, considering that. It sounded as if Reynolds had drawn in her *Zhigaaah*, but that was impossible. They hadn't had sex. She hadn't even touched him.

He touched me. Memories of his attack at the base club sent shivers down her spine. Reynolds *had* touched her. He'd burrowed his face in her hair. How much of her *Zhigaaah* had he inhaled? Was the change to him permanent?

If it has lasted this long, it likely is.

No. The doctors at SLAL can do something. If they made Zhigaaal for Evan, they can do something to reverse the effects on Reynolds. She prayed it was true and feared it wasn't so acutely that her stomach ached.

Reynolds started pacing back and forth, his voice and speed increasing intensity together. The first crash of glass against the metal bulkhead was so abrupt that Zondra had to swallow down a squeak of surprise.

The destruction went on, hiding any sound she might have made. Splintering stoneware and statuary overlapped with the splashing water that was probably from her beloved fountain.

It ended abruptly, and Reynolds laughed harshly at the destruction.

Most likely the pseudo-victory driving him. It wouldn't have been enough for a Dominant, but Reynolds wasn't a Dominant or even a true human alpha.

The tearing of fabric sent her heart skipping in a sickening non-rhythm. Zondra fingered the clothing hung around her. Would Reynolds attack only what he could see? Only the things that held a pungent scent? Or would he seek out every corner for more to destroy?

As if in reply, the cabinet door banged open.

For a long moment, they stared at each other. Reynolds panted hard, his hand fisted around the short work knife all members of engineering carried. The sheen of sweat on his skin and runnels of the same glistened in the shaft of light from the still-ajar corridor door.

The knife clattered to the debris-littered deck plates. Before she got her closer hand halfway to it, her wrist was trapped in one of his meaty fists.

Reynolds yanked Zondra out of the cabinet and to her feet.

A spearhead of glass sliced her, gouging from the ball of her foot to the height of her arch. She screamed and pulled the assaulted extremity up, shaking the shard loose.

He slapped her hard enough to snap her head aside. Zondra stumbled and fell onto a pile of quilt stuffing with a crunchy layer of shattered glass beneath it. In the next heartbeat, Reynolds was squatting beside her, his mouth pressed to hers. He tried to force her beneath him, and Zondra squirmed against his grip.

Her instincts warred with her training. Hiding had failed her, and without her mate to protect her, instinct dictated she escape and run to him. Her training was to do as much damage as she could to Reynolds on the way, to kill him if she could. He wasn't her mate, and he was touching her, hurting her, intent on raping her.

Both sides agreed she had to stop that last eventuality, whatever it took. Discounting the emotional damage a rape would do to both herself and Evan, she was carrying, and the physical damage was too much to risk.

For one mad moment, Zondra considered opening her mouth and using her hunting teeth against his tongue. The thought of tasting his blood made her physically ill, and the stench of him in close quarters prompted her gag reflex.

Instead she dug the fingernails of her free hand into his face and raked through his flesh with the crossbred talons. Reynolds reared back with a roar of rage and pain, giving Zondra the opening she needed to grasp the work knife and drive it into the hand compressing her wrist bones.

He released her with a howl of pain, and Zondra pushed past him, scurrying to the corridor. She hadn't considered where she'd go from there. Med Call was amidships; engineering was aft, just as she was. Evan was in engineering.

Zondra squeezed her eyes shut at the glare in the corridor. The overheads were set to low light for sleep, but even fifty percent was double what she considered a comfortable level. Movement behind her vetoed the idea of going back for her glasses, and she rushed toward the stairs, hobbling on her injured foot.

Working from her Xxanian memory, Zondra made the turns that led her to the stairs. She navigated the three levels down into the belly of the ship, then farther aft to the pressure tunnel.

The scent of oil and scrubbed air sent her stomach roiling, but she forced herself to breathe through her mouth. Without her eyes to guide her, she needed to tongue-scent. Halfway down the tunnel, she scented Evan. That was all it took to double her lagging speed.

* * * *

Evan looked around at the shouts from below, shaking his head in disbelief at the sight of Zondra.

There was no mistaking the green and gold *S'suuhhea* she wore that so closely matched her eyes. But why was she wearing it here? Though it covered her from beneath her arms to her ankles and had a thick loop of fabric around her neck, it wasn't something Xxanian women wore in public.

But the *S'suuhhea* wasn't the most disturbing part of the image. Her cheek was purpled and swollen, the tender flesh marked as even their roughest sex rarely did. Her left hand was coated in blood and gripping a blade, and she'd left a bloody trail into the engine room, most likely from the foot she was favoring.

The operators below had backed to their panels and were busy shooting nervous looks at one another. The JO on duty grabbed the code pad and summoned the Marines.

"Five minutes to defuse the situation or they'll kill her," he muttered. Evan dropped off the machine and sprinted to her, alarms blaring several decks away.

Zondra reached for him, sobbing.

He sidestepped the blade. "Knife, Zondra. Give me the knife." If she was unarmed when the Marines arrived, they had breathing room to solve this. *Whatever* this *is.*

Her hand came out, shaking hard, and she offered the weapon to him. Evan took it slowly, making a show of her willingness to release it. Once he had it, Zondra wrapped her arms around him and sank against his chest.

Evan stared at the work knife in confusion. His own was weighing down his right pocket, which meant she'd taken it from another crew member who used them. He turned it, searching out the engraved name and service number through the slick of tacky blood.

"Reynolds." *I will kill him for this.*

As if in answer to the challenge, the bastard stumbled through the tunnel doorway, blood coursing down his cheek and hand. "Guess I just have to kill him to have you," Reynolds mumbled.

Zondra fled to Evan's back, her breathing rasping and uneven.

"You scaly types get off on that, right? Two men fighting to the death for you. That's how you do it."

She shook her head against Evan's shoulder.

Evan took a step away from her, growling an order for her to stay where she was. Zondra sank to the deck plates, probably too exhausted to stand.

Or too injured.

Reynolds launched at him. That was the final blow, the one that shattered Evan's strained control. Evan dropped the work knife and laid a punch to Reynolds's chin that knocked the latter off his feet. He landed hard, and Evan came down over him, both fists raising bruises and crushing bone.

Someone grabbed him, and Evan threw the interloper off. Then there were two sets of hands pulling him off Reynolds...three...four.

When the rifle muzzle rammed into his chest, Evan put his hands up in surrender. He came back to his senses slowly, wincing at the amount of blood on his hands, splattered on his clothing, and soaking into the knees of his dungaree pants.

"Stand down," the Marine sergeant on the other side of the rifle ordered.

"Stood," he answered, unable to curb the inner smart-ass.

A second Marine reached a hand between them and searched out Reynolds's pulse. "Dead," he reported.

Evan closed his eyes, envisioning the trial to come. The best he could hope for was a military prison. If they handed down the death sentence, Zondra would pine to death after him, either taking the baby with her or leaving their son an orphan.

"Don't kill anyone."

Fucked that one up. Right, MacNair?

"Get the woman to Med Call." A dig of the muzzle into his ribs punctuated the order.

Evan opened his eyes as the second started moving. His fury uncorked. "You do not touch her," he thundered.

He tried to reason with himself. Zondra was injured. She needed care.

This wasn't a rational state. His bonded mate was injured and traumatized. "Reynolds assaulted her. Let me move her or—"

"You go to a cell in the brig, Duncan. Nowhere else. Not on my watch."

Evan scowled at him. "Then find a woman to help Zondra. She won't accept a man near her right now, and I won't accept one touching her." It was a blatant threat.

The two Marines shared a pained look. Finally the sergeant sighed. "Lieutenant, find out if Med Call has a female corpsman or doctor on duty."

"Roll one out if you have to," Evan added.

The Marine nodded his agreement, and the JO called it away. In the minutes following the call, more Marines arrived and took the place of the E-Divvers who'd restrained him.

Not that anyone had to muscle Evan into place anymore. He was content to kneel in the cooling puddle of Reynolds's blood and stare at Zondra.

She lay, curled on the deck plates, shivering, her eyes closed and inflamed. None of the men were stupid enough to approach her, which meant they'd all make it out of engineering alive...including Evan.

"Time to go, Duncan," the sergeant boring a hole in his chest announced.

"When the corpsman has Zondra," he countered.

"This isn't a discussion or a negotiation," the one at his right shoulder snapped.

"You're right. It's not."

The tension stepped up another notch, and the Marine who'd pronounced Reynolds dead waved them off. "Why fight him? You'll come quietly when she's gone?"

Evan managed one snap of his head in a nod.

"Then let him. What can it hurt?"

After a moment, the sergeant agreed.

The corpsman wasn't one Evan recognized, but she was female. Zondra roused to her call, though she seemed groggy, and she kept her eyes squeezed shut.

The light. "Give her my safety glasses," Evan requested.

"What?" the corpsman asked.

"My glasses." He jerked his chin down toward his shirt pocket. "They're shaded."

She liberated them from his shirt pocket and settled them on Zondra's face. "Come on, Mrs. Duncan," she urged, helping Zondra to her knees. "Doc is waiting at Med Call."

Zondra turned her head, assessing Evan's position. Her brows went up in surprise. "No. You can't. He—"

The Marine at his right shoulder tightened his grip. "Your husband is under arrest, Mrs. Duncan," he informed her.

Before she could protest, Evan did. "You're injured, Zondra. Go to Med Call and let them treat you. Contact Aleeks or MacNair. I want you safe at home. I can't protect you here."

The rifle gave another warning poke at his ribs. "That will be up to Captain Pira. If he lets her leave, she'll leave."

"He'll let her go home." Pira had to. Evan no longer believed she was safe on board.

Zondra hesitated and then nodded. She leaned to embrace him, and two of the Marines reached out to pull her back. Evan surged against the restraining hands, shouting a protest. Marines piled onto him, forcing Evan nearly to the deck plates. The corpsman yanked Zondra out of the fray and eased her down to her knees again at the periphery; both women stared at the scene, wide-eyed.

Evan forced a calming breath, his blood boiling. "Get her to Med Call before one of these idiots touches her."

The corpsman nodded, hauled Zondra to her feet, and ushered her to the pressure tunnel. Evan swallowed down his rage. Watching her go was the hardest thing he'd ever done.

Chapter Twelve

"Admiral MacNair?"

Matthew pivoted on his heel and headed for Pira, certain Zondra was in that direction. He was right.

Zondra lay in a secluded treatment room, soft cuffs around her wrists to hold her to the bed. Based on her stillness, Matthew guessed she was drugged into unconsciousness.

"What is the meaning of this?" he demanded.

"She wouldn't let the doctors touch her. She freaked, tried to peel one's face off for rendering aid. We had to sedate her and restrain her, for our own protection and hers. Don't worry. They checked with SLAL for the proper meds and dosage for a pregnant Xxanian."

Matthew forced back his fury. He would have her out of the straps as soon as possible, and Zondra wouldn't know she was restrained while she was out. There were more important concerns. "How is she?"

"We've healed the bruises, and the liquid stitches will have her foot healed in a matter of days."

Oh, Zondra. Matthew had seen the reports on the way over, but he hadn't been able to visualize the portrait of Zondra they painted: bloodied, beaten, frightened, and lashing out at every turn.

He peeled the blanket back from the lower corner of the mattress and cupped her foot up to survey the laceration Pira had referred to. Matthew winced. It would scar.

"Daahn will be furious," he grumbled. Xxanian warriors took attacks on a female or child very seriously. Her *gran-seir* would view Zondra as both. If Evan hadn't already killed Reynolds, Daahn would be here with his *zuahhhbeahhh* and *s'saahhta* in hand, ready to gut Reynolds and anyone who stood in his way.

Pira shifted nervously. "He won't—"

"No. Of course not. Not for Reynolds. He's dead." But if this cost Zondra her life, all bets were off and not even Matthew would be able to talk her *gran-seir* down.

Still, Pira lurked at the door to the room, as if he was afraid to leave his scent anywhere near her. "Good." He didn't sound like he thought it was.

"You can come closer, Pira," Matthew invited. "I assure you Zondra doesn't bite without provocation." He settled her foot on the mattress, laying a hand over the soon-to-be scar. As a rule, Xxanian females and children were sheltered from battle. She shouldn't have been scarred.

"According to Lieutenant Rice, Reynolds wasn't four-oh before Duncan got to him. She shredded half his face and drove a knife through his arm. And the doctors..." He trailed off uncomfortably.

"The reports said Evan warned your men that letting a man touch her in her state was not a good idea. He asked for a female to treat her...and he asked for Zondra to be sent home to her family."

"We didn't have a female doctor on call," Pira complained.

"Then you should have called one in or let Evan calm her while the doctors worked. Any injury they suffered was their own stupidity."

"But Reynolds—"

Matthew turned on him, and Pira shuffled a step backward. "If Reynolds hadn't broken into their stateroom, that never would have happened, Pira. Mated Xxanian females do not approach men without their mates for protection. It's hardwired."

Pira voiced a grunt that spoke his doubts.

"What do you intend to do about this?" He had to know to prepare for the fallout with Daahn.

There was a tense moment of silence. "I want her off my ship." There was an edge of violence in his tone.

"Release Duncan to me, and we'll be gone in—"

Pira darkened to crimson. "After what he did to Reynolds? We had to ID him with fingerprints. There was no face left to identify. Even his teeth were shattered."

Matthew turned to the bed, arranged the blankets over Zondra's foot again, and tucked them in as he had when she'd been a baby. Then he turned back to Pira and leaned against the foot of Zondra's bed. "Reynolds had been warned at least three times to keep his distance from Zondra. This was the second time he's assaulted her."

"And if someone comes on to her without knowing?" Pira challenged.

"Zondra will turn him down, and Evan will send him packing. Reynolds should have stayed away. Any intelligent man with a shred of self-preservation would have."

"You'll guarantee that? An isolated incident? No more mangled bodies? What happens when you're wrong, MacNair?"

Matthew managed a grim smile. "Ever wanted to kill someone, Pira?"

The captain stuttered and sputtered for a few moments. "I never have outside of a war zone."

"But you've wanted to. Come on. We're human."

"She's not." He grumbled the rest. "I'm not sure Duncan is anymore."

"He is...and he's not."

Pira glared at him. "Now you're talking nonsense."

"No, I'm not. Duncan can be very human, as human as we are. Until the moment someone endangers Zondra or his children. At that point, all bets are off, and he is more Xxan than human, a creature of instinct protecting his mate. I mistakenly trusted that military discipline would prevent any threat to her aboard ship. I was wrong about that."

Silence fell again. "He turned Reynolds's face into ground meat. I have no choice but to press for manslaughter at least."

"If you separate them, you kill Zondra...and the baby. If Evan outlives them, he'll kill every one of your men he comes in contact with. Even if he dies first, you kill them all."

Pira stared at Zondra. He swallowed hard, and his color dipped.

Matthew continued, using everything he had in a single barrage. "If Zondra dies because of the actions of the military in response to this very natural and instinctual Xxanian reflex, Daahn will sever all agreements and treaties." He let that sink in.

By the expression of pure panic, he could tell Pira was putting the rest of the chain of events together. If Daahn severed all agreements and treaties, it would mean war between the Xxan and crossbred Xxan on Earth and the humans.

Only these were Xxanian warriors with intimate knowledge of the planet and the inner workings of the government. They were soldiers who had built safety dens and armed themselves out of instinct. They were trusted allies with clearances to sensitive areas and information. They were acclimated Xxan who could fight in any weather, unlike the first wave that had invaded Earth, warriors who had shivered in the cold and had come bearing flawed intelligence reports half a century earlier.

"Oh, fucking hell," Pira croaked.

"That about sums it up. I'm sure there is a better option than that."

Pira stared at the wall, moving his feet aimlessly. "I've..." He cleared his throat. "I need to talk to the judge advocate about this situation."

"Absolutely." And the judge advocate would talk to the brass. The brass would talk to Interagency Command. IAC would probably get the world government on the line—

"If we do this, Duncan can never come back. You know that, don't you?"

His heart stuttered at that. "What are you saying?" Daahn wouldn't stand for his *gran-vvaash* being exiled from her home and nest any more than he'd accept her death.

"He's out, MacNair. Duncan is not stable enough to live and work in this environment. It would be criminally negligent of me to allow his wife to stay with him...and equally wrong to separate them."

Matthew grumbled a Xxanian curse he'd learned in his early days fighting with Daahn. "Do it. If it's the best we have, do it."

* * * *

Evan stared at the ceiling of the cell, flat on his back on the rack, his fingers hooked behind his head. In some sick irony, he had twenty times the space he'd had in berthing, though only a third of what he'd had in the stateroom he'd shared with Zondra.

Maybe I should have killed Reynolds off years ago.

He didn't laugh at that. It seemed all the joy had bled out of his life when the corpsman had led Zondra into the pressure tunnel the day before.

Where is she? Was she in Med Call? With MacNair? With her family? In another cell? Not knowing that was worse than watching her walk away.

Worse still was not knowing *how* she was. Evan was tortured by the possibility that she was badly injured. He hadn't had the time to examine her closely. What if the blood she'd tracked in hadn't been from her foot? What if she'd lost the baby? Would they tell him if she had? He doubted it. They were stupid, but not stupid enough to send him into another killing rage.

The urge to pace the floor was strong. The urge to test his abused fists against the bulkheads was stronger. Evan tried his best to ignore those urges and to focus on something else...anything else, but there was nothing else in existence to think about.

And I really don't want to break my knuckles this time. They are still healing from the last assault.

The bruising and cracked bones had been treated; the latter would be healed completely in a matter of days. The corpsmen had shot sideways glances at him. They'd whispered between themselves, opining that they'd expected that level of damage from a Xxanian warrior fresh from the battle he'd had with Reynolds. A human should have broken his hands.

He grumbled a curse at the true torture of that visit. The corpsmen had claimed they hadn't seen Zondra and had no clue what her condition was. They were probably lying, hiding something from him.

I can't know that. He pushed it away as a useless concern, when he had so many pressing ones.

What will happen to Zondra and our son? Could a crossbred Xxanian child live without its mother? Evan wasn't sure about that. Xenobiology wasn't his field. If it didn't involve turning wrenches and hooking up wires, it wasn't his specialty.

He'd heard the guards postulating on his punishment at change of shift. Apparently the rumor mill had settled on a good old-fashioned firing squad. The thought of what that would do to Zondra had stolen what little remained of his appetite. If he could just turn back the clock a day—

What? What would I do? Talk to him? Hold him off long enough for the Marines to arrest him instead of me?

Hell, no! I'd kill him again. I'd choke the life out of him, snap his neck, air lock him and evacuate to vacuum, throw him in the pressure tunnel and increase to crush depth, throw him into the closest turbine... The possibilities for killing Reynolds in engineering were endless, and every one of them sounded appealing.

The door latch clicked, and Evan prepared to turn away yet another tray of food.

It wasn't food. MacNair strode in, scowling at him. "I thought I told you not to kill anyone."

The door closed and latched again.

"Let some asshole try to rape your wife, MacNair. Let him beat her up, try to destroy everything you both own, try to kill you to rape her, and—"

"You're preaching to the choir. If Reynolds wasn't dead already, I'd go do it myself. I'd knock out the guards and break into his cell to do it, and I'd present his cock and balls to you and Zondra as proof that the asshole was gone."

Evan forced his muscles to relax at the show of solidarity. "Where is she? *How*...is she? And the baby. How is the baby?"

"In Med Call and healing well. She's sedated. And she is...as well as can be expected, given what happened to her."

He tensed at what MacNair hadn't said.

"The baby is fine," he hastened to add.

"Any word on what they intend to do with me?" His stomach clenched. He'd willingly spend the rest of his life in an isolation cell like this one if he didn't die and take his family with him.

MacNair sighed and scrubbed a hand down his face, abruptly looking twice the age he had moments before.

Evan levered up to sitting, staring at him. "That bad?"

"The good news is you *didn't* just kill your mate and son."

His body reacted to that as if it had been a threat. Evan tried to talk his rampaging heart rate and tensed muscles to a relaxed state, but this was a definite snafu. *Situation normal, all fucked up.* "Life in prison then. I guess that's the best I could have hoped for."

MacNair ambled to the sink and leaned against it, smiling weakly. "Even if they did that, it would kill Zondra unless she lived in that cell with you."

Words escaped Evan. Forcing them was a major test of willpower. "What are they going to do with me? They aren't going to lock Zondra up, are they?" How would he live with consigning her to that fate? How would a Xxanian deal with prolonged captivity? And their son... He couldn't raise his son in a jail cell.

"To save your family, you're going to lose your career. No complaints. No appeals. You walk out of here and never come back. At twelve years in, that means you lose your retirement and benefits. It's all gone, Evan, but it was the best I could do."

His heart sank. After everything MacNair and Zondra had done to make mating and his career work, Evan had screwed it up. He nodded. "Dishonorable discharge. I understand."

"No. Medical."

"What?" He couldn't have heard that right.

"Medical. Other than Honorable. The fact that mating has irrevocably changed you has been deemed a medical condition that adversely affects your job performance and makes you a danger to self and crew. You are no longer fit to serve in the military."

There was no answer Evan could formulate to that.

"You're out, Evan. You can't come back, but a medical discharge allows you to keep your clearance and get a job on the outside."

"I'll need it."

"Yes. You will. Now...are you ready to get out of here?"

Evan scrambled to pull his grippers on. He hesitated, running a hand over his bare chest.

MacNair laughed heartily.

"They took my clothes as evidence, and they only gave me pants. I didn't think to ask for another shirt." He hadn't asked for anything. *How Xxanian of me.*

"Where we're going, you won't need one."

Evan stared at him, working at that comment without hope of understanding it. "Where are we going?"

"To collect Zondra. After that, we're going where she'll be safe." He crossed the room to the door.

"Good enough for me." Safety was imperative. Anything else was secondary.

MacNair knocked, waited for the click of the lock, and pushed through the door. Evan followed in his wake, goose bumps rising as a complement of four Marines fell in around him.

Med Call had never felt so far. To make it worse, word spread in the usual shipboard fashion that Evan was being moved. Sailors and Marines appeared in doorways and corridors. A few offered nods that might have meant support or might have meant they believed he was being taken to an appropriate punishment. Others sneered or whispered.

"Why isn't that convict cuffed?" someone from the crowd called out.

Evan didn't look for the person who'd said it. He kept walking. This was his life now. It was time to get used to it.

He stepped into Med Call with a sigh of relief and followed MacNair to the isolation alcove where Zondra lay unconscious.

"Drugged?" he asked. He'd never seen Zondra so unaware, even when asleep.

MacNair nodded.

Evan pulled the blanket back, stopping cold at the sight of her in a different *S'suuhhea* than the one she'd been attacked in.

As if MacNair had been taking a stroll through his mind, he offered an explanation. "I changed her. I wouldn't let anyone else."

Her godfather. MacNair doesn't have sexual feelings for her. "Thank you."

Evan lifted her arms and crossed them over her softening abdomen. A discoloration on her wrist caught his attention, and he examined it. Realization came slowly. The sons of bitches had tied her down. He snapped a look at MacNair, forcing his muscles to relax at the warning look the admiral shot him in return.

Keep it corked. Get her the hell out of here. Evan couldn't do her any good locked in the brig.

He lifted her and turned to follow MacNair. To his surprise, there were a dozen Marines in Med Call. Now that Evan was paying attention to them, he noticed they were all in body armor. Realization that they expected a fight to get out chilled him.

"Maybe it would be best to have you take Zondra out, and I'll come out separately." It was unlikely that someone would fire on Zondra and MacNair—much less likely than someone attacking Evan.

"One move," MacNair ordered. "It gives anyone who wants to fight less time to organize."

Evan turned to argue with him and gaped at the old man suiting up in body armor of his own.

"If I can fight Xxanian warriors without armor, I can certainly fight humans with it." As if punctuating the point, MacNair tightened his leg armor down and stood to secure the chest plate.

"Is that supposed to make me feel better?" Evan protested.

"Actually...yes. It is." There was a hint of a smile on his face.

Evan shifted Zondra closer to his chest. "It would make me feel better if Zondra had body armor." He didn't request it for himself. Trying to carry Zondra while they were both armored would be worse than one set of armor, and he sure as hell wasn't taking armor for himself if Zondra didn't have it.

"Unfortunately there isn't any small enough to fit her on board. I checked."

Much as Evan hated to admit it, loose-fitting armor with large gaps would be worse than none. It would bog them down with weight without protecting her. "This is crazy, MacNair. If anyone does attack, they'll be coming for me. I can't be holding Zondra when—"

"We'll be protecting you both. Just duck if I tell you to and let us do the fighting."

Apparently there was no arguing with him. Evan gave up and tossed a couple of choice curses his way. The Marine guards gaped at him, understandably stunned by the audacity of talking to the fleet admiral that way.

MacNair laughed heartily. "Not much different than what Daahn said to me more than four decades ago. The elder is going to love having you as an addition to his nest."

Evan's heart stuttered. *Daahn's nest?* "We're going to—"

"Yes. Just do me a favor and repeat that litany to Daahn the first time he pisses you off." He reached for the helmet a Marine was handing off to him.

That made little sense. "You're not setting me up for the kill, are you?"

"And kill Zondra with you? Not a chance."

His cheeks heated. "Sorry, MacNair. I know you wouldn't."

"Might as well make it Mac from now on." With that, his helmet went on and the darkened visor down. He drew a stun stick smoothly and glanced their way.

Evan managed a stiff smile. "All right, Mac. Let's get my mate and son the hell off this ship."

A nod was the only reply.

The corridors weren't made for more than two men abreast. That left a space to either side of Evan that only the Marine guards' weapons filled. It would have been more comforting to be shoulder to shoulder with armor, but beggars couldn't be choosers and any protection was better than none.

"Why didn't you just call for a lockdown?" Evan groused.

One of the guards snorted. "Pira wants to prove his men are *human* enough to control the urge to kill you."

Something in his tone caught Evan's attention. He looked from one uncovered face to another, noting the sea of dark glasses. Several of their necks and foreheads undulated, ridge plates extending and retracting in fierce anger.

Xxan. Mac brought in a dozen crossbred Dominants.

"Being human is overrated," he quipped. "I'm glad to have you guys on my side."

Smiles appeared on two of the faces, just a quirking of the mouth in response to his compliment.

One guard offered a tip of his head. "You and your mate are safe under our protection."

Evan nodded his thanks.

Walking the corridors was nerve-racking. There was no longer a question of what people felt about Evan.

"Where are you taking him?" an onlooker demanded.

The stress on the last word, as if Evan was something loathsome, raised a sour wave in his mouth. Pira thought these men weren't a threat? He either wanted someone to kill Evan or was terminally stupid.

The sailor who'd spoken reached for the guard ahead of Evan and to the right. "Hey, I asked you a question, Marine."

The Xxanian in question shoved him back before the sailor could connect with his shoulder. "Prisoner transfer, fireman. Stand back."

"Prisoner transfer?" another challenged. "With the woman along for the ride?"

"Keep moving," one of the guards behind him instructed Evan.

Stopping was the last thing Evan wanted to do. He'd only stopped because the men in front of him had.

"The brig's the other way," someone farther up the corridor shouted.

Someone across from him retorted with: "Scalies guarding scalies. They always protect their own, you know."

"Don't answer," Evan's adviser whispered.

He nodded, though the reply stuck in his throat like a small wad of food, choking him lightly.

"Back off." Deacon's voice came from one of the side corridors. "What if it had been your wife? Your girlfriend? The woman is the mother of his child, man. That's a sacred trust. A man protects his wife and children. At least a *real* man does."

Evan met Deacon's gaze over one of the guard's shoulders and nodded his thanks.

The sailor beside him shoved Deacon against the bulkhead. "What're you? A scaly-lover like him?"

In the blink of an eye, the closest Marine to them had a shock stick at the attacker's throat. "Stand down or the brig is your next stop."

"Drop."

It wasn't Mac, but Evan complied. He hit the deck plates on his knees and shielded Zondra with his body.

Weapons unlocked and powered up in every direction.

Shit. This is about to get ugly. I should have taken the armor for me. At least it would have shielded Zondra better.

Mac's voice was amplified by his helmet. "You've got one chance, son. Hand the weapon over and face 'assault with a weapon' charges or die here."

One of the weapons ramped up to a higher setting, and Evan prayed it belonged to a Marine guard tired of this bullshit rather than the one attacking their group.

There was a moment of tense silence, then grumbled curses.

"Back off." The voice was rough, probably fighting its way past an extended set of ridge plates.

Shuffling feet announced someone complying, and Evan breathed a sigh of relief.

"Your men failed, Pira," Mac called out. "Guess they aren't so superior after all. I want a lockdown. Now."

The alarm blared, and the crowds shuffled back into rooms and side corridors. Pressure doors sealed in every direction. Moments passed, and two of the remaining sailors were shoved to the emergency rail and cuffed to it.

"Cameras show all clear, MacNair." Pira's voice echoed off the stark metal.

The Xxanian Marines secured their weapons, and two of them lifted Evan to his feet.

"You protected your mate well," one of them complimented him.

"You, too. Thanks."

Deacon looked around, more than a little rattled by the chain of events if his wide eyes and ragged breathing were any indication.

Mac opened his visor with a puff of released air and waved Deacon along with them. "You're with us. If you stay here, it's going to get ugly." He pointed to the prisoners. "Pira will deal with you."

"Better than scaly justice," one shot back.

The guard between him and Evan scowled at the sailor. "I guarantee I would have killed you quickly for pointing a weapon at a female."

Mac took over from there. "Captain Pira put his reputation on the line in the belief that none of you would be stupid enough to try this. What he does to you will be lasting, I'm sure."

With that, the procession started moving again. Two of the Marine guards broke ranks to place themselves between Evan and the new prisoners, then shuffled back into line around him.

The rest of the trip was uneventful, and Pira met them at the forward hatch.

Mac took a packet of papers from the captain's hand. "Make a transfer packet for Petty Officer Deacon. Captain Seaver will be glad to have him."

Pira nodded grimly.

And Pira will regret losing both of us this way.

It took a moment for the significance of sending Deacon to Seaver's ship to sink in. That was where Aleeks was stationed. Gratitude that Mac was taking care of Deacon welled up in his chest, and Evan closed his eyes and thanked him silently.

"What do you suggest I do with the two below decks?" Pira asked, seemingly weighing his words carefully.

Evan opened his eyes, watching the interaction for signs that it was all going south again.

Mac handed the captured weapon over. "Assault and two counts of assault with. That will land one in the brig for a week or so and the other in Leavenworth for at least six months, by my estimation. I'd tack a drop in rank on the second...or a dishonorable. Your choice. Oh, and I highly recommend race relations training. Your command is full of bigoted idiots. You know that, don't you?"

"Just that?" His surprise was impossible to miss. "You're not going to press for the limits?"

Mac offered a cold smile. "Tell them the scaly-lovers suggested it."

With that, he led the way to two nine-man vans guarded by two Xxanian Marines each.

Chapter Thirteen

The trip to Daahn's nest didn't take long. In less than an hour, the vans had dropped Deacon off at his apartment and Mac, Evan, and Zondra off at a rambling ranch-style house. Evan glanced at his truck, already parked in front of the home, seemingly packed with everything he'd left at the house he'd been sharing.

Everything left after Reynolds's attack. He hoped Zondra had a decent amount of belongings here. Evan resolved to replace what he could...and erase what he could of the attack from her memories.

Mac cleared his throat. "I couldn't be sure how much would survive the mob." He didn't apologize for the invasion of privacy.

"Thanks, Mac."

The Marines took their leave. Several tipped a head to Evan and wished him well. One uttered a Xxanian phrase that held the reverence of a prayer and turned away with a deep bow.

"What did he say?" Evan asked.

Mac clapped a hand on his shoulder. "May you have many daughters."

His brow furrowed. "Dau—" Evan snapped a look at the retreating vans. The son of a bitch was wishing himself a prospective mate. "That bastard."

"Cut them some slack, Evan. Human women don't agree to become mates often. Other Xxanian females are more likely to. But look at Zondra. If she chose a human, others might."

Mac turned toward the house, bringing Evan's scrutiny to it again. It looked deceptively normal and human. He wouldn't have guessed that the highest-ranking Xxanian elder on Earth lived here if he'd been shown a picture of it.

The code pad flashed a welcoming green, and Mac opened the door, waving Evan and Zondra in ahead of him. The room was akin to a locker room: there were two long benches and hooks, some of which had brightly-colored cloth hung from them.

He expected to move on, but Mac started stripping off his armor and storing it beneath the farthest hooks on the right.

"Mac?" What in the world was he doing? Was it against some Xxanian household rule to enter Daahn's nest in armor?

"Toe off your shoes."

"What?" What were the rules? And what would Daahn do if Evan violated them?

Mac pulled off his shirt and hung it on an empty hook. He brought the blue cloth from the neighboring hook back in his empty hand. The cloth looped over one shoulder, leaving most of his chest bare, and covered him from hips to knees.

"Shoes," he repeated. "Even if you refuse to wear the *S'suumea*, you cannot enter the nest in shoes."

Evan toed off the grippers, reasoning that it was good form to do so in any household. "The...thing you're wearing is called a *S'suumea*?"

"Yes. This is the formal *S'suumea*; Daahn insists on the formal version. It's the traditional dress of a Xxanian male." Mac stripped off his boots and socks, then his trousers and underwear, leaving himself nude beneath the *S'suumea.*

"Insists for whom?"

"His descendants. He'll likely try to talk you into it. Hell, he'll demand it if I know the old buck, and I do." Mac shot him a sly grin. "Remember you cursing me out?"

Evan nodded.

"May be the time to pull that out on Daahn."

"Check. I'll keep that in mind, but if he pisses me off before that, all bets are off." He meant it to be a joke, but the recitation was as dry as his throat.

Mac smoothed his *S'suumea.* "Don't back down. If you say something and back down, Daahn will see it as a weakness."

"Got it. Anything else?"

"Zondra is Daahn's *gran-vvaash*—his granddaughter—but she is your mate. You are the head of your own nest. This is his nest, and he will try to order you."

"Can he?" Evan asked nervously.

Mac chuckled darkly. "That is up to you. As Zondra's mate, Daahn finds himself—for the first time in her life—not in complete control of the particulars of her life. Do you intend to give him that control willingly?"

Evan fisted his hands beneath Zondra's sleeping body. "No fucking way."

"Right answer."

The discussion temporarily ended, Mac opened the door at the far side of the room. Behind it was an indoor garden. The air was hot and moist, and the smells of green, growing things and spice were pungent.

There were few walls separating the inside of the huge structure, and the roof was farther overhead than seemed right. He wondered if the changing room had been built on a gradual slope, but there was no way to be sure without using a level.

Evan could see through the first few doorways and wondered if there were blast doors installed to drop during invasion, compartmentalizing the structure. It was likely. He'd heard Xxanian warriors believed in defensible homes.

Here and there, columns emerged from thick stands of bushes or trees and reached for the heights. The structure was deeper than it had looked from the front. Evan had assumed it was no more than four rooms deep, but it seemed he'd underestimated it.

By far.

Evan bit back a moan of pleasure at the moss beneath his feet. It was softer than carpet, lush, and soothing. For a man who'd spent the better part of twelve years sucking oil and scrubbed air and walking on deck plates, it was a slice of paradise.

Daahn knows how to live.

Dripping water and insect noises put him instantly at ease. If there were fans, he couldn't hear them. He understood now why Zondra had brought the fountain with her onto the ship. The sound of machinery must have been intolerable for her.

The floor sloped down at a twenty-degree or so angle. In the space of three large room lengths, they were a full story underground and still descending. Evan hadn't been able to see the far reaches of the building, but he suspected the tunnels might extend past the outer walls. There was no way to be sure. The tunnels twisted and turned, winding through more garden caves. A set of rock stairs led up, and Evan peered into the darkness. If he had to guess how deep they'd come, his best estimate would be about three stories below ground.

"The sleeping chambers," Mac informed him. "Though family members can choose to sleep in the center nest, sometimes a little privacy and human comforts go a long way."

Evan filed that information away for later use. "Do you have a sleeping chamber?"

He smiled. "I *am* family. I'll probably sleep here tonight."

The next cavern was at least ten meters high and twice that width, with what appeared to be a natural pool in the center. The water wall at the far side certainly wasn't natural. Evan suspected much of the cavern had been built and not discovered as it was.

Movement caught his eye, and Evan looked around. Aleeks closed from one direction, and a hairless man that was probably Zondra's *seir* from the other. Both wore the formal *S'suumea*.

Where is Daahn? The hair on the back of his neck rose, and Evan whirled around to face the *Grea* Elder.

The fucker was huge, easily half a meter taller than Evan was. He was wider, too. Evan's best estimate was that the elder weighed in at no less than two hundred and twenty kilos of green-black scales, with eight-centimeter-long talons on the tips of his digits.

Rumbles and hisses left Daahn's mouth, and Mac answered them. A different set emerged from the elder.

Aleeks appeared at Evan's shoulder. "He has welcomed you to the nest. Thank him."

"Thank you for offering us a safe place." He meant it.

Daahn's ridge plates extended, and his frill spikes fanned out around his head and shoulders. Evan could fully understand why the first troops who had faced Xxanian warriors in battle pissed themselves.

Forcing himself not to retreat was difficult, but Evan managed it. He stood his ground, staring up at Daahn, weighing how strong he wanted the elder to think he was. With Zondra in his arms, he suddenly felt like he was using her as a shield. "Mac, you may want to take Zondra."

The *Grea* Elder's frills wavered and then straightened.

Mac leaned toward Evan. "You're insulting him by saying he'd attack you with his *gran-vvaash* in your arms."

That kicked Evan's anger into high gear. "On the contrary, if he intends to fight me, I plan on having both hands free to give it my best shot. Having Zondra out of the line of fire goes without saying."

"Ballsy, boy," Mac breathed, but he didn't take Zondra.

Evan glared at him. "Aleeks, would you please—"

Daahn's frills folded against his skin, and his ridge plates retracted. He put his hands out for Zondra.

Evan took a step back, shooting a questioning look at Mac.

"Do it. There are... It is a Xxanian custom to honor a woman by bathing." He hesitated and looked up at Daahn. "All of us will enter the pool with Zondra and bathe her with clove oil."

His gut reaction was to tell them to shove it. Instead, he forced his answer from between clenched teeth. "Zondra expects this?"

Aleeks answered that time. "Only from relatives. If we had another sister with a mate, her mate wouldn't be allowed to touch Zondra."

"And doing this doesn't"—Evan stared up at Daahn. It was clear the elder understood English, even if he didn't speak it—"obligate us to anything?"

The Xxanian's eye slits narrowed, but the elder didn't respond.

"What are you saying, Evan?" Mac inquired. "Be specific."

"If Daahn thinks this gives him some hold over us or rights to tell me how to live my life, he can screw that. Zondra is my mate, and I'll dig a fucking cave to shelter us before I—"

It took a moment for Evan to identify the seal-bark sound as laughter. Daahn's hand thumped down on his shoulder, sending shards of agony Evan tried not to show down his arm.

The wide mouth full of serrated hunting teeth opened, and Daahn spoke slowly...and in muddled English. "I greet the brother warrior. Welcome to the nest."

"Again...thank you." Hopefully this time it wouldn't offend Daahn.

Time for a show of trust. Evan offered Zondra to him.

The elder took her solemnly and tucked Zondra beneath his chin. A series of trills and coos left his lips, odd sounds for so fierce a creature to make.

"The soothing sound the Xxan make for their young," Aleeks imparted. "*Gran-seir* has held every child of his line like that and welcomed them to the nest."

Evan made a mental note to have Zondra teach him that to use with their children. For that matter, he needed to learn Xxan. The constant translations—or lack of them—was likely to drive him insane.

The cooing turned to a hummed note, and the other men joined the chorus. Evan tried to match the pitch, and Mac offered a nod of encouragement.

It was a slow procession down to the pool. At the edge, everyone except Daahn started removing the *S'suumea*. Evan hesitated, then stripped his pants away and dropped them to the rock edge.

Daahn settled Zondra in Evan's arms and motioned them down the slope and into the pool. The other men followed. When the water reached halfway up his thighs, Aleeks told him to stop and kneel. The water covered his lowest ribs, and Zondra's dark hair floated along on the surface.

Ripples slapped his back, a sure sign that Daahn had entered the water. Evan didn't look his way, unsure of Xxanian mores on nudity and propriety.

Zondra's *gran-seir* went to his knees near her feet. The scent of clove was nearly eye watering in its intensity. Daahn passed a small bottle to Mac, then lifted one of Zondra's feet and massaged the clove oil into it.

Mac took a handful and passed the bottle along to Aleeks. Mac worked the oil into her lower leg through the silk. Aleeks started at her hand and his *seir* at her shoulder.

Aleeks spoke without looking up. "When her legs are done, lower Zondra into the water. Cradle her head to your chest, so we can—"

He stopped short at Daahn's roar. Evan skittered to the side, running aground on Zondra's *seir*.

The older man steadied him. "Don't move," he ordered.

Daahn roared again, and Evan stared at him, swallowing a lump of fear. The ridge plates and frills were out and the latter shaking in warning. The hisses escaping his mouth left no question that he was furious and intent on harming someone.

"Tell him," Zondra's *seir* urged him.

"Tell him *what*? I don't speak Xxan, remember?" *Shit. Please tell me he doesn't want me dead.* It wasn't dying that scared him; it never had. But what his death would do to Zondra was enough to curdle his stomach.

"You killed the one who scarred Zondra? If you did, tell him now," he ordered.

"Yes, I killed him. I pummeled him into a puddle on the floor...literally. He was dead within minutes of me reaching him."

Daahn's roaring became a growling...then subsided. His frills came down slowly, but his ridge plates remained extended.

Evan loosened his hold on Zondra, trying to force his ragged breathing smoother.

The elder's attention to Zondra's injured foot was even more out of place than the cooing sound had been. He brushed his mouth over it, nuzzled the liquid stitches, then made a sound that Evan might have called a sob if he wanted to chance Daahn killing him. In the next moment, he was spreading clove oil over that foot gently, not massaging as he had the other.

The sounds he made were stilted. The ones Mac made in response had a soothing note to them. Daahn jerked his head up and stared at Evan for a moment. His nod was slow and precise.

"Is something wrong?" Evan asked, his pulse jumping.

Mac smiled. "Just a sign of respect."

He preempted Evan's move to ask more questions by telling him it was time to shift Zondra. Evan complied, and the men moved into a tight ring around her, shuffling to place Daahn at her back. He tensed at the move. Mac warned him down, and Evan nodded in response. He didn't know the meaning of Daahn's placement, but he suspected he was about to learn it.

"Remove the *S'suuhhea*," Mac instructed. "The female always removes her clothing in the water, where the other males cannot see her."

Evan peeled the silk up. It clung to her body and came away in a slide that was far too sensual for his piece of mind, considering the other men surrounding her. When the garment was in Evan's hand, Aleeks took it and tossed it out of the pool.

Daahn made a rumbling little sound, and Evan stared at him over Zondra's shoulder, waiting for the other shoe to drop. The elder didn't speak again. He raised one taloned hand, palm up. His son poured the clove oil in it. Aleeks raised her hair and held it away from her shoulders and back.

At the first stroke of Daahn's hand against the back of her neck, Mac started talking. "Daahn will bathe Zondra's back. After that, he will hold her for you while you bathe her chest and...intimately. While you do that, Aleeks and I will leave the pool. Andy will stay to translate."

Andy. Her *seir.* Evan hadn't known his name. "I understand."

"Typically we would all leave, but with Zondra unconscious, this is going to go a little differently than usual."

"In what way?" Based on Mac's tone, he could guess it was something he wouldn't like.

"Andy will leave the water before you and have a drying cloth ready for Zondra outside the pool."

His jaw tightened down, and Evan forced it loose. "Okay. So he's going to help me get Zondra dried and dressed since she can't do it for herself."

"Sort of. He'll hold her while you dress in the *S'suumea*, then—"

"I'm not dressing in it."

Daahn stopped moving and raised his head to glare at Evan.

He didn't back down. Mac had told him not to. "I realize this is your nest, but I am not one of your descendants. Maybe someday, I might wear it...for holidays or ceremonies. But I am human, and I will dress as I always have."

There was a moment of silence. Daahn offered a single grunt and went back to work bathing Zondra.

"What did he say?"

Mac smiled. "You don't really want to know that."

"I'm not wearing it," Evan repeated.

"He doesn't expect you to."

"I take it that grunt was some sort of insult then?" The hair on the back of his neck bristled in response.

Daahn's nostrils flared, and Evan wondered if he was gauging his enemy's state of mind by the move. The Xxan were very scent oriented, he knew.

"You could say that."

"Good enough. I'm sure I'll offer a few of my own before we're done."

Daahn snapped a look at Evan, snorted, and collected more clove oil.

Something in that move made Evan want to laugh, but he restrained himself. "So Andy will hold her while I put my dungaree pants back on. What then?"

"Daahn will hold her while you dry and dress her. Tonight he insists that you both sleep in the center nest."

"Insists?" His anger took notice at that.

"Cool down. The center nest is calming and healing for an injured Xxanian. He wishes Zondra to wake to the calming effects. I highly suggest you don't refuse this order."

Evan forced his muscles to ease. "If it will help Zondra, I will do whatever she needs." He focused on Daahn's oversized head. "You don't have to make orders for that. Just explain it to me."

The elder raised his head again, met Evan's gaze, and offered a tip of his head in seeming agreement.

Daahn let out a series of hisses and trills, and Mac and Aleeks rose and left the water without a backward glance. When they were gone, Evan eased her back into her *gran-seir's* arms. The other two men didn't look down at her. That was something of a relief.

Andy passed the clove oil into Evan's hands, and Evan set to work bathing her.

Halfway down her chest, Daahn started speaking in Xxan again.

Andy's translation was slow and measured. "This bath is ceremonial. It will only be repeated if Zondra is ill or injured...or after she gives birth."

Zondra would be awake for those baths. It wouldn't be as awkward or as intimate. "I understand."

Daahn continued, and Evan listened to the cadence. It wasn't short and gruff. Nor was it the cooing tone he'd used for Zondra. Already Evan could pick out the tone a Dominant used with another Dominant. It was a tone of respect.

"You will bathe Zondra with the clove oil once daily for two months. It doesn't have to be here in the center nest. It can be in your rooms."

"Is there a reason for this? Will it help Zondra?"

He nodded. "The spice is very important in a Xxanian mating. You don't need Daahn's permission to use the spice, but when he orders you to use it to bathe Zondra, you should."

It grated on his nerves, but Evan grumbled his agreement.

The bathing grated on his nerves as well. Touching her intimately in the presence of other men wasn't something he wanted to do. Worse, he was hard and wanting, with no way to sate himself. His breathing ragged, Evan tried to focus on finishing the torturous bathing.

Andy started talking, what was clearly a communication from him and not from Daahn. "I know. It's arousing. We won't think you're some sort of deviant."

Finding the words to answer that was nearly impossible. He stared at her *seir* for a long moment, then nodded.

"Finished?" Andy prompted.

"Yes." Not nearly, and I won't be until Zondra is awake and comfortable enough to be receptive. After what had happened, who knew how long that would take.

Andy rose and strode out of the pool. Fortunately, he wasn't erect. That would have snapped Evan's patience. He did likewise, and Daahn steadied him with a hand on his shoulder. Evan wanted to protest that he didn't need the help, but this was for Zondra's safety, he was sure. He let it slide.

Her *seir* had a brightly colored sheet in his arms, and Evan settled Zondra into it and wrapped it around her. That accomplished, he snagged his pants from the floor and pulled them on.

That move short-circuited halfway up his legs, at the moment Daahn reached out and placed his hand over Zondra's womb. A series of sounds left his lips, his mouth opened, and his forked tongue extended for what Zondra called a tongue-scent.

Evan shot a look demanding answers at Andy. He wasn't going to attack Daahn, but he sure as hell wanted to know what the elder was doing.

The explanation came immediately. "My *seir* is evaluating your child. An elder always knows what the child will be early in gestation and plans accordingly."

"It's a boy. We already know that." Keeping the edge out of his voice was impossible, it seemed.

Daahn offered a crooning sound and turned his gaze on Evan.

"A young Dominant." It sounded as if Andy was offering correction. "Daahn is most pleased with the addition to the nest."

"And if he wasn't?" Evan challenged.

Andy smiled widely, showing his hunting teeth. "Any young are rejoiced. But a young Dominant confirms that you are a strong enough warrior to be an asset to the nest. Of course, in the future, if you bring female young to the nest, you will be most prized."

"I'll keep that in mind," Evan offered dryly. He finished donning and fastening his pants, watching as Andy passed Zondra into Daahn's hands and took his leave.

No translator. Either Daahn had nothing left to say to him, or they felt whatever he did say would be impossible to mistake.

Evan retrieved the clean *S'suuhhea* from the thronelike chair set before a water wall. Daahn didn't presume to uncover Zondra for him. He let Evan handle dressing her and even lowered her for Evan's comfort.

Once she was dressed, Daahn motioned with his head, and Evan lifted her out of the wet sheet. The elder started to turn away.

"Is there any particular place in the center nest that we should sleep?" he asked.

Daahn turned toward them, made an expansive motion with his hand, and tipped his head. With that, he disappeared behind the cover of the high plants that circled the pool.

"Anywhere we want," Evan interpreted that move.

He chose a soft patch of grass five meters from the pool and settled Zondra on it, then wrapped himself around her. In moments, the calming sounds of the center nest, the feeling of Zondra in his arms and her scent, and the stresses of the day herded him into sleep with her.

Chapter Fourteen

The sounds of the center nest surrounded her, and Zondra smiled at the tricks her mind played on her. Although she rankled at the fact that they'd given her drugs, this side effect was a pleasant surprise. It was a lush hallucination, complete with scent.

Scent? Zondra had never realized hallucinations could be so detailed and involved.

She forced herself toward what passed for consciousness, hungry for every sensation that connected her to home and family. *Even if it's fake.* Fake security was decidedly better than the reality she'd face when she opened her eyes.

It was so realistic and vivid, Zondra swore she could hear the insects that pollinated the plants. She sighed, wishing she could hold on to the hallucination.

A movement brought a potent and very familiar scent.

"Evan," she breathed.

"Thank the stars." He sounded relieved.

Zondra forced her eyelids up, focusing blearily around at the center nest. "How did I get home? I don't remember..." Anything past the female doctor asking me to relax for the scan plate.

Evan pushed himself up on one elbow and stared down at her. "You were drugged unconscious by the doctors. Mac and a bunch of Xxanian warriors escorted us here."

He stroked a hand along her cheek, bringing a strong smell of clove. The center nest always smelled faintly of the spice, but it seemed Evan was nearly bathed in it.

Bathed. "You bathed me with clove?"

His jaw tightened. "Me...and Mac, Aleeks, your *seir*, and your *gran-seir*."

A smile curved the edges of her lips. "That must have been a tense moment." For everyone involved. She wished she'd been awake to witness it. Watching Dominants posture and jockey for position was usually quite the show.

"You have *no* idea."

"You didn't kill any of them, did y—" The rest died in her throat, and memories of Reynolds made her shudder.

"No. I doubt your family would give me reason to. You're safe here. You know that."

She nodded. A Xxanian nest was probably the only safe place for them on the planet, for the time being.

But there were other concerns. "What about you? You're not in a cell, but I've never heard of the military returning justifiable homicide as a ruling...or releasing someone that did kill someone aboard ship on bail, no matter what the situation was."

His smile was strained and lopsided. "Mac's doing. I have a medical discharge."

"Good." He was out and not facing charges. That was a relief.

"It is. I still have my clearance." But his expression didn't make it seem like it was good.

He needs to work. He needs to feel he's providing for me. Maybe she could help with that.

"Did I ever tell you what Daveed Raashh does for a living?"

His brow furrowed. "Who?"

She knew she'd never mentioned him to Evan. There'd never been a reason to. "Daveed is my *gran-seir's* second-in-command's eldest son."

When he didn't reply, she continued.

"Daveed owns Spice Luxuries."

"The Xxanian-style catalog you had on board ship," he murmured.

She'd been intending to use some of her earnings as a translator to purchase things from it. "Yes. And his younger brother Arren owns Spice Automotive."

His eyes glittered at the name. "Most guys I know would sell their mothers to own a Spice performance machine."

"The entire Spice Enterprises is owned by Raashh's nest. They are very picky about who they hire, and the pay would be...well, at least double what the military paid you...maybe more. That's not counting performance bonuses. The Xxan are big on paying well for those who work effectively." She knew how prized Evan had been as a technician.

His eyes narrowed. "Are you trying to set me up in the family business?" There was a challenge in that. She'd offended him.

"No. For one thing, they aren't family. And I would have nothing to do with your decision to apply with Spice Enterprises or the process of it. You are simply...uniquely qualified to apply."

The look of confusion returned. "I am?"

Zondra nodded.

"My security clearance makes a difference?"

"Spice also has a space division. They build some of the equipment you were maintaining aboard ship. Having a security clearance means you are able to work in production on military projects. That and being human means you can do on-site maintenance without the...difficulties the Xxan face in the same situation."

He didn't reply to that. Evan's face was studiously neutral. "And that will be the only reason they want to hire me? No...strings?" He searched her face for a response, even as he waited for her words.

Oh, he was astute. "If a bunch of Xxanian Marines helped transport you, it is possible that Daveed's son Marcus was one of them."

"And?"

"Daveed will know your connection to my *gran-seir.*" He opened his mouth to speak, and she hurried on. "It wouldn't be a favor to either of you or to me to hire you. The Xxan do not practice nepotism."

"Then what would it be?"

"Our nests are allies. You would be seen as a trusted ally."

"Nothing else?"

Answering that was difficult.

Evan must have seen the struggle in her expression. "Zondra?" He paused only a moment. "It's the daughter thing again, isn't it?"

That forced a gasp from her, and she nodded dumbly. How had Evan learned that?

"I am not making that promise to them." It was a solemn vow.

"What promise?" What promise did he think someone was asking him to make concerning any daughters they might have?

"That one of theirs can take care of her quickening if we have a daughter. Or that we'll convince her to mate with one of them."

She smiled and pressed a hand to his bare chest. "No one would dare ask it."

"Or expect it?"

"No. Not even expect it. Even my *gran-seir* would only suggest several for you to choose from for her. My *seir* would have considered Marcus for my quickening, I'm sure."

His muscles eased beneath her fingers. "Good. Then we should get some food into you."

How Xxanian. "Not yet."

He tensed at her outright refusal. "And the reason why is...?"

"I assume my *gran-seir* ordered you to bathe me with clove daily for a period of time?"

"Two months. I'm not sure if it's a punishment or—"

"A cleansing of violence for me and a bonding ritual for us as a couple. Sometimes it is a punishment for neglect, but that isn't the case here."

His expression spoke his relief. The lines in his forehead eased, and he offered a tense nod of thanks. "But we can do that later," Evan decided.

Zondra shook her head. "The first bathing wasn't completed correctly."

The tension, adrenaline, and musk rolling off him were enough to make her nipples go hard and her musk flow. *This is going to be so good.*

"In what way? For that matter, how could you know it wasn't completed correctly?" There was an edge of violence in his tone, no doubt at the idea of the other men in the pool with them again. Or maybe it was a promise to gut Daahn and the others if they'd taken liberties.

Zondra wrapped her arms around his neck. "The family bath ends with a private bath between the mated couple."

"I did that." He sounded offended by her statement, as if she'd accused that he hadn't bathed her.

"Not really. Any formal spice bath between the couple ends with making love in the pool or on the grass or stone surrounding it. Here or in our private pond upstairs. But always here first."

His eyes went hot in interest, and his musk was potent in the promise of precisely what she was asking for. "I think food can wait for a bit. I wouldn't want to offend, after all."

"You're probably right." She sighed as if conceding an argument.

One eyebrow arched. "*Probably* right?"

"Maybe? Definitely?" she teased.

He shifted his position so that he leaned over her. "Definitely," he informed her.

"Definitely."

"So your *gran-seir* sentenced me to sex once a day with my mate?"

The thought seemed to amuse him. It was good that he wasn't offended by it. Dominant males tended to posture and hold grudges. Neither would help them.

"At least once a day," she corrected him. "You'll want to scent our rooms properly."

His smile said he was about to take up the challenge. "How properly?" He knew already.

And she knew how much Evan loved a mating frenzy. They'd indulged in a dozen of them so far.

"Mating frenzies as many evenings as you feel my condition will allow." Stroking a male's ego and protective instincts could never hurt.

"Are you saying you want or need careful handling in that department?" It was delivered in a soothing, almost crooning voice.

"No, but if I do, I trust you to know it."

He lifted Zondra into his arms and took her to the bathing pool in the center nest. There, he settled her on her feet. She glanced down at his dungaree pants, wondering at the fact that he wasn't wearing a *S'suumea*. Had Evan refused to? Or had no one told him *Gran-seir's* rule in the confusion of their homecoming?

His head swiveled to the left and right, and his eyes narrowed. "No one will be watching us, right?"

She shook her head. "*Gran-seir's* cavern is through there." She pointed to the cave on the far side of the pool. "He will hear us and know all is well between us, but no one would dare watch another man with his mate."

Evan started stripping off her *S'suuhhea*. "I wonder if Spice employees get a discount," he murmured.

The change of subject shocked her. Zondra would like to claim it hadn't offended her. That would be a lie. She planted her hands at her hips, stopping the flow of silk down her body. "You're thinking about a performance car *now*?" she demanded. He is not dominating his way out of this one.

He placed his hands over hers. "No. That thought would have come later. Much later."

Mollified, she nodded.

"Your hands," he hinted.

Zondra started unbuttoning his dungaree pants. Evan released her *S'suuhhea* and let it drop to the boulder they were standing on.

"What were you thinking about then?" *I sound like a pouting child.* But she couldn't seem to help herself.

He planted two fingers under her chin and tipped Zondra's face up toward his. His eyes were warm and inviting.

Soothing.

There was no bite of displeasure in his expression. It appeared that he was pained by her mood. She relaxed, and Evan rewarded her with a kiss.

"I'd started saving up to buy you the leather and emerald choker from the Spice catalog," he informed her.

"I know the one."

And she knew why he liked it. Zondra had simply found it pretty. He'd likened it to an ornate sub collar, right down to the heavy silver rings decorating the lower edge that could have a leash hooked onto them.

"With the raise in pay and a discount, I could give it to you very soon. Not as soon as I want to, but soon."

Zondra knew what he was asking. "I will wear it proudly, whenever and wherever you want me to."

Though it looked like a sub collar on close inspection and could doubtless be used as one, it was ornate enough to pass for jewelry, even if Evan wanted her to wear it out around town with him. *And the emeralds are a close match for my eyes.*

His kiss left no doubt that he was about to reaffirm his dominance in their relationship. "You won't regret that choice," he vowed.

"I know I won't."

Evan stripped his pants off and led her into the pool, snatching up the clove oil on the way in.

The water was warm and smelled lightly of the spice, despite the filtering systems that cleaned the water constantly. The water wall covered the hum of machinery, lending natural sounds that soothed her.

Waist deep, Evan turned toward her and popped the top on the clove oil. He started at her neck and worked his way down her body, sealing his mouth to hers in a heated kiss. The clove stung pleasantly against her musk ducts, not unlike a weak *Zhigaaal*, and her nipples rose in response.

Evan massaged them with the clove oil, testing her responses. His hands were rough against her breasts, soft against her womb. He poured more of the clove oil into his hand and reached around her body to work at her neck and her mating stripe. The need to have him follow through was pressing, and Zondra tipped her hips against his ready cock.

Evan released her mouth. "Are you sure?" His scent announced that a positive response from her meant nothing would stop them.

"Oh, yes."

He turned her, washing her back while he urged her into shallow water. The clove oil did delicious things to her buttocks and thighs. By the time he reached her slit, Zondra was murmuring pleas for more.

Evan helped her to her knees, solicitous even though he clearly wanted to dominate her. He sank to his knees behind her, but Evan didn't rush to more. He took his time, stroking handfuls of water down her body to wash the excess oil away. That left a slick sheen between them that she was certain would feel wonderful during sex. As if in confirmation, Evan trailed his hands up and down her body, ruthlessly arousing her.

Just when she thought she could take no more, he slid his cock inside. Her breathing hitching, Zondra tried desperately to clear her head. Evan held her, stroking leisurely circles over her clit that launched her toward climax.

"The next time, it will be a frenzy," he vowed.

But there was nothing frenzied about what he was doing to her. Every movement was torturously slow. Every breath he took warmed her mating stripe. Evan couldn't have proclaimed his place in her life more clearly if he'd screamed it to the nest.

Zondra pressed back against his length, urging him on.

"Scream for me."

The order sent shards of pleasure up her spine. Zondra didn't doubt that he wanted her *gran-seir* to hear it. It was a very Xxanian instinct to want the other males to hear how sated his mate was.

The sound stuck in her throat, and Evan prompted her with a sharp little pinch to her nipple. That not only prompted the scream but launched her into a mind-altering climax. His name echoed off the stone walls, and Evan roared his own climax out.

His cum was hot and potent, a promise of what was to come when they reached their rooms upstairs. Evan held her loosely to his body in the aftermath, his cock bucking against the walls of her sheath, prompting groans from both of them.

They parted slowly, and Evan rose, helping Zondra to her feet after him. Her knees shaking, she gratefully accepted his support out of the pool. He stopped and reached out for something, and her gaze snapped to the bottle of clove oil floating on the water.

That was all it took to get her laughing. She stifled the response, so as not to offend Evan. If his smile was any indication, he wasn't offended.

"At least I closed it," he pointed out.

"Good thing, too. If you hadn't, you'd be paying for a new bottle and a new filter."

He raised an eyebrow and guided her to her *gran-seir's* chair. Before she quite had her breath, he had her wrapped in the drying cloth someone had left there for them. He rubbed the oil into her skin, then pulled down the *S'suuhhea* from the back of the chair and helped her into it. His turn toward their discarded clothing ended abruptly, and Zondra looked down at the *S'suuhhea* she'd slept in.

The S'suuhhea. *His uniform pants aren't there.* She bit her lower lip, torn between telling him it had likely been a joke and laughing outright at the jest.

Evan wasn't amused in the least. He turned his attention to the back of *Gran-seir's* chair and glared. Though she didn't need to see it, Zondra turned her head. She sighed at the sight of the *S'suumea.*

His muscles strung tight, Evan wrapped the drying cloth around his waist and tucked it in tight, muttering curses. Zondra opened her mouth to tell him it was a joke, but Evan turned on his heel and marched toward the main door.

She hurried to follow him. "Evan?" He couldn't be considering leaving. *Can he?* That thought made her panic, and she moved faster. "Evan?"

He didn't answer her. Instead he made the turns toward the *s'sanuea,* his step purposeful. He pulled the door to the preparation room open and strode through without closing it. Without preamble, he unlocked the outer door and strode through.

Zondra shut the door between the *s'sanuea* and the nest, then rushed to the doorway. "Evan? What are you doing?"

He reached into the back of his truck and pulled out a seabag. Slinging it over his shoulder, he turned and waved her back into the *s'sanuea.*

She complied, at a loss to explain his actions. Evan came back into the nest and shut the

armored doors. He slung the seabag down on the
closest bench and opened it. He pulled out a pair
of jeans, let the drying cloth fall, and pulled them
on.

"I am not wearing that damned *S'suumea*," he
grumbled. "Not a chance of it. Not ever."

"Have you already told *Gran-seir* that?" she
chanced asking.

"Yes. And I intend to stand by that, no matter
what tricks they try to pull or jokes they make. I
will walk outside nude next time if I have to." Evan
worked the button fly closed.

At least he knew it wasn't a serious bid to
make him wear the traditional dress. "Then he
won't force the issue."

He shot a look of disbelief at her.

"I'm guessing this was Aleeks's idea of a joke. I
never said my brother had a good sense of humor.
Did I?"

Evan fastened the last of his buttons, then
tossed the drying cloth over one shoulder and the
seabag over the other. At last he offered Zondra
his hand. He whipped open the door between the
s'sanuea and the inner nest, tensing at the sight
of Daahn behind the door.

Without giving the elder time to ask what the
uproar was, Evan shoved the drying cloth at him
and drew Zondra along with him. Half a room
away, Daahn recovered enough to roar out
Aleeks's name.

"Hopefully Aleeks is in the nest now," Zondra
imparted. "It will go easier if he faces *Gran-seir*
now rather than later."

And he *would* face their *gran-seir*. A simple prank between Dominants—even a scuffle between them—would have been beneath *Gran-seir's* notice, but Aleeks's prank had upset Zondra, and no Dominant worth his scales would allow that to pass without punishment.

"His problem," Evan replied simply.

"Yes, it certainly is." Zondra smiled up at him. "You know... The drying cloth wrapped around your waist looks quite a bit like an informal *S'suumea*."

"I'm not wearing the *S'suumea*."

"You looked really good in it." He did. *Positively scrumptious.*

He turned at the base of the stairs and glared at her. "I'm not wearing the *S'suumea*."

"They are very accessible." She let the tease hang between them.

His eyes narrowed. "I am not wearing the *S'suumea*...in the center nest. Not for your family."

"I can live with that."

Section 2:

Aleeks

Close Enough to Human

Dedication

To Tamer, the man whose killing rage would rival even Aleeks's.

To the military men and women of the past, present, and future.

Chapter Fifteen

Three years later

"What do you think, Daahn?" Jacks asked.

"You know what I think. This is fucking stupidity."

Commander Aleeks Daahn forced his jaw to unclench. There was something wrong with this whole setup. Even his *gran-seir* had agreed that the Xxan didn't negotiate this way.

The Xxan don't negotiate at all. They were hunters; they took what they wanted, as they'd tried to take Earth fifty years earlier.

But the councilors had refused to listen. They'd claimed that since Daahn the Eldest had been away for half a century, things might have changed for the Xxan in that time.

Barking unlikely, in Aleeks's opinion. According to his *gran-seir*, the Xxan hadn't changed significantly in millennia, his own decisions and those of some of his command notwithstanding.

The councilors had agreed to this meeting on *Xxania Hethhh*, the Xxan sister-moon, a festering hunk of rock that had been all but mined out of its precious ores and minerals. Now it was up to Aleeks and three squads of other elite troops to keep the fools alive, agree or not.

The Xxan entered from their side of the mountain range, streaming into the amphitheater in triple rows. They were massive reptilian humanoids, the Dominant males with their ridge plates fully extended in show and their serrated teeth bared as a warning to rival males. Not that Dominant Xxanian warriors saw humans as rivals. It had taken his *gran-seir* two years in captivity to develop that much respect for humans.

The *Grea* Elders took the higher seats, the lesser Dominants below, and the Subdominants as a buffer between them and the humans across the theater.

Just as *Gran-seir* postulated. Their opinions of the untouchable humans hadn't changed.

Then why are we here? It was a setup, but it was a damned odd one. Most of the human Council was present—all but the three female Council members, by his count—and all the Xxanian *Grea* Elders. The former made sense to him; the latter didn't compute.

Aleeks forced himself to breathe through his nose alone, keeping his mouth shut tight. The tongue-scent of so many rival Dominants would make it nearly impossible to control his need to raise his ridge plates in response.

As it was, they'd hidden his Xxanian eyes behind dark glasses and trusted the confusion of Xxanian and human scents to mask his own mixed heritage. It was a safe bet that the Xxan would assume the worst if they discovered Aleeks among the humans.

When the Xxan were seated, Councilor Allen greeted them in the traditional manner. While many of the other soldiers listened to the conversation on translators, Aleeks chose to do his own translation.

184

"Honored Grea *Elders, Dominants, and all, I greet you and speak as negotiator for Earth's leaders. I am Councilor Ian Allen."*

One of the *Grea* Elders stood, motioning expansively. *"The Xxan welcome our human guests. It is an honor you show us, learning our language. Perhaps you would allow us to show you the same honor."*

Aleeks motioned his men to covert readiness. After nearly fifty years of disdain for all things human, the Xxan wouldn't offer such a magnanimous show unless there was a trap involved somewhere.

This entire thing is a trap. The question remained: where was the switch to activate it?

A murmur in the human ranks swelled into a cacophony of voices overlapping.

"It can't be."

"She's human."

Aleeks examined the slight female making her way to the center of the dirt floor between the delegations. She was dressed in black pants and a button-down shirt, not unlike those worn by Earth's soldiers of two generations ago, though hers bore no insignia of rank and affiliation. Her dark blonde hair was pulled back in a braid behind her head. She was barefoot and wearing a pair of dark glasses not unlike Aleeks's pair. In fact, they might have been a pair of standard-issue glasses taken from a human prisoner of a few decades earlier.

Curious, he tasted the air, using her female musk to separate her from the other bodies crowding the amphitheater. His mind rebelled, and Aleeks forced his ridge plates back, almost painfully.

Jacks jostled him. "She's human, Daahn. Some of the prisoners must have—"

"She's not." Aleeks knew precisely what she was, but she started speaking...in English, stealing his chance to say it first.

"Honored councilors of Earth, I greet you and speak as negotiator for my *Grea* Elders Xxan." She bowed her head first to the Xxan and then to the human delegates. "I am known as Mirienne Johns. I am of your Marilyn Johns, formerly of planet Earth."

Jacks started to ask a question, and Aleeks motioned him for silence.

Councilor Allen recovered his wits enough to speak. "You're human?"

Aleeks rolled his eyes. Though he didn't trust this, the idea of crossbred Xxan-humans should hardly come as a shock to Allen.

She hesitated, then removed her glasses, meeting the councilor's eyes across the five meters that separated them. Aleeks didn't question what the councilors saw. No doubt, Mirienne Johns had retained the Xxanian eyes, just as Aleeks had.

But why is she called Johns? She should carry the name of her seir *or* mate. Barring the possibility that Marilyn Johns herself had been pregnant with a son when she was captured, and that son had taken a Xxanian female to mate, producing Mirienne in the bargain, her naming made no sense to Aleeks.

Mirienne didn't put her glasses back on. The amphitheater was dark enough for the Xxan and those with Xxanian eyes. He wasn't certain why she'd worn the glasses at all.

It's theatrical. Something is very wrong here.

"I know this must be a shock for you," she continued.

Hardly...if it's real.

"But I hope you can see past—"

The first blast came without warning, mowing Allen down. Taken off guard, the human troops and councilors scrambled.

Mirienne turned, seemingly horrified at the attack. Her weapon came up as Aleeks's did, both locked on the Xxanian shooter. Her blast hit home a split second before his, both killing shots.

Blasts came from every direction in response. Aleeks shifted his attention from the Xxanian warriors attacking them to the "negotiator" taking down those she "represented" and back again.

She was shouting in Xxan, ordering them to stand down, shooting one warrior after another as their weapons came up. Her head snapped around at a command from the *Grea* Elder who'd called her forward.

"Kill the crossbred abomination."

Aleeks's heart stuttered in fear and then smoothed. They didn't mean *him*; they meant Mirienne.

The *Grea* Elder was dead before his words echoed...then two more went down. They weren't three in a row, which would've indicated she wanted to kill the entire forum. Rather, they seemed chosen at random. Something told Aleeks they weren't random.

The uproar from the Xxan seemed to support that theory. Mirienne abandoned the next elder she'd targeted and started dodging blasts, bolting for a tunnel opposite Aleeks's position. Suddenly, none of the Xxan were interested in firing at the retreating humans. Every Xxan with a weapon in hand was firing at a single crossbred woman.

Aleeks provided her cover, ordering his men to cut down every Xxan in fighting stance, letting instinct rule him in the manner that had served him so well in battle thus far. Still, the Xxan didn't turn on the humans again.

He let out an explosive sigh as she disappeared down the shaft. Aleeks cut down the first five Xxanian warriors trying to run her down. If he could give her a decent enough head start, she might just escape them.

Jacks pulled at his shoulder. "The councilors are gone, Daahn. We're pulling out."

He nodded, covering his men to the darkness on their side of the mountain range. Not that there was much to cover them from. Some of the Subdominants had followed Mirienne Johns down the tunnel, but the rest of the Xxan had retreated to their own side of the range.

There were only two transports left when he reached the touchdown point. Aleeks ignored them both, heading for Admiral MacNair. Only MacNair would understand, and only he had the power to keep them from pulling out completely.

In the distance, Aleeks noted several Xxanian transports lifting off and speeding farther into their space.

"Daahn," MacNair greeted him.

"I need a transport and my team," he stated bluntly.

MacNair gaped at him. "Denied."

"We need Mirienne Johns."

"We do or *you* do?" he challenged.

Aleeks forced his ridge plates down, aware that his forehead undulated in the battle to keep them retracted. "*We* need her...and she needs our help. We would have been sitting ducks in there without her."

He didn't add that he'd warned them it was a trap. That might push MacNair too far, especially since MacNair had agreed with that assessment. Though politics went against Aleeks's Dominant male Xxanian side, his human side could rein that in...usually.

MacNair sighed. "Captain Seaver," he shouted.

Seaver's head came up. "Sir?"

"You have a mission, Captain."

Seaver scowled at Aleeks but didn't comment.

"Bring her in for questioning, Daahn. You have eight hours. After that, I'll leave you on this rock, your *gran-seir* and *seir* be damned."

Aleeks bit back a smile. "Understood, sir." He turned away from his 'godfather.' "Jacks! I want the team suited up for stealth and ready to roll in thirty or less. Less *is* preferred."

The lieutenant grumbled but complied.

* * * *

Miri hissed a series of curses in Xxan and human English. Damn her *gran-seir* and *seir* alike. Damn her entire family, the *Grea* Elders, the

Dominants...and anyone else who had even a passing knowledge of this shit.

It had all been a lie, from conception... She ground her serrated back teeth at the unintended pun.

From conception to execution, and if I am not mindful, it will mean my *execution.*

That eventuality firmly in mind, Miri crept along the darkened tunnel, her senses open to scent and sound and movement of air as much as they were to sight. If she could find her way back to the surface, Miri could hide herself in the old growth, lose herself in the sacred areas no one else cared to tread.

The ambush came without warning. The six humans had been shielded from every sense: wearing dark clothing to blend into the tunnel walls, unmoving, silent, and masked in breathers to still their air.

Her hand shook, and she rested her thumb on the weapon lock, torn on the point of readying the weapon for a firefight.

On one hand, she had no wish to harm the humans. Miri had been raised and trained to be a negotiator to them. She hadn't been raised as a weapon.

Yes, I was, and now I know it. And so do they.

That fact was the one reason she kept her thumb on the lock. Innocent of the plan or not, Miri had been used by the Xxan to stage the attack. She might have to fight her way out.

"Lower your weapon, Johns," one of the humans ordered.

She spied the black on black insignia of a lieutenant, the only protection he'd have on a world that obeyed the Interstellar War Pact. Failure to display rank and affiliation could see him dead.

I have no insignia. No doubt, the Xxan had planned it that way. She hadn't questioned it, because this had been presented as a diplomatic mission and she as an honored representative of the Xxan. Now she was a combatant. They could kill her without pause. *And likely will.*

Miri took a step back into the tunnel she'd come out of, her trembling more severe. She'd passed a crosstunnel ten meters back. If she could reach it—

The arms suddenly encircling her were as strong as her *Xxan-Dree* trainer's. Miri didn't waste time questioning who he was or how he'd managed to sneak up on her. As he ripped the weapon from her hand, Miri moved—down, then in a flowing movement around his body.

He was quick...and skilled. Her trainers had never put her through her paces so strenuously. Every move to escape was met with a block. Every move to incapacitate him for a moment was countered skillfully. Miri was considering doing him real harm when the end came.

It was a move she'd never encountered before, either with her *Xxan-Dree* trainer or her human martial trainer. One moment, she was on her way to freedom. The next, Miri was facedown on the stone, her wrists captured behind her back, locked in his larger hands. The length of his body pinned her down, spikes of pain from her injured abdomen making her gasp for breath.

"Concede," he grumbled.

Miri pressed her forehead to the smooth stone floor, abruptly weary. "It would seem...I have no choice in the matter."

His laughter was low and dark...but not cruel, as she usually experienced. "An accurate assessment."

"If you're through dancing with her," another voice interrupted. "Perhaps you would verify her identity, Daahn?"

Miri braced herself for the sting of a blood test that never came. Her captor nuzzled at her neck, and she jerked at his hold, panic driving her to flee. He pushed her down with a wordless growl, stroking his tongue up the side column of her neck to her jaw.

Every muscle in her body tightened in fury. How dare he examine her so intimately! A hiss of warning escaped her lips.

His next move stunned her, rendering Miri a babe in his hands. His tongue stroked over her mating stripe, and her body responded fiercely. Even before she felt the press of his erection to the back of her thigh, Miri's body had slicked to welcome him in, the pains fading into the background for once. Her glands released *Zhigaaah*, the female sex pheromone, making her head swim.

"You are mine, little blue," he whispered.

She shivered in delight, needing him to finish what he'd started. Another voice buzzed at the edges of her consciousness, drowned out by the cascade of *Zhigaaah.*

"She's the one," the male over her attested.

Miri's blood went cold at that pronouncement. Her eyes pricked in tears she couldn't bear to shed. She swallowed down a sob, then forced words out, feigning confidence she didn't feel and pride she had no right to display. All the while, she nursed the loss of the illusion stoically...as she'd done before.

"I suppose you should kill me now, though I am hardly worth the energy. If my—" *They aren't my people. I have no people.* "If the Xxan find me, they will kill me, and I have no information to give you. I am worse than useless to either side now."

There was a moment of tense silence. Miri forced her breathing to even.

"Are you?" the one over her challenged.

Daahn. They said his name was Daahn. And she thought she'd spied the insignia of a commander on his uniform. *Commander Daahn.*

Her muscles ached. "Yes, I am." She prepared for the blast that would kill her. Or would he break her neck? It would save them the energy of killing a useless prisoner.

There was another moment of silence. "I see. Jacks...the shackles, please."

Miri didn't fight the restraints. She didn't intend to fight anything they did. If they wanted to question her, even to beat nonexistent information from her, it would still be a gentler death than the Xxan would grant her.

Chapter Sixteen

Aleeks stared down at his prisoner, wondering at her reaction. He'd seen Mirienne Johns take down two dozen of the Xxanian command, three of them *Grea* Elders, to allow all but the first slain human—*Councilor Allen, may the stars welcome him home*—the chance to escape the trap set for them.

Still, Mirienne wasn't fighting his hold on her arm. She wasn't attempting to slow them. She wasn't even examining her captors and her situation for possible corridors to escape. She was silent, biddable...but still proud.

But why? Was this just another step in the plan? Was she meant to be captured, in order to attack later? Or had she truly been surprised by the Xxan's duplicity and deception?

"Ahead," Arris directed him, pointing the way, no doubt because Aleeks had veered off slightly in his inattention.

Aleeks nodded, tugging Mirienne toward the waiting warship. She glanced at it, then away, matching his long-legged gait. She winced, half closing her eyes, dropping her chin back to her chest as it had been for nearly the entire trip back.

"Jacks," Aleeks called out, not taking his eyes off the prisoner, though he was certain she didn't mean to attack him.

"Yeah?" the human replied distractedly.

"Glasses." He put his free hand out for them.

"But you have—"

194

Aleeks glared at him, knowing full well that it unnerved humans, even with his dark glasses in place.

"Got it," Jacks grumbled. He pulled his own glasses from the padded case at his back and settled them in Aleeks's hand.

Aleeks pulled Mirienne to a stop. She hesitated, then raised her head slowly to meet his gaze. He settled Jacks's glasses on her face, shading her eyes.

Mirienne moved her mouth as if to speak, then closed it. Her nostrils flared, and her tongue appeared at her lips, taking in his scent. The sour smell of adrenaline poured off her, and her muscles tensed. Aleeks grasped her other arm, shaking his head slightly in warning, and she looked away. A tremor worked through her body, then went still.

"Daahn, we're out of time," Jacks reminded him.

"Right." He turned her toward the waiting ramp.

From above, Captain Seaver's voice bellowed out, "I hope this madness was worth it, Daahn."

"It wasn't," Mirienne breathed.

"We'll see," Aleeks answered his CO. "It was worth a try."

Despite her statement and her fear, she preceded him up the ramp.

Seaver scowled down at her. "Lock her down. We'll get to her once we're clear."

Aleeks started to lead her away.

"Not you," the captain ordered. "Hand her off to Jackson."

Aleeks released her as the human lieutenant took hold of her opposite arm. He watched long enough to ensure that Jacks would treat her fairly...and long enough to see her single peek back at him.

Seaver didn't address him immediately. The captain had more important things to do...like getting them the hell off *Xxania Hethhh* and into human-controlled space, where they could dock with their carrier. At that point, Mirienne Johns would be transferred from the lock-seat to a cell aboard the carrier.

Luckily, the trip to the rendezvous point didn't take long. With a transport still out, their carrier was the one guarding the fleet's back, lagging behind the rest, though not by much.

Aleeks spent the time at tactical. The others probably thought he anticipated problems with Mirienne. He didn't, but it didn't hurt to appear vigilant.

On their way down the ramp into the carrier's primary landing bay, Seaver finally broke the silence. "Well, we've got her, Daahn. Now explain to me why we *want* her."

He considered that. "If it was a setup, she would have taken out only cannon fodder. She went not only for the Subdominants and Dominants, but also for the *Grea* Elders."

"It could have been a coup," Seaver suggested, handing off a docking order to a waiting deck chief.

"No. She ran from the Xxan, and though she had ample time to do it, Johns didn't try to harm us."

Seaver's eyes narrowed. "She allowed herself to be taken?"

"No, but she didn't attack me, either. She just tried to escape me...at first."

His captain's raised eyebrow asked the question silently.

"Mirienne...Johns expects us to kill her, eventually. She thinks one side or the other will. Once she was caught—"

"She should have fought," Seaver surmised. "She had nothing to lose."

"She had nothing to *gain*," Aleeks countered. "Not against seven of us and without her weapons."

The captain sighed. "And if she doesn't have information about their military?" he asked.

"If she turned against the Xxan that way, Mirienne Johns would be a good ally. Military information or not, she has information from inside *Xxania Uuaahht*, current information. And she's well trained."

Saying that sent an atypical spike of annoyance through him. It made little sense that he could fathom. He worked with female soldiers every day, but the idea of Mirienne Johns fighting was different somehow.

"If we could trust her," Seaver cautioned.

"If it comes to that, I can assure it." But if it came to that, she wouldn't be permitted to don a uniform.

It could go that way. The residue of *Zhigaaah* in his bloodstream had Aleeks semierect and aching to follow through. Just the scent of *Zhigaaah*, that of a female not related to him and untainted by *Zhigaaal*, which would indicate mating, was enough to catch a Dominant's attention, but Mirienne was a potent female. The sight and taste of her blue mating stripe, confirming her in her fertile window, had been too enticing to let pass without a sample. How she'd made it this long unmated...

Well, that probably went without saying. She wasn't Xxanian. If his suspicions were founded, the Xxan had never created a natural crossbreed like he and his *seir* were.

"How...? Whoa—" Seaver's face paled, and he swallowed hard. "You mean, you'll...? Uh..."

Aleeks smiled at the captain's inability or unwillingness to face the fact that one of his officers was a crossbreed with very Xxanian mating habits, that he could—and ultimately *would* bind a female to him until they were nearly inseparable. Once mated, Aleeks and his mate would crave each other. If he died, she would pine to death. If she died, it would send him into a killing rage, and if he survived long past it, it was unlikely he'd mate again.

The captain's fear of and distaste for the idea of such a commitment was common among humans, and so they pretended it wasn't a reality in their crossbred associates. It was a mental block many humans suffered from.

Aleeks was aware that Seaver could see the serrated hunting teeth surrounding his very human incisors and canines. Smiling a big, toothy grin wasn't an expression he indulged in often. Seaver's shudder of revulsion illustrated why he usually stifled the urge.

"You'll—" Seaver took a step away from him. "You'll want to handle her questioning then."

"I insist."

The captain waved him away.

Aleeks headed for the primary cell block, anticipating seeing her again. He coded into the block, nodding to the guard on the way past the desk. The door lock clicked open for him, and Aleeks pushed it wide, then stopped in the doorway, horrified.

Mirienne lay curled on the bunk, her eyes squeezed shut and weeping, her cheeks red and ravaged.

Damn you, Jacks. The lieutenant had taken his glasses back and left her in agony in a fully lit room.

"Fifteen percent," Aleeks ordered. "The lighting is never to go above twenty percent, but no more than fifteen percent in the next three days." She'd need at least that long to heal from this assault.

"Yes, sir." The guard punched Aleeks's orders into the console before him without question, and the lighting inside the cell dropped to a comfortable level for Xxanian eyes.

Aleeks strode inside, closing the door behind him, noting in annoyance that the lock engaged. She was hardly a threat in this state.

He didn't waste time. Aleeks wet a cloth with cool water and went to her, pressing it to Mirienne's swollen face. A half-swallowed sob escaped her lips, and her shivering form jerked in response to the touch.

The effects of tears on her sensitive crossbred skin would be nearly as agonizing as the light was to her fully Xxanian eyes. It was one of the few reasons Aleeks didn't curse his own inability to tear.

At a loss to comfort her, Aleeks searched out a parent's soothing rumble in the Xxan language. It was surely something she'd heard before.

"Do not insult me," she snapped in English.

Startled, he fumbled for words in his primary language. "I didn't mean to insinuate that you are a child," he offered by way of apology.

"No. Of course not. Instead, you insult me by assuming I wish to speak Xxan." There was a note of hurt underlying her anger.

"Would an Earth lullaby be more to your taste?" he asked in exasperation.

Mirienne hesitated, her brow furrowing against his fingertips. "I don't know what lullaby is," she admitted.

"Then you weren't—" Aleeks bit off the rest of the retort, aware of how hurtful it was to suggest she hadn't been raised right. "I'll refresh the cloth."

He could hear her moving on the bunk, see wisps of that movement at the corner of the mirror, and he removed his glasses to see better in the semidarkness. It was no surprise to find her upright and leaning against the wall, her lower legs hanging over the edge of the narrow sleeping surface. The fact that her eyes were open, however, was surprising.

Mirienne was in misery. Aleeks went to her, wasting only a moment to take in her red-gold, slitted eyes before he pressed the cloth to them again.

"I'm sorry," he whispered.

Her jaw tightened. "That I'm Xxan enough to require darkness or that I'm human enough to cry salt tears when the light—"

"I'm sorry that Jacks did this to you."

For a moment, she was silent. "Why...are you doing this?"

"Caring for you? You're injured."

"Do humans always care for their prisoners?"

"I'm not human," he reminded her.

"More than I am." She sighed.

"I can't cry."

People believed that made Aleeks cold, but he felt as deeply as anyone else did. He simply couldn't express it the same way they did. He didn't sweat. He didn't blush or pale...unless he was ill. He often chose not to smile.

"The Xxan would have loved you."

Aleeks's move to question that was cut short.

"I don't need my eyes to answer the charges against me," she stated, her spine stiffening.

"Should there be charges against you?" He kept his tone cool and nonjudgmental.

"Would you believe me if I claimed there shouldn't be?" The bite of cynicism was no surprise.

Yes. "Maybe. You did kill three of the *Grea* Elders."

"That doesn't make me your ally," she pointed out. "You have no choice but to assume me part of the plot against you. I know that."

"And you allowed me to bring you here. What does *that* tell me?" Aleeks wasn't certain what it told him, but he wanted to hear what *she* thought it did.

"Should I have killed you to escape deeper into the tunnels?" she countered.

"You could have *tried.*" *And failed.* Mirienne was good, but she wasn't that good. She was a much better shot than she was at hand-to-hand combat.

She faltered, something incoherent emerging before words did. "I don't understand you."

"You didn't know what the *Grea* Elders intended," he stated confidently.

* * * *

Miri took a calming breath. She didn't understand why he bothered to play this game, but she'd answer honestly, nonetheless. "No. I knew nothing about the deception."

She counted the heartbeats, hardly daring to breathe. Commander Daahn had no reason to believe her. No sane warrior would.

That left him with only a few choices. Would he call her a liar? Would he try to prove her a liar? Would he try to beat some other truth from her? Or would he simply kill her?

"You've trained extensively," he noted. "Enough to attempt to escape me without harming me...in at least five different forms, including high Xxan."

So he wants to prove I'm lying. Miri chose not to answer him. What would be the point?

"You didn't even take the lock off your weapon," he continued.

"I was ready to. I would have, if forced to it."

"Would you really?" That was a taunt.

She forced down her urge to strike at him.

The cloth left her face, but he didn't move away to freshen it again. Miri opened her aching eyes, locking on the gold-green of his. The intensity of his gaze unnerved her, and her heart fluttered as if she were his prey.

"What were you trained for, Mirienne?" he asked bluntly.

"To be a negotiator. I believed it, until..."

He tossed the cloth into the sink without looking in that direction. "Until the Xxan started shooting at us."

"Yes. So...you see, there really is nothing I can tell you." Miri steeled herself for his decision to kill her...or to torture her for information she didn't have. Master S'sie would have already done so.

"You can tell me why you were trained for war," he replied in a voice that announced his patience was wearing thin.

"Sometimes negotiations fail." *I've always been told I would fail. I thought they were just unkind words; I didn't know I'd been set up to fail.*

A smile turned his lush lips upward. "I suppose that's true enough."

Miri shivered at the memory of Daahn over her in the corridor on *Xxania Hethhh.* She stared at those human lips, wondering what they would feel like beneath her sensitive fingers...or on her mating stripe for an extended stay.

As if he knew what she was thinking, his eye slits narrowed and his nostrils flared, his lips parting slightly to bare the tip of his tongue. "Why you?" he asked.

She looked at the closed door, a thousand unkind words ringing in her ears, certain she would be blushing if she were truly human.

"You are weak, Mirienne."

"If the negotiations were not so important, I would kill you now for your incompetence."

"You are a hateful thing...weak, unappealing..."

"Mirienne?"

"Do not call me that," she growled. Miri tensed to fight, wincing at the cut of the shackles into her wrists. She sank back to the wall, forcing her muscles to ease.

Commander Daahn rose, coming face-to-face with her. "Why *you*?"

"Because I was convenient," she exploded. "Because, weak as I am, I survived."

His eye slits widened, then narrowed again. "Weak?"

Tears pricked at her eyes, and Miri blinked them away. Commander Daahn was lucky that he couldn't cry. "Yes, weak." She'd always been too weak for Xxanian tastes. Perhaps he was only seen as strong because he was compared to real humans. "Too...human, they said. Not to be trusted."

Were they wrong about me? That was a question she didn't want to examine too closely.

Daahn grasped her by the shoulders, turning Miri toward the head of the bunk. She lowered her chin to her chest, preparing for death.

Miri started trilling the death song under her breath, then abandoned it. Surely, the Xxanian

Seir-God had forsaken her, and she didn't know the names of the human gods or how to appease them. Her soul would face the vacuum alone.

One metal cuff unfastened, then the other. She held her position, even when he backed away. Confused, afraid to meet his eyes, her heart pounded so fiercely that her head spun. It was another of her human frailties.

"Are you hungry?" he asked.

Her stomach roiled in warning at the thought of food. "No." Actually, she was ravenous, but she'd bring up whatever she tried to eat, and it would be far too long before another meal would be forthcoming to waste food when she was certain it wouldn't stick.

"When you are, let the guard know. I'll leave orders. You eat a Xxanian diet, of course."

She nodded. Miri wouldn't recognize a human diet, if presented with it.

"What should I call you?" he pressed.

What was he asking? "Commander Daahn?"

"That's my name."

There was a tone in his voice she didn't recognize. It was akin to a taunt, but different enough that it didn't stoke the urge to strike back at him. Miri turned to him, uneasily noting his wide smile. She backed into the corner, bracing for attack.

His smile disappeared into an expression of irritation. It was an expression she'd seen often in her life. She'd always found a scowl less threatening than a smile. A scowl meant a simple beating; a smile meant something worse.

"It was a joke," he snapped at her.

Miri shook her head, at a loss. She'd thought she'd learned English, but there were so many words he used that she didn't understand: lullaby, joke... How many more would there be?

His expression softened. "You don't know what a joke is either?"

She chanced addressing him. "No. I don't."

"I'll try to remember that. In the interim, you protested me using your name. What should I call you? Did they call you Johns?"

"Miri."

"Mary?"

"If you insist." What did it matter? She was a prisoner. Soon enough, she'd be dead. What he called her was immaterial, as long as he didn't call her that hateful name.

"Is it your name?" he asked, seemingly perplexed.

"No. My name is Miri."

"Then why would you accept Mary?" His irritation spiked so abruptly the ridge plates on his forehead and neck raised.

Miri's breath went choppy at the warning of a Dominant male. Her abdomen ached, a stark reminder of what happened when a Dominant was angry. She averted her eyes, lowering her head in the submissive show, her hands out and palms up. "It doesn't matter," she managed to say. "Call me what you like." The Xxan had often enough.

"Then why shouldn't I call you Mirienne?" It was clearly a challenge. If there was one thing a Dominant enjoyed, it was prevailing in a challenge, and no one could mistake that Daahn was a Dominant.

She glanced at his extended ridge plates, noting the way his hair crested over the top of his head, resuming the submissive immediately. He wasn't mollified. "Call me whatever you like," she repeated. *Please, let my capitulation be enough. If it isn't...* She didn't know what he'd do, but it wouldn't be pleasant.

Commander Daahn sighed. She saw his hand rise and peeked up at him. He ran the hand over his forehead, grimacing. His ridge plates eased back slowly, and her breathing eased with them. He was content with her answer. With a Dominant, content was often the best she could hope for.

"It's been a long day," he stated. "I believe we both need rest."

Miri didn't respond to that. His swinging emotions kept her off balance. *Perhaps that is his plan.*

He turned toward the door and pulled out his darkened glasses. "Until tomorrow," he dismissed her. Then he was gone, with a swift knock, a grunt of a word, and a single shaft of stinging light.

She forced her heart rate and breathing to normalize, sliding down the wall to the lush mattress. Miri curled in on herself as she had when she was a child. *As I have every night since that last beating.*

That wasn't something she wanted to consider. The realities of her situation were troubling enough. For the first time in years, Miri allowed herself the solace and weakness of real tears.

Chapter Seventeen

Aleeks speared at a chunk of warm, raw beef, his thoughts and emotions in turmoil.

Miri Johns was a minefield. They'd told her she was training as a negotiator, but her understanding of human nuances was nonexistent. She didn't understand jokes or lullabies or even compassion and caring.

He paused with the fork halfway into his mouth, realization slamming home in his sleep-deprived brain. The Xxan cared for their young. If anyone knew it, he did.

Then why doesn't she know it? She was raised by them. She should know it as well as I do.

He chewed at the *z'haahn*, considering it. Smiles were perceived as a threat. She hated her own name. She'd obviously been berated often.

"Because, weak as I am, I survived." Convenient...

That was what she really believed her only value was to them.

His appetite deserted him, and Aleeks placed the fork on his plate, kicking himself for missing this all night. How many times had he rolled this problem over and let the obvious slip him by?

She'd been a distraction for them, a human decoy. She'd been trained to fight, in the belief that, when the reversal came, she would protect the Xxan.

How bad was it? His ridge plates had sent her into a panic. His smile had forced her to a defensive posture. She'd taken the submissive at the first sign of his status as a Dominant male.

Questions coursed through Aleeks's mind. They were questions only Miri could answer.

Determined to have those answers, he took to his feet, turned—and came face-to-face with Jacks.

The lieutenant glanced at the half-full plate, his smile wide. "Off your feed, Daahn?" he teased. "The little lady Xxan getting under your skin?"

He'd lost track of how many times in the last day he'd had to fight his ridge plates back. This time, he didn't fight it. Aleeks let them extend fully.

Jacks stared at them, his eyes going wide and his face paling. He scrambled back two steps, running aground on another table.

"You tortured her," Aleeks informed him. "You didn't even turn down the lights for her when you took your glasses back."

"She's a prisoner, Daahn," he protested weakly.

"Oh? Then I suppose you'd want a cell kept at forty-five degrees Celsius? Or at five? You'd accept it without bringing charges of abuse of a prisoner?"

Jacks darkened, and he didn't reply.

"Don't do it again, Lieutenant Jackson. Next time, I won't be nearly this forgiving."

"Understood...sir." His lip curled in disgust at using the title for Aleeks.

That's right. Remember my rank. I won't hesitate to pull it, if you try this again. Aleeks forced his ridge plates back and headed for Miri's cell, punching in the code for the outer door so hard his fingers ached.

He paused at the desk, her situation tumbling around in his mind. "Has she requested food?" Aleeks asked the guard on duty.

"Not on my watch."

"Check the logs."

The guard tapped at the screen. "Not at all. In fact, she hasn't requested anything. Not toiletries. Not a change of clothing. Not food or drinks. Nothing."

Though he'd expected as much, Aleeks felt his temper rise. This time, he kept his ridge plates fully retracted, but it cost him in effort. "*Z'haahn.*" *No. She's been raised by the Xxan.* "A meat tray...just meat, prepared as I like it."

"Yes, sir." Unlike Jacks, there was no disrespect in the term.

Aleeks strode to the door, opening it when the lock clicked, pulling off his glasses as the light behind him disappeared.

Miri lay, curled on the bunk again, her hands drawn up under her chin. Her face was raw and swollen, so much so that he initially thought someone had disobeyed his orders and turned up the lighting.

Closer inspection showed she'd been crying. Even now, she wasn't still. Tremors racked her body, and her muscles tensed and released.

She murmured a protest in Xxan, then another in English. Her breathing went ragged, and a weak cry escaped her lips.

Her eyes opened, and Miri lunged at him, wild-eyed, hissing a warning. Aleeks turned her beneath him, pinning her wrists to the floor near her head and her hips beneath his. A second cry...one of pain, rattled his nerves.

The door opened, and she squeezed her eyes shut to the light. Aleeks endured it, gauging her responses in her half-awake state.

"Do you need assistance, sir?" the guard asked.

Miri winced, no doubt envisioning punishment for attacking him.

"No. It was my error. Miri was sleeping, and I startled her."

"If you're certain..."

She opened her abused eyes, lost again.

By the stars, she has no concept what understanding and kindness are. "I am," Aleeks replied. "Close the door, please; it hurts our eyes."

"Yes, sir. I'll log the incident for you, sir." The guard withdrew and shut the door, before Aleeks could protest the report.

It's probably better to let him report it. If I try to stop him, it won't look good.

Still, there were answers he needed. "What were you dreaming?"

Miri closed her eyes, relaxing beneath him. "The attack."

"The attack on *Xxania Hethhh*?"

She hesitated for a long moment, opening her eyes, the slits widened in some strong emotion she'd masked otherwise. "Was there any other?"

Yes, but why won't you tell me about it? Aleeks eased off her, kneeling on the floor by her feet. "Did I injure you?" He motioned to her midsection, piecing together that she'd cried out when he landed over her.

Miri scurried to the corner where the bed met the wall, then folded her knees to her chest. "No."

Her eyes called her a liar, but Aleeks decided not to press the issue. A hundred questions fought for his attention. "Who were the three *Grea* Elders you killed?"

"Uuumaal—"

"No," he interrupted her. "Who were they to *you*?"

Her breathing hitched. "The first...was my *seir.*"

The one who ordered her killed. Her own seir *ordered her death.*

Damn, he never claimed her. Why wasn't she named Mirienne Uuumaal?

She waited, tense, adrenaline tainting the air around her. Did she expect him to condemn her for killing the *seir* who had wanted her dead?

"Go on," he invited.

"The second was the one that...mixed the genes to create me. Me and the many others who didn't survive it."

Aleeks nodded grimly. "You're not a natural phenomenon then." He'd suspected as much.

She bristled visibly.

"I only meant that your parents didn't—"

"No. They never mated. They said my mother chose to...donate to me...to carry me, but I doubt that now."

"Did you ever meet her?" Aleeks pressed.

"No. I never did. They said she didn't survive carrying me. She was old by then. It might be true."

He considered that. "Who raised you?" It was a safe bet that her *seir* hadn't.

Miri shrugged. "My trainers."

"Trainers? What are trainers?" It wasn't a term his *gran-seir* had used.

She furrowed her brow, seemingly seeking a translation. Before he could suggest she use the Xxan and let him translate for her, she spoke again. "The ones who taught me. Is there another—"

"No, Miri. Who *cared* for you?"

"When I was ill, there were physic—"

"No." Why was this so difficult? Aleeks tried to order his thoughts. "Who...fed you?"

Her expression announced clearly that he'd offended her. "I assure you, I am more than capable of feeding mys—"

"By the stars!" he cursed.

Miri pressed herself farther into the corner, watching him as if for an attack.

"When you were a child, who fed you?"

She shook her head, looking young and lost.

"Before you could feed yourself?" he qualified.

"You remember such a time?" Miri asked.

Aleeks bit back a string of curses. "Did anyone...bathe you?"

Her eyes narrowed in suspicion. She shook her head in a negative response.

"Send you to bed?"

She glanced to the mattress and back, her confusion deepening, if her expression was any indication.

"Comfort you?" he continued.

"I don't understand. Why should I require comfort?"

Aleeks put up a hand, motioning for a moment of peace. He was getting nowhere; he had to face that she didn't remember a time when anyone had cared for her as a child was typically cared for. "Who was the third?" he asked.

Miri shook her head, lost by the abrupt change of subject.

"The third *Grea* Elder you shot?"

She averted her gaze, wrapping both hands around one small foot. "One of my trainers," she grumbled. "Master S'sie taught me *Xxan-Dree*."

"And?" he pressed. "Why one trainer?"

"The next would have been Master Haauulen, my human martial trainer," she admitted.

"Why S'sie first?"

She peeked up at him, her adrenaline level rising alarmingly, refusing him an answer.

He's the one she fears most. But why?

A knock on the door broke the tension.

"Come in," Aleeks ordered.

Miri looked to the far corner of the room, narrowing her eyes but choosing to leave them open.

The tray settled before Aleeks, and he waved the guard away, watching her reactions. Miri's nostrils flared, and she bit at her lower lip. She shot a look of longing at the platter but averted her gaze almost before he'd noted it. She made no move to take the offered food.

"Aren't you hungry?" he asked.

She didn't answer.

"I know you haven't eaten in at least a day."

"I haven't eaten in three. What has that to do with it?"

"Your system..." No. It was unlikely. None of the crossbred had eaten on a Xxanian cycle, even the first generation, like Aleeks's *seir.* "They only allowed you food weekly?" He'd thought she was thin because they'd fed her only meat. He hadn't realized she'd been deprived of a proper eating schedule as well.

"It is how the hunter eats," she countered. "Hunger makes the senses keener."

"Hunger weakens you. It makes you sick and—"

"The Xxan didn't seem weak to me," she grumbled.

"But you were. You were sickly and weak, off balance as you came due for another meal." He didn't question it.

Miri didn't answer it.

"Their systems are made for that abuse, Miri. Ours are not. Don't you understand? You aren't weak. They *made* you weak."

Her breathing hitched, but she didn't reply. She didn't look around at him or the food.

"Eat, Miri." Why wasn't she taking what he was clearly offering?

She glanced at the platter, then locked on his eyes, waiting, tense for a reason he couldn't put a name to but wished he could.

"You're refusing to eat?" he asked.

Her jaw tightened in anger. "You taunt me," she accused. The tears she cursed so vehemently pooled in her eyes, and she blinked, doubtless trying to banish them.

Aleeks worked at that, realization making him ill. "The Dominants ate first. Since you weren't their young, you ate the scraps they left, as a Subdominant would."

"The weak eat last," she confirmed.

Changing her perceptions was going to be harder than he thought. "Not when a Dominant views you as his own."

Females were never treated the way she'd been raised. They were always fed with the Dominants...instead of the Dominants, when food was scarce. Even young, unmated females were pampered.

Miri didn't offer an answer to that.

Aleeks moved into her space, and Miri planted her hands on the floor, preparing to strike. He plucked a cube of meat from the tray and tried to offer it. She stared at it, wary.

* * * *

Miri hardly dared breathe. The scent of meat had her stomach grumbling, jarring her injury so that food almost became unappealing again. Her head spun in the combination of pain and hunger.

Commander Daahn cocked his head to one side, assessing her as the Xxanian physicians often had. "Maybe I should feed you," he suggested.

"What?" What was he talking about?

"You have never been fed correctly, as far as I can tell. If you learn how a proper Dominant feeds his young, maybe you'd learn not to fear me."

"I don't fear you," she lied.

A slight smile pulled at his lips. Daahn placed the offered meat in his mouth, chewing it. Miri chanced another peek at the platter out of the corner of her eye, calculating that there would be little or none left for her at the end of the meal.

He leaned toward her, and she gasped in surprise. His meat-heavy breath washed over her face, making her hunger more acute. It was torture, but she didn't run from it. For a moment, neither of them moved, beyond her trembling and their tandem panting.

"Open your mouth, Miri."

She did so, and Daahn sealed his lips to hers, pushing the chewed meat into her mouth with his tongue. It was warm, spiced...and tasted of him. His lips retreated slowly. Miri savored the meat, then swallowed it down.

The next cube was already in his mouth. Miri watched him chew in a sense of anticipation.

He didn't order her to open for him that time. Daahn met her lips as they parted, pushing the meat across the join. His tongue lingered, stroking, affecting her as a light touch across her mating stripe might. His tongue and lips eased back, and Miri swallowed.

She glanced to his lap, wondering at the bulge of his cock. Was this why Master S'sie and Master Haauulen had never mouth-fed her? Because it might cause a sexual reaction? Miri knew well

217

enough that the very hint of that was distasteful to them.

Or perhaps it was just as Commander Daahn said. Since neither of them was her *seir*, perhaps they felt no compulsion to show her such care.

Daahn's lips nuzzled at hers, seeking entry. Miri admitted him, but he didn't press the food into her mouth. She drew the meat from his mouth with her tongue, shivering at the low growl from him.

He withdrew, and Miri stared at him, trying to feel out his state of mind. He was tense, but she was fairly sure Commander Daahn wasn't angry. She swallowed slowly, caught in the intensity of his gaze.

Another cube disappeared into his mouth. Miri savored the overlapping flavors, aware that her body was more than passably aroused.

Again, Daahn waited for her to take the food. Miri did so, but the commander stroked his tongue along hers, scattering the shredded meat through both of their mouths.

His hand circled the back of her neck, and one finger rested on her mating stripe. Their tongues entwined, sending pleasant waves along Miri's thighs. Her eyes slid shut.

A swift move later, she was seated across Daahn's thighs, his cock pressing to the outside of her leg. He stroked at her mating stripe, his large hands overlapping the edge to caress the line of her shoulders and neck as well, inflaming her.

Their mouths parted, and Miri swallowed the meat she'd retained, fighting the need to gasp for breath. She could taste his musk, feel his arousal.

"Miri?" he rasped out.

"I am certain a Dominant doesn't feed his young that way."

"No. Not that way," he agreed. "But you are hardly my child."

There seemed no safe answer to that.

A cube of meat touched her lips, and Miri parted them to take it. The next few bites passed in a similar manner.

Daahn's tongue stroked at her lower lip, likely cleaning away a drop of blood. Still, she opened for him.

He surged inside, exploring, scenting her...inside and out. His hands ranged over her body, taking her measure. He pressed at her abdomen, and she shied, gasping into his mouth. As much as she wanted his touch, she didn't want anyone or anything touching that spot.

Daahn's mouth left hers, seeking out the beads of *Zhigaaah* he'd raised. His breath fanned over her throat. Then his tongue was there, bathing the pheromone from her body. He stroked his lips along to pick up more. He buried his face in her neck, inhaling her scent, fisting her hair.

She didn't protest it. Visions of Commander Daahn buried to the hilt inside her danced behind her closed eyes.

His head came up, and she forced her eyes open, abruptly aware of his fingers lying against the heat between her thighs, stroking idly. His eye slits were narrowed to near invisibility.

Daahn licked his lips slowly, with a meaning that wasn't lost on her. His cock was hard and long, ready to thrust home inside her. By all the constellations in the night sky, she wanted him there.

"Will you eat, Miri?"

"Eat?" Her mind moved slowly. He was feeding her. Whatever else it had become, he'd set out to feed her. "Yes, I'll eat."

His eyes closed. "Then you should." Daahn set her aside, distancing himself. He pushed the half-empty platter of meat between them. After a moment of hesitation, he stood and headed for the door, putting his darkened glasses on.

He stopped, a step away from his goal. "I expect you to order a platter no less than twice a day. Three times would be better, but your body may not take to that change quickly. It...it will be difficult for you, but to be healthy, you have to start eating fruits and vegetables. We can typically do without grains, but the rest is necessary."

Miri forced a hitching breath back as best she could, nursing old hurts and new. "I understand, Commander."

That's what Daahn was...another Dominant in authority who didn't want her. When all was said and done, was there a difference between a *Xxan-Dree* trainer and a human commander?

As if in answer, he knocked for the guard and then walked out the door.

Chapter Eighteen

Aleeks cursed himself solidly as he made his way back to Miri's cell. He had no right to do this. No matter how much he wanted her, there was little question that she had no idea what was happening between them.

He'd had to leave her earlier. The alternative would have been to follow his Xxanian blood and screw her on the closest flat surface, which would have been the floor of her cell.

Even now, Aleeks's senses were muddied and his endocrine system in a firestorm. Miri was potent, so potent that changing and washing his clothing, wiping down his gear and showering hadn't erased the effects of her *Zhigaaah* from his mind and drives. Every atom in his body screamed at him to bind Miri to him, and given much more time with her, he was going to do precisely that.

He nodded to the evening guard on the way past and pushed the door open at the first indication of the click. His gaze swung from the empty bed to the wash station. In the time it took her to startle, Aleeks had slammed the door behind him and was halfway across the room to her.

Miri turned from the mirror, nude from the waist up, wide-eyed, pulling her shirt up to cover her palm-sized breasts. She half tripped away from him, coming up against the far wall with an audible smack of skin to metal. Her gaze cycled between the door and his expression, as if she was weighing her odds of escaping him.

Aleeks took her arm, guiding her away from the wall and to the sink again. He ran his hand over the discolorations on her back, wincing at the telltale heat radiating off them and the ridges of scar tissue. She didn't move and barely breathed as he examined the healing bruises.

"They did this to you?" he demanded. "The Xxan? Master S'sie?" *No wonder she killed him.*

Miri didn't reply. She held herself rigid, as if she expected more blows to rain down.

Aleeks stifled the urge to shake an answer out of her. "Why didn't you ask for medical attention? You have that right, whether the injuries were done in our care or not."

"I'm not sick," she replied weakly.

"That's all you've had medical aid for?" Why that should surprise him was a mystery.

"That and broken bones," she confirmed.

His ridge plates came up. Aleeks couldn't have stopped them if he wanted to.

Miri stared at them and swallowed hard. "What else would require—"

"Stop," he ordered.

She started to sink to her knees, and he grasped her by her arms, dragging her back up. Aleeks ignored her little gasp of fear, pulling the shirt from her hands.

Miri crossed her arms over her breasts. He draped the shirt around her body and held it up for her, shaking it in silent order. She eased one arm away from her chest and slid it into the waiting sleeve, then the other, baring her breasts and bruised ribs to him. Aleeks scooped her up in his arms and headed for the door.

222

Miri pulled the shirt closed around her body, shaking her head. "Commander Daahn, this is not necessary," she pleaded.

"Knock," he instructed her.

She raised a shaking hand and knocked, burying her face in his chest before the door opened.

Aleeks's primary cock came up hard and fast at that move. He was a Dominant, and she was turning to him for protection. The fact that it was protection from light was immaterial to him. It was a rush he enjoyed.

The guard looked from Miri to Aleeks in concern.

"Your glasses," Aleeks ordered. "And inform Med Call that we are on our way."

The guard didn't question Aleeks further. He slid the standard-issue dark glasses from the pouch on his belt and settled them carefully onto Miri's lap. She pushed them on but didn't look around at the corridor; her face stayed hidden in Aleeks's chest.

He strode toward Med Call, the guard opening the cell block door for him, then rushing back to comm ahead.

* * * *

Dr. Geery looked up from the bed she was preparing for them. "What is it, Commander Daahn?" she inquired.

Miri stiffened at that question.

"Be still," Aleeks growled at her. He settled Miri on the bed. "I want a full workup, and I want

223

it now." He should have done this upon her arrival. The delay...the oversight was inexcusable.

Geery raised an eyebrow. "If you would," she hinted, motioning to the exam room door.

Aleeks leaned against the wall, making it clear that he was staying.

The doctor darkened a few shades, and she cleared her throat before she started speaking. "Is this acceptable to you, Johns?" Geery asked.

"She prefers 'Miri,'" Aleeks informed her.

Geery ignored him. "Is his presence acceptable, or do you wish privacy?"

Miri stammered out an answer, probably scenting an ally in the other woman. "I wish to be left in peace in my cell."

"Unacceptable," Aleeks snapped...literally. His teeth clicked in warning as he clenched his jaw shut.

Miri shrugged. "Then you can do what you like."

"I can force him to leave," Geery continued.

Aleeks tensed for a fight.

Miri glanced up at him, seemingly assessing his state of mind. She lowered her face in a partially submissive show. "Let him stay."

Geery nodded her agreement. "Very well. I'll start with blood tests."

Miri snarled but made no move to interfere with or evade the draws.

Geery placed them in the analyzer, then reached for the shirt. She fingered the open front, shooting Aleeks a look that demanded an answer.

"It was already off," he defended himself.

She stripped the shirt off her patient, then pressed lightly at a bruise over Miri's rib cage. "You're very underweight, and..." Geery turned away and grabbed down a sheet, then covered Miri with it. "Take off the pants and hand them to me."

Miri didn't hesitate to do as ordered.

Geery set up a scan plate. "Lie still. This won't hurt."

As ordered, Miri held still for the slowly moving plate.

The doctor started reading off the results. "Two old fractures of the parietal plate, one of the frontal, just over the sinus cavity, cheekbones, nose... By the stars! Jaw, upper and lower."

Miri didn't react to any of it. She stared at the ceiling, her expression unreadable.

"Scapula...both of... Oh, my. The humerus of the right arm, radius of the same. First, second...six ribs, multiple times? Damn it, these types of injuries are no accident, and some of them are fairly fresh."

Miri clenched her jaw.

Geery glanced at the screen, then did a double take. She pulled up at her side of the sheet, settling her hands over Miri's abdomen. Miri winced but didn't cry out.

She did cry out! Earlier, when I landed over her, she did. What did I miss?

"Who did this?" Geery demanded. "With what?"

Miri said nothing.

The doctor looked to Aleeks for an answer.

"The Xxan. I would imagine it was one named Master S'sie." It was possible that it was her *seir* or one of the others she'd targeted, but Aleeks was banking on S'sie.

As if in confirmation, Miri shuddered.

Geery startled at the movement, looking to her patient then back to Aleeks. "Why?"

"Why, what?" he challenged in return. "As yet, you haven't told me what you've found."

Geery darkened. "Someone has induced a blunt trauma to her abdomen so severe that Miri may have lost one ovary in the aftermath."

Aleeks fisted his hands in impotent rage. "What can be done?"

"Luckily, her body has already healed much of the damage. Luckily, because it seems no one treated her for it. I can heal the rest."

"How long ago?" he asked.

"Several weeks, I would say. It had to be agonizing for her."

"Finish your examination."

Geery didn't question him. "Broken fingers, left wrist...left femur, tibia and fibula on both sides, tarsals..." She reached up and pressed a button on the main console without looking at it. The screen before her changed. "She's malnourished, an—" Geery bit at her lower lip.

"And, what?" he prompted.

"Anemic. How does someone who eats nothing but meat—"

Aleeks stared her down.

Geery flushed in anger. "I take it Miri was starved?"

"As a matter of course." His extended ridge plates made his voice rough, but forcing them back was currently beyond his abilities.

She nodded grimly. "Her hormones are also off, even for a crossbreed. They are seriously off balance. Can you explain it?"

"Reproductive?" he asked.

Geery nodded.

"How long have you been blue, Miri?" He knew from experience with his sister that it often took more than a month to settle into a smooth transition.

At first, he was certain she meant to remain silent.

When it emerged, her voice was cold and clipped. "Several weeks, I would say." Her eyes challenged him.

Aleeks's blood ran cold in understanding.

Chapter Nineteen

Miri shifted, swallowing down the urge to
vomit. For hours, they'd poured drugs and
nutrients into her system. She'd attempted to eat
the foods Dr. Geery claimed she needed. She'd
even endured the healing of Master S'sie's attack.
The only positive move had been that Geery had
dimmed the entire Med Call to a comfortable level
for her, so Miri had been able to dispose of the
dark glasses.

For a precious time, she'd felt better than she
could remember ever feeling in her life. But now,
she felt like her entrails were being seared inside
her.

She kicked the blankets away, hot and
uncomfortable beneath them. Even the light knit
gown she wore irritated her. Miri wanted to be
naked and immersed in water.

With that thought firmly in mind, she eased
off the bed and staggered toward the door,
collapsing to her knees after a few steps. Master
S'sie's voice echoed in her mind, telling her she
was useless, weak, unappealing. Miri reached a
hand toward the corridor, trying to stay conscious
long enough to crawl to a water source.

Daahn's arms encircled her, and he drew Miri
to his chest, enveloping her in his delicious scent.
She wanted to taste his spice, to feel it burn on
her sensitive tongue.

One cool hand stroked along her cheek, and
he brushed his lips along her mating stripe. His
tongue sampled, teased, wrung a moan from her.

"Daahn, release her," Geery demanded.

"She's fevering."

Miri fisted her hand in his shirt, hoping he'd take her to water. He would know. He *had* to know that she needed the soothing effects.

And him. She snagged at his shirt with her hunting teeth, and his musk increased, making her head spin and her body wet.

"Get her into bed. I'll administer—"

His arms tightened around her, and his voice went rough and hard in authority. "No. We need a shower."

Miri heaved, trying desperately to control her body. She groaned, her throat bobbing against her attempts to swallow down her dinner a second time.

Daahn's voice caressed her forehead. "If you have to, don't stop yourself."

"Commander Daahn," Geery protested.

"Med Call has a shower!" he shouted. "Where is it?"

There was a moment of tense silence. "This way."

Daahn scooped her from the floor. His jogging forced Miri past her endurance, and she emptied her evening meal onto his clothing and hers. He didn't slow, didn't complain, didn't express anger or disgust.

He stopped and settled Miri on a countertop. She gripped the surface with one hand, pushing the foul clothing off her shoulder with the other.

"What do you need, Daahn?" Geery asked.

"Time."

"What?"

"Get out. This is a crossbred thing."

Miri forced her eyes to focus, her mouth going dry at the sight of Daahn's bare back. He tossed his vomit-stained shirt on the floor, then went to one knee and started working on his boots.

Geery tapped one soft shoe on the floor. "This is highly—"

"Out, Geery. Trust me. Water is healing for us." He pulled off the first boot, switched which knee he rested on, and started on the other.

Miri dragged the gown off her body, wiping idly at the slick of soured meat and vegetables.

"I don't like this, but I trust you."

"How magnanimous of you," he replied dryly.

"I want to see Miri when you're done...better or worse."

"Fine. Now go." His second boot hit the floor. "We'll need clean clothes," he added. Daahn stood, working at his pants, heedless of the doctor's presence.

"Going," Geery conceded. The door closed behind her.

Miri forced her breathing to a steady stream, watching the last of his clothing slide away, baring taut buttocks and hairless legs. He was beautiful, graceful, sculpted. Next to him, Miri felt awkward and, as Master S'sie had accused, unappealing.

He turned to the shower, spinning the dial and testing the temperature against his wrist. She shifted, trying to see more of him, but he was turned just far enough from her to deny her the view.

Another wave of nausea assaulted her, and Miri wavered, nearly overbalancing off the countertop. Daahn turned abruptly, and her gaze locked on his semierect cock as it brushed against the smooth, hairless plane of his thigh.

* * * *

Aleeks ambled toward her, watching her hand splay over her smooth mound and then slide away to settle on her thigh. Her breathing was quick and uneven, her musk flowing freely, and her *Zhigaaah* in overdrive. It was the quickening of her change, and there was only one way to ease it.

He dragged her to his body, chest to chest, walking them both into the hot spray. Miri tipped her head back, reveling in the cascade of water. She eased down his body to her feet, her heat brushing against him in invitation.

Her skin teased at his as she turned, bringing his primary cock up. If she laid a hand anywhere near his secondary, he'd bind her to him tonight.

No. She can't control this. This is biological.

Aleeks stroked his hands down her chest and abdomen, washing away the remnants of her rioting stomach. Had she realized what was happening to her, Miri would have known to forgo food, but she was clearly innocent of the realities of the quickening.

She arched into his hands, in a frenzy, her *Zhigaaah* mixing into the steam. Pushing her hair over her shoulder, Aleeks nipped and sucked at her mating stripe, drinking pheromone and water from her, in bliss that was fast rising to a fever pitch. He traced the edges of the blue, from nearly the apex of her shoulders to halfway down her shoulder blades and from one side to the other, ten centimeters out from the midline of her back, in either direction.

Miri reached a hand up and back, fisting it in his hair. Her body stroked up and down his, a female Xxan in need of a cock at her finest. His primary was more than prepared to oblige her. Little hisses and mews escaped her lips, both an invitation and a warning that he might have to subdue her.

He ranged his hand down her abdomen to her mound, pressing her buttocks to his length. At her moan, Aleeks stroked at her clit. Her body undulated against his, and Aleeks thrust his fingers inside her.

"More," she pleaded. "Daahn, pl—"

"Aleeks," he corrected her. "Call my name, Miri." By the stars, he wanted her to say it. It was a Dominant thing, he was certain.

What did S'sie order her to call him? Master? He pushed that thought away, unclenching his jaw. That was a discussion for another time.

"Aleeks, I need," she whispered.

He needed, too. Aleeks forced her down to her knees, sliding his hand free of her body. He bent Miri forward at the waist, and she raised her ass, baring her swollen slit to him.

Aleeks pushed inside her, reveling as she rose up against his length, taking more of him. For a long moment, they held that position, locked together, water streaming over their bodies, her musk coating his cock, making his length sting pleasantly.

Miri ground against him, and Aleeks started thrusting.

There was nothing soft and gentle about it. She was in her quickening, her first true mating frenzy, and Aleeks was a Dominant. Had there been another Dominant to witness it, he would have fought the rival down for her. Aleeks would have won.

Though Geery didn't know it, her push to treat Miri and not let the quickening run its course had endangered her life. By the grace of his human side and his military training alone, the doctor still drew breath.

Their mating was fierce and fast, their sounds and musk rising, surrounding them in the cloud of steam.

Aleeks didn't question that it would take more than once to sate her. It had taken his sister Zondra hours. *Hours!* He shivered in delight at the thought of it. No human woman could take his fervor that long.

Of course, Zondra had taken a human as her first. Evan, potent and talented as his sister proclaimed him to be, might not have been able to sate her as quickly as a crossbred male might have. In order for them to bind and produce young, the human doctors had to manufacture *Zhigaaal* of Evan's musk. Zondra still argued that he didn't need it, that he could stay erect without massive amounts of her *Zhigaaah*, and that his cum alone was nearly enough to bind them.

No. It will be hours. And they were going to enjoy every moment of it.

As if in agreement, Miri slid off his length and turned to him, tracing one finger down the ridge plate at the left of his neck, bringing it up in Dominant show. She dipped her head, chasing water droplets down his chest with her lips, flicking her tongue over one flat nipple, bringing it up for her. Miri moved to the other, trailing her hands down his abdomen toward—

Aleeks gripped her wrists, stopping her. He wouldn't bind her in this frenzy. At the same time, they both needed more.

He guided her to the shower wall. "Wrap your legs around my hips."

Miri complied, using the wall to balance herself. Once her legs were out of the way, Aleeks forced her to the wall, pinning her arms above her head, thrusting into her again.

She screamed in pleasure, her voice echoing off the stark walls. Encouraged by her show, Aleeks pounded into her.

He was vaguely aware of the door opening, but it was a minor annoyance. Miri was more important.

"Commander Daahn!" Geery protested. "I cannot allow—"

He turned his head, glaring at her in the dim light, his ridge plates coming up fully. His move to order her away was cut short by Miri's climax, her rippling grip on his primary setting off his own. Instead of an order, a groan escaped his lips.

"Commander!"

Miri nuzzled at his throat, oblivious to their audience. "Aleeks, please. I need." She licked a taunting line up his extended ridge plate.

Aleeks beat back the urge to rip out the well-meaning doctor's throat. *Diplomacy. I have to convince her to leave us, without harming her.*

"I know you do," he soothed Miri, searching all the while for the words to defuse the situation, without the waste of too much time. "Doctor Geery, you have my vow to explain this. But not now. I'm asking you to be patient long enough for me to care for her." She would have to be patient, because he was incapable of it.

"And if she conceives?" the doctor challenged.

"She can't. Not yet." If she was quickening now, there was no way her womb had been ripened for it.

I hope. Please, let him not have gone that far. Aleeks wasn't certain if an insufficient amount of *Zhigaaal* to bind, given before quickening, was capable of forcing the change.

Miri nipped at his chest, drawing a thin stream of blood in desperation for more. The move was expected, and it fired his instinctual urge to dominate her. Aleeks thrust his hips up, and Miri's head rocked back, a drop of his blood on her lower lip.

Geery's words came from a retreating back. "If I don't get a satisfactory explanation, Captain Seaver will be contacted."

Fuck Seaver. A completely irreverent thought gripped him. *No, fuck Miri.*

* * * *

Aleeks stared down at Miri's sleeping form, his cock sensitized, wishing against likelihood that she'd wake needing more of him.

As it was, he'd tasted her body as he'd dressed her in a fresh sleeping gown, testing the end of her frenzy greedily, gorging himself on their mixed musk. She'd moved against him, but she'd remained largely oblivious to his attempts to rouse her from sleep, so he'd left her to her recovery.

Her pheromone coursed through his system, making an admittedly dangerous Dominant lethal. If another man challenged Aleeks for her now, there was a very real possibility that the upstart would find himself dead.

A Xxanian *seir* would typically remove the female from her first male at this point, with or without—usually without—the younger Dominant's agreement. Separating them allowed their fire to cool and each to approach the subject of binding with a clear mind.

There was nothing rational about Aleeks's state of mind. Beyond the fact that he was going to make certain Miri was sane enough to refuse him, there was no question he'd pursue her and bind her as his own, were she willing to be bound.

He licked his lips, savoring their mixed flavor, imagining what her *Zhigaaah* mixed with *Zhigaaal* would taste like, skating his fingertips along the length of his primary cock through the clean pair of pants he wore.

Near the end, his secondary had emerged. Had her frenzy gone on much longer, Aleeks would have had to resort to condoms to catch his *Zhigaaal* so as not to start the binding accidentally. He'd resorted to the devices when dealing with human women interested in the kink of sex with a man with two cocks. Sex that included both appendages was a bonus plan for Aleeks, condom or no condom.

"Are you ready to explain?" Geery inquired.

He nodded, not taking his eyes off Miri. "It was her quickening, the first—"

"I know what the quickening of a young Xxanian is, Commander. Miri is too *old* for a quickening. It comes at sixteen, eighteen at the latest, in both pure Xxan and crossbreeds. She's twenty-five Xxanian years, twenty-one in human. By either scale, she should have done this years ago. Don't try to bullshit me."

"She was starved and constantly wasting her reserves to heal. A few famine seasons can push quickening back a full year. Miri has had nothing but famine in her life. It wasn't the right environment to produce young. You heard her. Miri has only been blue for a month or less. They stunted her development. Believe me, she's so potent, even I hadn't realized she was prequickening, until the quickening took hold of her."

Geery settled into the chair beside him, looking from Miri to Aleeks. "Why did the Xxan...? Why the blunt trauma? It was targeted; it had to be."

Aleeks sighed. "She's potent, much more than any crossbreed I've ever met." Not that there were many on Earth. "I imagine..."

Why was it so difficult to face his suspicions? S'sie was dead. He wasn't a rival Dominant she might choose to mate with, to bind herself to.

Because I know she fears him. I know this might be why she does.

"Go on," the doctor urged him.

"The Xxan would have been appalled by an attraction to Miri. Rather than admit she was an enticing female, they would have punished her severely for tempting them, for arousing their interest."

"But she has no choice," Geery protested, her hands fisting on the arms of her chair.

"She has no choice in the fact that her eyes tear when exposed to light, either. That didn't save her from them."

She paled, her eyes locking on Miri. "Did he...? This S'sie...?"

"I don't know. If he did, before she had reached the quickening, his disgrace would be all the deeper."

"And the punishment to Miri all the more severe," she guessed.

"Yes. As you said, it would have been agonizing. He wouldn't have sent for a doctor. He'd want it to be agonizing."

"And...he wouldn't want proof of the crime revealed to them when the doctors might interpret it?" she ventured.

"No doubt."

Chapter Twenty

Miri looked around the room in confusion. "It's not a cell," she noted, peeking up at Aleeks.

Commander Daahn! He hadn't repeated the offer to call him by his given name since she'd awakened in Med Call two days earlier, aching but sated, her fever broken.

"Yes and no," he replied cryptically. "There will be a guard posted at the door...for now. You won't be permitted to leave your quarters without me as an escort."

"My..." Her breathing caught on the rest. The main room was easily twice the size of the cell. She could see the bathing area through the right-hand doorway and assumed the other led to a bed. There were padded chairs and carpets on the floor.

"Yours...until permanent quarters are arranged. Unless it is deemed a matter of security, you say who enters here."

Miri stared at him, her mind grasping at and slipping from that idea. She'd never had a space of her own. She'd never had control over who could enter that space...or not.

He cocked his head, working at some problem. "What is it?"

She shook her head, turning toward the second door, trying to hide her confusion. That reaction seemed to frustrate Daahn.

As she suspected, the door led to a bedroom. The bed was wide, easily three times the width of the bunk in her cell and longer, too. Miri had considered the bunk an extravagance. She wondered if the *Grea* Elders slept in such a space, different as their dreaming mats were from beds.

Daahn's heat at her back made her all-too-aware of how convenient that bed was.

Or the bath. Though the shower had been invigorating, the idea of being immersed in a tub of water with Daahn was enough to dampen her tender body again.

"Is it acceptable to you?" he asked.

"More than acceptable," she managed to say.

He turned her gently, his expression earnest. "I do have questions," he stated.

"If any answers I possess can be of help," she promised.

Daahn took her hand and led Miri to the long, low seat in the front room. Once they were both settled on the plush material, he raised her chin so Miri met his gaze.

"Did S'sie have sex with you before your quickening?"

Miri pulled from his hold, standing and walking to the food counter. Her heart pounded in the rush of unwelcome memories.

"Useless, unpalatable, human female."

If I was unpalatable, why did he?

Daahn's arms encircled her, and she startled. His hold was gentle but insistent. "Tell me."

"Yes." She cringed, anticipating his anger, his disgust that she'd taken another Dominant before him.

Her understanding of Xxanian mating was limited. The only knowledge she truly had was the description of the quickening Geery had given her the morning after hers, an encounter that Daahn had been blessedly absent for. Miri did know, from that discussion, that the Dominant who sated her quickening expected to be her first. She had no clue what Daahn's reaction to the fact that he hadn't been would be.

He buried his face in her hair, holding Miri to his body. "Why did he beat you? Do you know?"

"I couldn't," she forced out miserably.

"Couldn't what? You weren't aroused?"

She lowered her face, afraid of his reaction to the truth. The words stuck in her dry throat.

"I see. You were."

Miri braced for his condemnation.

"That is to be expected," he continued. "I will assume he was aroused."

She shook her head. That had been the problem, after all. Master S'sie hadn't been aroused.

Daahn rotated her toward him, his lips turned down in a scowl. "Did he or did he not come erect for the act?"

"His primary," she whispered.

His eyes narrowed, and his eye slits widened, a disconcerting combination. "And his secondary? Did it extend, at all? Did you encourage it to?"

"A bit but not fully."

"Did you encourage it to rise?" he repeated.

"I..." How did he mean that? "How did I encourage the primary to rise?"

"Did you touch his cocks? Did you touch anywhere around their bases?"

She shook her head. "He was already erect when he..."

"When he what, Miri?" His voice was low and soothing, but his eyes held the promise of violence to come.

Miri took a calming breath, trying to decide if refusing him an answer was more or less dangerous than offering an answer he wouldn't want to hear.

"Did he take what he wanted, without asking?"

She fought for clarity. "How does a male ask—"

"He aroused you and thrust inside." He didn't question it, but she sensed it was something he wanted her to confirm or modify, to make clear to him.

"Yes. He did." *Was that asking?*

Daahn pulled her to his chest, stoking at her hair. "If you did nothing to entice the secondary to rise, it is a testament to your potency and S'sie's arousal that it rose, no matter how minutely it did. If he told you it was some deficiency in you that it didn't rise fully, he lied."

Miri squeezed her eyes shut, trying to shut out the rest of the memory. *No. I need to hear that it was wrong. I need to know it.*

"He stroked at my mating stripe. He licked at it."

"Miri," Daahn breathed, his chin working back and forth at her hair.

"It was so unexpected, I tried to turn to him."

"You don't have to—"

"I do!" She forced her voice to calm. "I...need to."

Daahn rocked her back and forth, swaying with her in his arms. It was oddly comforting.

"He forced me over the edge of the table and used his claws to rip my pants at the seams...the inner seams."

A growl rose from deep in Daahn's chest.

"It felt so good. He smelled so right."

"But you know better now," he interrupted gruffly.

"I knew better then...well, just after. He came in me. It felt so good, I moved against him, seeking more."

"And he battered you." He didn't question it. His ridge plates shifted against the top of her head.

Miri nodded. "He told me I was worthless, unappealing, unpalatable, that he couldn't even come fully erect for me."

"He lied," Daahn attested.

"Yes. Then he washed me."

His head came back, and Daahn stared at her, his fury imperfectly masked. "He tried to hide it by washing his cum out of you?"

She considered that. "No, just outside. He scrubbed at me. It was..."

"What?"

"I hurt. I hurt so that I could barely breathe and couldn't stand, and I still wanted him. I wanted him in a way that defied reason. As time went on, I tried to understand why—"

Daahn released her, his eye slits widening and his muscles tensing. He uttered a series of curses in both languages, his Xxan long and trilling, perfect to her ear. "How long did this...attraction last?"

She fought for a clear memory, though the days after that beating flowed together, making a precise determination impossible. "Several days, as I recall it."

He turned away, rubbing a hand along the back of his neck.

"Daahn?" she called out nervously.

"And he told you that you didn't arouse him," he growled. "Did he continue to beat you while the attraction lasted?"

"Yes. He did." Daahn didn't believe she wanted Master S'sie now, did he? She considered assuring him that it wasn't so.

"Unbelievable. Truly unbelievable."

"It is the truth," she managed to say. She fought back tears at the fact that he didn't believe her, but one escaped and spilled down her cheek.

He looked back at her, his expression unreadable.

"You don't trust me," Miri surmised, her heart sinking. He had no reason to. He never had. He likely never would.

And now this. The sex had been a Dominant show, no doubt, and by S'sie's attack on her, she'd offered offense to Daahn's Dominance.

It was a completely enjoyable show of Dominance, unlike S'sie's. She wanted him to repeat it, but that was unlikely, considering the turn of events.

As if drawn by that thought, Daahn was abruptly before her, his body crowding hers to the countertop, his hand tangling in her hair. "Do you want me to trust you?" he asked. "Implicitly? Completely?"

She nodded, at a loss for words. Why she'd want such a thing was beyond her. How she'd accomplish it was a mystery.

His hand released her hair and slid lower, settling on her mating stripe. His massage set off waves of heat and musk. Miri felt *Zhigaaah* bead up. Daahn licked first at the tear track on her cheek, then worked at collecting the pheromone from her throat. His cock and musk rose in response.

Miri pulled at his belt, loosening it, moving along to the buttons beneath. His cock thrust toward her, stroking over the back of her hand. She sought out the sensitive flesh at the base, encouraging him. He'd asked if she'd done that for Master S'sie; it must be the way to arouse him.

Daahn unbuttoned her shirt one-handed, his fingers brushing between her small breasts and down her stomach. His other hand worked diligently at her mating stripe, and his mouth closed around the lobe of her ear, suckling lightly at her. He paused at her belt, flattening a hand against her abdomen and stroking upward, teasing his thumb at her nipple, forcing Miri against him in pleasure.

Her fingertips found an indentation beneath his cock, and Daahn shivered in response. Did he have a full secondary, a vestigial secondary, or was it simply pleasurable to be touched there?

"Bring me up," he ordered. "Take me fully."

Miri hesitated to admit she didn't know how to. She hadn't succeeded in bringing Master S'sie up fully, after all. She hadn't even been given the chance to try. She needed to think, but his circling thumb was driving her mad, and—

She pressed her thumb to the spot, circling as he was at her nipple. Daahn arched toward her with a moan that sounded of delight, the nub extending past the flap of skin, seeking more. Miri played at it, circling the soft tip more purposefully.

Daahn dragged her shirt off her free hand, letting it settle around the hand working him. He thrust up into her touch, now three finger widths extended, a full finger width farther than she'd risen the master.

"You're so good," he whispered.

Miri's confusion was cut short by his move to disrobe. His chest, appearing from behind buttons, had nearly her complete attention. She lowered her face, kissing at the cut she vaguely remembered leaving the night of her quickening, moving on to one flat nipple, licking at his smooth skin. His still-rising secondary played at the back of her mind.

His shirt left his body and dropped to the floor. Daahn cupped her head to him, encouraging her. "You want something to lick?"

She moved to the other nipple in answer. Oh yes, she wanted to lick him. She wanted to collect his musk on her tongue, as he did hers.

"Then you'll have it," he promised.

Daahn backed away, his secondary cock sliding from her grip. He worked at opening the belt and the buttons down her pants. "Take them off." When she hesitated, he removed her shirt and tossed it away.

Miri pushed the pants down her hips then thighs, her heart skipping at Daahn's tongue darting out to scent her, his eye slits narrowing. At midthigh, she released the pants and let them fall, stepping out to stand naked before him. When he didn't move, she started to turn, offering him her body.

Daahn took her arm, shaking his head. "Not this time." He led her to the wide bed, pushing his pants to his lower thighs. Without a word, he folded himself onto the edge of the mattress, his cocks standing tall, jerking toward her.

Miri stared at them, hungering to feel the primary buried inside her, the secondary stroking her clit at every thrust. Master S'sie's had only found the mark a few precious times. Daahn's would more often.

He leaned back onto one elbow, his eyes issuing the order to his soft-spoken words. "Lick, Miri."

She sank to her knees between his ankles, glancing up at Daahn in hopes that she'd interpreted his order correctly. At his nod, Miri stroked her tongue over the primary head, gathering his musk.

His breathing hitched and then smoothed. "Now the other," he instructed.

The secondary was softer to the touch, pliable, bending and undulating against her passing tongue. The taste was different, more pungent, enticing her to taste more. She stroked her tongue along the length, circling the head at the apex of every trip, enjoying the way the shaft and head followed her movements, playing against her tongue much as his tongue had played against it while he fed her.

It was thinner than his primary by half, but when she'd started licking at it, it was half the length, as well. Miri hadn't realized how long a properly stimulated secondary would grow. And it was still growing. Daahn's secondary nearly matched his primary in length.

Drunk on his fluids, Miri risked asking an impertinent question. "How long will you get?"

He hummed a self-satisfied note. "Do you wish to find out as you are or by taking me in?"

"The secondary?" Her words slurred, and her heart thundered in her ears.

Daahn smiled, showing his hunting teeth. The sight of the predator usually frightened her, but Miri found it exciting on Daahn...in this situation.

"A few more licks, little blue," he directed. "Then you'll learn what I can do with two hungry cocks and a willing female."

She complied, bathing him, base and shaft and head, first the primary and then the secondary. Daahn watched her, moaning as she sucked at the tip of the secondary, his fingers massaging at her mating stripe, drowning her body in pheromone and mating hormones.

"You feel it," he crooned. "My *Zhigaaal* is making you mine. Do you want that?"

Miri sucked at the secondary again, taking down as much of his fluids as she could, hungering for more.

"Massage the base as you suckle."

She did as he instructed, moaning at the wash of *Zhigaaal* in her mouth. This was why he drank her *Zhigaaah*. It was pleasant, drugging, arousing.

Daahn eased her head back, meeting her gaze. "Massage the base, but do not drink this time."

He jerked at her touch, and Miri looked down to the secondary, aching for it. Her mouth watered, and yet she was thirsty. The *Zhigaaal* was thick and pungent, a creamy fluid that trailed down the sides of his secondary at her massage.

"A little more, Miri. When it reaches the base, your education continues."

Her channel throbbed in time with her heart, and her head took up the beat in a light spin.

"You need to feel it," he surmised. "You need my cocks filling you with cum and *Zhigaaal*."

"Yes. I need it."

"Unbuckle my boots. The less time I waste disrobing, the better for both of us."

Miri switched her dominant right hand for her weaker left, unbuckling his boots as quickly as possible. *Zhigaaal* ran over her massaging fingers, making them tingle and burn lightly. It wasn't an unpleasant sensation, though it was mildly surprising.

"Stand," Daahn ordered.

She obeyed without question, her hands leaving his body. Daahn didn't look at her. He toed his boots off, then divested himself of pants and socks.

Then he looked at her, ranging his gaze up her body, licking his lips. "Stroke the *Zhigaaal* over your nipples."

Touching herself for him was bold, but she felt sensual, appealing in a way she hadn't felt since—

Pushing that thought away, Miri played at her nipples as he had, moaning at his intent staring, hissing at the slight burn of his pheromone on her skin. Her nipples came to hard points, and she stroked harder, enjoying the way the *Zhigaaal* sensitized them.

"Now your clit."

His voice was falsely calm, she knew. Every sign, from his partially extended ridge plates to his taut muscles, said he was poised to strike from his reclined position. By the stars, she wanted him to pounce on her.

"Your clit," he reminded her.

Miri spread her legs, circling her lightly coated fingertips over the nub, crying out at the musk escaping down her thighs, at the maddening need for his touch instead of her own.

"What do you want, Miri?"

Snips of memories assaulted her. There was something..."That night, you ate our mixed climax."

"You remember that?" A dangerous smile graced his face.

She nodded.

"You want it again?"

"Oh, yes."

He flowed to his feet, rippling muscle in motion, the predator, the silent hunter. Her entire body burned and pulsed, a drumbeat of pure anticipation.

Daahn guided her to the warmth he'd abandoned at the edge of the bed, sinking to his knees, his eyes locked with hers. His hands pressed at her shoulders, urging her to her back. He raised one leg and then the other, settling her feet to the edge of the mattress, spread wide around her body. She was open to him, exposed. The very air around them vibrated in the rising tension between them.

The first lick started at the inner apex of her left thigh, stroking toward her knee, following the trail of her musk. He repeated the move on her right.

The next three licks brought her hips up off the bed. They were soft, bathing licks, removing every drop of her musk from the surface of her body. He followed it with a fluttering of licks inside her. Miri moved restlessly, her head pitching back and forth, moaning when he retreated.

His fingers explored the same path, and the bite of heat announced that he was spreading *Zhigaaal* over her. Holding herself still for it was a physical impossibility, but Daahn didn't chide her for her weakness. He patiently found every fold and hollow, anointing the outer lips but not inside. Finally, he did the same for her anus.

Daahn braced his hands on her knees, staring down at her writhing form. Just when she was about to question this form of torture, he moved, thrusting his tongue inside her. Miri's leg muscles tightened, forcing her hips up.

The burning intensified, playing delicious counterpoint to his busy mouth. The need clawed at her, setting off the same searing sensation in her gut that the quickening had.

Water. She needed the bath.

No. She needed his cock inside her, quenching the flames from the inside out.

"Daahn," she gasped out. "I need you inside me."

His mouth left her, and he straightened, looking down at her. "My name," he demanded.

"Aleeks."

He nodded. Aleeks moved toward her, seating his secondary at her seam instead of his primary.

Miri shook her head, at a loss to form the words to refuse. His secondary was dripping in *Zhigaaal.* She wouldn't survive being coated inside as well as outside. Already, it felt as if her vital organs were ablaze.

The secondary stroked inside her, filling her yet not, painting his *Zhigaaal* along the corridor to her womb. The need slammed into her, and Miri bowed up from the bed, tears escaping her eyes, burning against her sensitive cheeks as his *Zhigaaal* burned the rest of her. She cried out harshly, lunging for Aleeks, her Xxanian drives dictating that she escape this torture.

His hands circled her wrists, pinning them to the bed near her head. He rose up over her, pushing her along the soft sheets, his strong thighs forcing against the insides of hers, his primary stroking sensitized flesh with every movement. In the end, they were both on the bed, Aleeks staring down at her, her legs loosely wrapped around his thighs.

Aleeks transferred both wrists to one large hand and reached the other between their bodies. The *Zhigaaal* stroked along her inner thighs was such a shock, her muscles tightened down, drawing his secondary to her *os*.

"That's right," he crooned to her. "You want me deep."

Miri shook her head, denying it. "I want..." Her breathing was ragged, her senses in a riot.

"Yes?"

"Your primary," she replied thickly.

"You'll have it, as soon as you're prepared for it."

The room seemed to spin around her. "You didn't prepare me during the quickening."

He didn't smile at the reminder. "That was your quickening. This..."

He released more *Zhigaaal* onto the surface of her *os*. Miri gasped at the sensation of his secondary extending past the mouth of her womb. Aleeks's body was still, which meant the secondary was growing longer.

"This is mating, Miri," he breathed. "You are mine. Already, you *want* to be mine."

With that pronouncement, he came. His primary spewed cum over her abdomen, while his secondary jetted *Zhigaaal* inside, heating her womb. Her climax crested, and his continued, coating her womb in his potent pheromone. Miri fought for an easy breath, groaning; she could feel every millimeter of her womb, outlined in acid heat and aching for his primary to fill it with cooling cum.

Every muscle in her body relaxed. Miri stared up at Aleeks through a pleasant haze. He released her wrists, feathering his fingertips along her cheek.

He backed out of her, her legs sliding away
from his. His secondary reappeared, half again as
long as his renewed primary.

Miri licked her lips, her sense of smell and
taste overpowered by *Zhigaaal*. Everything was
Aleeks. She craved his touch, certain that every
stroke and lick would be an ecstasy.

Aleeks straightened, coming up on his knees.
Slowly, deliberately, he massaged the base of his
secondary, making his *Zhigaaal* flow again.

She numbly wondered how many times Aleeks
would fill her womb with *Zhigaaal* before he felt
her "prepared" for more. The droplets of his cum
sliding down her mound invigorated her. It could
be two times or ten times, and she wouldn't care,
as long as Aleeks was touching her.

* * * *

By the stars, her show was enough to make
him weep *Zhigaaal* without the massage. Drugged
on his pheromone, Miri lay in a near stupor, but
that wouldn't last long. Soon, her frenzy would
take hold again.

As if in agreement, Miri started to move her
legs, seeking release of her drives. Aleeks braced
them apart and back toward her abdomen,
positioning her for the next step in the binding.

Aleeks seated the soft head of his secondary at
her anus, easing inside. Miri went silent and still,
staring at him, her eye slits dilating as the
Zhigaaal penetrated layers of porous skin to her
bloodstream.

She bowed up, her breathing ragged, crying out wildly as he thrust deeper. The move brought his primary to her swollen pussy. Pleas for his primary cock left her lips on ragged sobs.

"Every way possible," he vowed. He slid deeper, seating both cocks in her.

"Yes," she whispered. "Every way."

Aleeks didn't doubt that she didn't know what she was asking. Nor did he question the fact that she'd love it when he educated her.

One of the conditions Evan had insisted on when he bound Zondra to him was that the *Zhigaaal* bladder and pump would always be carried on his human cock. If he pierced her with two, the strap-on would take the place of his primary. That meant he didn't wear the fake cock at all when he was anointing her body or filling her womb with *Zhigaaal*...or when Zondra was sucking him off. When Evan was filling his wife's ass with the pheromone, she was getting a load of cum, too, the fake cock filling her pussy. According to both Zondra and her husband, the arrangement had proven quite enjoyable for them both.

Just the thought of pounding his primary into Miri's tight little ass while he planted a second load of *Zhigaaal* in her womb had him at the edges of control. Aleeks thrust hard and fast into her, driving Miri to another orgasm. Her inner muscles gripped at both cocks.

Aleeks climaxed, smiling as she went boneless beneath him again. He placed a kiss on her forehead, noting her changing scent in satisfaction. After three days of frenzy, she'd carry his scent for the rest of her life, and what a frenzy it would be.

"The next time will be in the water, Miri." They might even make it to the tub in his...their quarters sometime tomorrow. As a Dominant, he wanted their mixed scent marking their living space as soon as possible. But first, he had to sate her into a slumber to move her that far.

Chapter Twenty-One

Miri went still at the sound of the tone from the doorway. Aleeks had left to attend to his duties for the first time since their mating frenzy had started, more than three days earlier, and answering a summons intended for him felt wrong.

The tone sounded again, and she bit at her lower lip lightly. Would it be considered an offense not to answer it? She would have to ask Aleeks that question when he returned.

She was Aleeks's mate now. There was no reason she knew of not to answer it, and likely many reasons to do so. Resolved, she marched to the door, slipped on a pair of dark glasses, and opened it.

The sight of Lieutenant Jackson in the corridor caused an immediate reversal of her position. She took a guarded stance. "Aleeks Daahn is not here," she informed him.

"I know. I came to speak to you."

"I cannot allow you inside." Subdominant though Jacks might be, a rival male didn't enter a Dominant's lair without an invitation from the Dominant himself.

He shifted uncomfortably. "I don't want to come inside. I need your help...as a translator."

Her heart stuttered. "You have a Xxanian prisoner?"

"Several of them. Daahn is occupied, catching up on the work he missed while..." He looked down the corridor as if discomforted by the concept that Aleeks was now a mated man. "We need a way to communicate."

Miri considered that. The last thing she wanted to do was face the Xxan. Moreover, Dominants were possessive of their mates. If she did this, Aleeks might be angry that she'd gone near a Xxanian male rival.

"Daahn said you'd help."

She nodded. "I will then." If Aleeks said he wanted her to work as a translator to the Xxan, she would bend to his wishes in it. Her reservations were, after all, largely rooted in his reactions and not fears for her own safety.

Jacks waved her down the corridor. Miri closed the door to their quarters carefully, listening for the click of the lock, then padded along with him.

The light tunic and pants Aleeks had provided for her brushed against her body. They weren't a warrior's clothes. Aleeks had decreed that a Dominant didn't allow his mate the dangers of a warrior's life. Before she met him, Miri would have taken such a sentiment as a reason to fight, an insult to her training. Now, his protection was a precious gift, and the clothing was just one outward sign of that protection.

"Do you ever wear shoes?" Jacks inquired.

Miri feigned no notice of his rudeness. "If Aleeks requests it of me, I will learn to wear them."

At the same time, she suspected such a thing would be highly uncomfortable and would steal her stealth, at least temporarily. Miri couldn't imagine Aleeks asking her to submit to it...or him risking her safety by compromising her ability to hide from danger.

The lieutenant's snort of laughter accompanied something of a sneer. "He wants you barefoot, pregnant, and in the kitchen, huh?"

"He accepts that I have never worn shoes. I am certain he would love to be a *seir*. But I cannot imagine why he would wish me to be 'in the kitchen.' It is the male's place to provide food for his mate, and we do not cook our food. True, mouth feeding is a very sensual exchange, but why would we engage in that in the food preparation area, when a bed or cushions are much more comfortable?"

He gaped at her, then turned away, red-faced.

The remaining trip passed in silence, a happenstance Miri found she enjoyed. Though she couldn't account for the warrior's silence, she was grateful for it.

Her peace dissolved into unease at the sight of the empty guard desk in the cell block. She stopped, grasping at Jacks's arm.

He shook her off, shooting a nervous glance around, as if Aleeks waited to tear his throat out. "What is wrong with you?"

"The desk is empty."

Jacks looked around at it, his eyes narrowing.

"Call for more warriors," she counseled. "Call them now."

"My men are—"

"Dead or captive. You cannot secure their release alone."

He glanced at the doors to the cells, nodding his agreement, grinding his teeth in frustration.

"You're right. Let's go. With this many, we'd better come in armored."

Her heart skipped in fear. She looked to the lights, thankful that the Xxan wouldn't be able to leave their cells without being blinded.

Jacks punched in the code to unlock the cell block door, and the attack came. Miri smelled the Xxan coming from the two closest cells before she saw or heard them. She grasped Jacks's sidearm and whirled around, thumbing the weapon lock and cutting down the three closest.

The return shot hit her upper arm, sending Miri falling into Jacks. They went down together, the human grasping at the gun as it slipped from her tingling fingers.

The unlocked door opened, spilling them into the main corridor, just as the security doors slammed shut, isolating the combatants from the rest of the ship.

Jacks started to bring the gun up. He stopped halfway.

Miri stared up at him, noting his shifting eyes in terror. She turned her head, her mouth going dry at the sight of the two Xxanian males. One was a young Dominant. The other—

"Master Haauulen," she breathed.

The human martial master lunged for her, dragging Miri up by her injured arm, nearly bringing her feet entirely off the floor. She panted back a scream of pain, refusing to give him the satisfaction.

"No!" Jacks brought the gun up.

The Dominant did the same.

"No," Miri ordered. She switched back to English. "Put it down, Jacks."

"They'll kill us," he protested.

"Faster if you do this than not. The security doors mean they know?"

"Fuck." His gun clattered to the floor.

She met Haauulen's eyes through both sets of dark glasses. *"Where are the other guards? Are they dead?"*

"They were more trouble than prize."

A sob rose in her throat, and Miri swallowed it down. "Dead," she whispered. "They're dead already."

"We are completely screwed," Jacks decided.

Haauulen propelled her past Jacks and toward the security door. *"Open it. Open it, or you both die."*

* * * *

"Welcome back, Daahn," MacNair greeted him. "I understand congratulations are in order."

Aleeks smiled, all-too-aware of the pleasant aches of an extended mating frenzy.

"Damn, but you all get that same look on your faces afterward, even Evan after Zondra."

"You've read the file?" Aleeks asked.

"Completely. She'll be a good ally, especially now that we've got prisoners."

Aleeks's smile faded. "Xxanian warriors?" Just the thought of them on the same ship with Miri made him want to fight.

"Yeah. Five tough customers. A *Grea* Elder, two Dominants, and two Subdominants."

"Why didn't anyone tell me they were on board?" He'd have to warn Miri. Maybe he'd have a guard assigned to their door until the Xxan were transferred.

"You were busy at the time."

Aleeks's retort was preempted by the screaming of alarms and the bark of speakers. He dimly noted weapons fire in the primary cell block. If their men were firing, the situation was pretty bad.

"Security doors?" Aleeks shouted, knowing a Xxanian threat meant his team was in charge.

"Door seven open. All security doors shut tight," the recruit at the board reported smartly.

The chief at his side nodded, confirming it.

"Get me a visual," Aleeks ordered. The corridor door was open? That was bad news. One of theirs would have had to enter the code. With any luck, all five Xxan were still inside the lockdown that surrounded the primary cell block.

"Coming up," the recruit offered. "Camera one."

Three dead Xxan lay on the floor.

"Down to two," Aleeks noted. That was good news. He'd much rather take down two than five.

Sounds of a scuffle whispered from the speakers—a shout of "No!" in English, then something he didn't catch.

"Get me the other view, now," Aleeks shouted.

"Camera two online now."

Jacks lay half collapsed in the corridor, his jaw clenched tight, in an armed standoff with a Dominant. He glared at the *Grea* Elder, then the lesser Dominant, throwing the gun at the latter with a clear "fuck." His eyes flicked back to the elder, a move Aleeks was certain meant the Xxan held one of their own hostage behind his larger body.

"What the hell is Jacks d—"

The voice emitted from the speakers stopped his heart for a few beats. He listened, firmly rooted in disbelief, numb to all but the most basic information. The guards left on duty had been killed without a shot. Miri was inexplicably in the middle of an uprising, trapped by those ordered to kill her.

Aleeks's gaze locked on Jacks. *I'll kill him.* He didn't question that the lieutenant had done this. Miri knew better than to approach another Dominant without her mate.

The elder shoved Miri through the door and into the corridor. A burn mark on the white of her tunic caught his eyes before she disappeared.

"Corridor view," Aleeks ordered. He had to know how bad her injuries were.

"Camera ten," the recruit offered.

Miri laughed, a manic sound, cradling her injured arm. *"I cannot. They aren't controlled from here."*

"Ah, shit," MacNair breathed.

The elder grasped her by the arms, pulling Miri up and to him, until her toes barely touched the floor. "You will—" He stopped, scenting her, burying his face in her throat.

Aleeks tensed.

Miri brought her left hand up for a blow to his unarmored chest. The hand faltered, then fell short; she screamed in agony. By the blood streaming down her right arm, Aleeks deduced the elder had purposely reopened her blast wound.

A hand settled on his shoulder, and Aleeks shook it off with a growl. He dimly heard MacNair warning the interloper away.

On the screen, Jacks lunged for them, shouting out an order to halt. The younger Dominant threw him to the wall and pinned him there with a rumbling and a head movement that warned Jacks was exceeding the amount of trouble the Xxan would put themselves to in order to keep him alive as leverage.

"What is he doing?" Jacks asked, clearly horrified, probably believing the elder meant to rip her throat out.

She shied from the elder's examination, choking on another cry of pain.

"Talk to me, Miri Daahn," Jacks ordered.

The *Grea* Elder dropped her. Miri backed away from him, trembling hard, her jaw clenched and her hand clamped over the open wound. She didn't look around at Jacks. Her gaze stayed locked on the greatest threat...the elder.

"Where is your mate, Mirienne?" he inquired.

She shook her head, glancing to the active camera and then away, as if she knew Aleeks was watching.

"Is he Xxanian?"

She hesitated for a moment. *"No."*

"Miri, what is he saying?" Jacks demanded.

"Quiet," she cautioned him.

Cruel laughter escaped the elder's lips. *"A human, but he will come for you. He will come for your* Zhigaaah.*"*

Miri straightened. *"Yes. He will."*

Aleeks nodded. "Good. He thinks I'm human. That will make killing him—"

The words stuck in his throat at the sight of the younger Dominant handing one of the captured weapons off to the elder.

He shook his head in sick disbelief. They couldn't mean to kill her. Aleeks's killing rage wasn't something the *Grea* Elder would want to fuck with while he was still in the midst of— *They think I'm human. They don't know even humans can have a killing rage.*

Miri tripped away from him, colliding with the wall, her knees buckling as the weapon came up.

And farther up. The first light bank flashed, then went dark. Miri covered her head with her uninjured arm.

Jacks surged against the Dominant holding him, going down hard around the fist planted in his chest. He landed next to Miri, a grimace of pain on his face and his arms wrapped around ribs that were likely broken.

The elder shot out the second light bank, then the ones in the cell block, plunging the corridor into darkness.

A cry of pain from Miri ended on a strangled gasp. Jacks rasped out her name.

The elder's voice broke the near silence from the speakers. *"Let him come."*

Aleeks pushed away from the console, marching toward the lockers in tight-lipped fury. MacNair fell in beside him.

"I'm going," Aleeks informed him.

"I know it. She's your mate." He shot a dangerous smile at Aleeks, the same one Aleeks had seen MacNair shoot his *gran-seir* many times. "Let me come along."

"No. You'll give my position away."

"That could come in handy," MacNair pointed out. "More to the point, I could give my position away, at the right moment."

Aleeks considered it, weighing three trained men, one injured, against Miri's life. "No. Too risky."

"I stood with your *gran-seir*." And fifty years later, MacNair still took pride in it.

"Against humans." Aleeks coded his locker open and started suiting up.

"May I remind you that I brought your *gran-seir* down myself? Alone? Without your high-tech armor?"

That did factor in favorably, Aleeks had to admit. "Can you be invisible?" he challenged. "If you give me away before I'm close enough to—"

"Boy, I trained at it before your *seir* was born. I taught every unit commander, including you, and as I recall, you couldn't find me."

Aleeks felt his lips twitch at the reminder and fought the smile down. He'd been a recruit, but he remembered how good MacNair was. "If you cost me Miri—if you even endanger her—I'll leave you for dead, my *seir* and *gran-seir* be damned."

MacNair grinned widely. "Understood," he offered Aleeks's typical reply to that threat.

Aleeks coded him into Arris's locker, noting the similar body type and height. "If you get yourself in it, you're on your own."

"Your mate is your only goal," he translated.

"My primary goal." That was a lie. The fact that protecting his mate meant doing his military duty of eliminating the Xxanian threat to the ship and crew was a coincidence he'd happily exploit. Miri came first; the ship and crew could be damned for all he cared.

MacNair swallowed down what looked suspiciously like a chuckle. "Of course."

In less than five minutes, they were suited up and ordering the chief at security to let them through one door at a time. It was nerve-racking, but with the lights out in the cell block corridor, they couldn't be certain where the Xxan were. Though it was unlikely, they had to assume the prisoners were outside the containment area. Only updates of silence over the mics kept him sane. No weapons fire, fighting, or screams meant Miri was safe for the moment...and likely precisely where he expected to find her.

At the final door, things were more complicated. The two guards trapped between the doors were evacuated, and the door behind them closed them in again. Using the punch pad on his wrist, Aleeks ordered the lights extinguished and the air normalized between their section and the section they had to enter.

While they prepped for that change, Aleeks removed his glasses and set them aside, sealing his face mask to still his air and hide the last of his scent. MacNair's mask was already in place. Though Aleeks had taken Miri down without the mask, he wouldn't take that chance with a

Dominant who was using her as a shield. This time, involuntary sounds were a real possibility.

A tone in his earpiece let Aleeks know the conditions were ideal. He tapped an order to unlock the door. Using his fingertips, Aleeks eased it open, using the ventilation flow to hide the shifting barrier.

That accomplished, he flowed toward the elder on the pad of sound-absorbing boot soles. Aleeks tried not to fixate on the weapon barrel planted beneath Miri's chin, on the streaks of dark blood on her white tunic and hand, on her trembling.

While MacNair needed his light-gathering goggles to see what was happening, Aleeks, Miri, and the Xxan could see as well in the near-total darkness as a human could on a lightly starlit night. In short, the only reason the Xxan couldn't see them was the uniformly black clothing and gear blending into shadows in darkness, shades of black on black that rendered them invisible.

The Xxan weren't similarly protected. Nor were they stilling their air, believing they were facing a single human.

In a few tense moments, Aleeks was situated behind his prey. He met MacNair's eyes through the masks and nodded slightly.

The admiral kicked the young Dominant's weapon away from Jacks, following with a fist to the Xxan's unarmored heart, taking the hulking reptile to the deck plates. The elder's gun left Miri and swung toward MacNair.

Aleeks didn't waste a moment. He grasped the elder by the wrist and wrenched, snapping the bone. He let the weapon fall, noting Miri landing on her knees as the elder twisted around and went for Aleeks with his uninjured hand.

It was the wrong answer. With his mate endangered, the killing rage had his blood boiling to avenge her. Aleeks hissed out his intentions in Xxan, cursing the face mask that compressed his extending ridge plates.

The elder's eye slits widened in surprise, his gaze panned to the misshapen hood of Aleeks's uniform, and he faltered in attack. Aleeks didn't. His punch crushed his adversary's windpipe, and the elder's head rocked back.

But the Xxan was still a threat to Miri. There were any number of attacks the elder could use before lack of oxygen incapacitated him.

As if in confirmation, the bastard made a grab for her. Aleeks grasped the elder's jaw and snapped his neck, pushing him away to die silently.

The remaining Dominant and MacNair were in motion, their weapons swinging toward each other. MacNair got a shot into the Xxanian warrior's shoulder, just as Aleeks took him down with a head shot.

"We wanted to question him, Daahn," MacNair complained, the protest muffled, thanks to the mask.

Aleeks ripped his mask away, stepping over the elder to kneel before Miri. "She's my mate."

MacNair sighed but didn't respond. If any human understood Aleeks's drive to protect Miri, MacNair would.

Miri pressed to him, and Aleeks hummed a soothing note, rocking her.

"How bad is it, Lieutenant?" MacNair asked.

Jacks gasped out his response. "Broken ribs, sir."

"You don't lunge at a Xxanian Dominant unarmored, son."

"Yeah. I remember."

"A painful lesson." MacNair stood and started addressing his comm unit instead of Jacks. "We'll need the doc down here and—Daahn, get some glasses on."

Aleeks fished a pair from the floor, sliding them onto Miri's face. "I need a second."

They flew at him from MacNair's position. "What were the damned things doing with glasses, anyway?" the admiral snapped. "Don't you young bucks know better than to give Xxanian prisoners glasses?"

Jacks coughed harshly. "Daahn said—"

"The cells," Aleeks interrupted him, sliding the glasses on his own face. "I darkened Miri's cell."

"I never went to her cell again," he admitted. "And she's had glasses every time I've seen her since."

"Lights up," MacNair ordered.

Light spilled into the corridor through the open security door. MacNair moved away to check each of the prisoners.

Aleeks assessed Miri's condition, sighing in relief that the wounds were relatively minor, certainly less dangerous than the damage she'd come to him with.

Her tear-stained face pulled at his heart. He shouldn't have allowed this to happen to her. A sob half escaping his lips, he wrapped his body around hers, closing his eyes as the security doors swung open nearly in unison, no doubt at MacNair's word that the prisoners were dead.

"What was that?" Jacks asked. "You crying, Daahn?"

"Shut up, Jacks. I haven't decided whether or not to kill you yet." The last thing he needed was the lieutenant's shit right now.

There was a moment of silence. "It's okay to be human, you know," Jacks grumbled.

"I'm not human."

"Close enough. That bastard Haauulen touched my wife, I'd've broken his neck too."

Aleeks nodded, his gaze straying to the *Grea* Elder, Miri's other trainer. She shuddered at the mention of his name, and Aleeks laid a kiss on the top of her head in comfort.

"Guess so," he offered. "Close enough to human. That's not so bad."

Epilogue

Homecoming

Two months later

Miri fidgeted in the passenger seat of Aleeks's transport, peeking up at the passing scenery, her heart hammering.

Aleeks sighed. "You are my mate, Miri. You're welcome in our nest."

She pulled her legs to her chest, nodding miserably. Aleeks was her mate. He would protect her, even at the cost of his own life. If only she didn't suspect that would be the price, Miri might be able to relax.

Assimilated to Earth or not, Daahn the Eldest was a *Grea* Elder. It was more than likely that he would kill her once her disgraceful choices were laid bare for him. *Once my dishonor is.* If her own *seir* had ordered her killed, why would one not related to her accept her?

Aleeks pulled up in front of a long, low structure and turned off the transport's engine, sending her heart into a skittering non-rhythm. He exited, rounded the vehicle, and opened Miri's door, offering his hand to lift her to her feet. Miri unfurled, pressing to his chest as Aleeks closed the door behind her.

She shifted uncomfortably in the grippers he'd provided to protect her feet from the frosted ground. Aleeks claimed he'd chosen them because they were lightweight and comfortable. She agreed with the former, but if the latter was true, Miri would hate to wear any other type of shoes.

A bitter wind pulsed through the long coat he'd provided, and she shivered. Though Miri had read about the weather on Earth, she hadn't believed the reports of sub-zero temperatures. She wondered at the fact that the Xxan wanted Earth. The winter temperatures alone would stop them cold. Miri winced at the unintended pun.

Aleeks guided her into the house and shut them into a room she recognized as a *s'sanuea*, a preparation room. Before Miri could catch her breath, Aleeks had stripped off her coat and hung it reverently on a hook. He went to his knees, slipped the grippers off her feet, and then removed his own.

He came to his feet, and Miri took over, unbuttoning his shirt. Aleeks buried his face in her neck, scenting her anew, though she carried his scent by virtue of their mating.

Miri didn't have to question that. It was a promise of protection. Moreover, it was an announcement that she belonged to Aleeks. There were certain to be other Dominant males in the nest...at least Daahn the Eldest if not Aleeks's *seir* and Zondra's human mate. Although all of the aforementioned were mated and wouldn't be interested in her, a Dominant always laid scent claim to what was his own.

Dressed only in his jeans, Aleeks pulled Miri under his arm. On some level, it surprised her that he didn't wear a *S'suumea*, but being born and raised on Earth, she supposed not all the traditions were deemed necessary.

"You will greet *Gran-seir* beneath my arm," he instructed.

Miri took a calming breath at that.

"They are my family, Miri. They are *your* family."

But she'd heard that elders didn't always approve of the mates chosen by young Dominants. Miri hadn't asked what happened when the elder didn't approve. Until Aleeks, she hadn't thought a Dominant would ever choose her. If any Xxanian did, she'd thought it would be a Subdominant, and even that had been highly unlikely.

She supposed the couple joined the female's nest, in such a case...if they survived the displeasure of the male's elder. But Miri had no nest. Would they live apart from a nest, if it came to that? Would Aleeks become bitter at the loss of his family?

He stared at her, waiting for a sign of Miri's acceptance. She nodded, her heart thudding against her ribs. Aleeks raised his arm, and she buried her face in his chest then faced the door sliding aside behind Aleeks's hand.

The air beyond it was hot and moist, and the lights were dimmed to a lounging level. Miri shook her head in disbelief at the first scent of the pungent spice she'd only smelled twice in her life on *Xxania Uuaahth.*

Aleeks stopped, staring down at her, his brow furrowed. "What is it?"

"*Saahaal?*" she questioned. Where would they get the precious spice?

He slid the door shut behind her, a smile curving his lips. "On Earth, it is called clove."

"It grows here?" she asked, calculating how the *Grea* Elders would respond to that fact. It wouldn't be a pretty sight.

"It does." He started forward again, then paused. "Though my entire family can speak English, only Xxan is spoken in the nest."

"Of course." She switched to Xxan to answer him, taking that warning to heart. Miri was glad to know it. Offering offense to his family was the last thing she wanted to do.

The floor sloped down into underground gardens not unlike those on the home world. The first two rooms were empty, and Miri relaxed, lulled by the stillness and physical comfort of the environment. It wasn't until someone moved in the shadows that she remembered the Xxan hunted the night.

Aleeks caught her against him when she scrambled for his back. "Still," he soothed her in rumbling Xxan.

Miri peeked past his chest, staring at the man emerging from the shadows. He was dressed much as Aleeks was, and his eyes were human, identifying him as Zondra's mate.

Aleeks addressed him in Xxan, confirming that even the humans in the family spoke the *Seir*-tongue. "We greet the nest mate."

"You are most welcome, brother warrior."

"Our thanks, Evan."

Aleeks offered his hand for a human handshake, and Evan took it. Evan met her eyes, cocking his head to one side, assessing Miri.

"My mate," Aleeks informed him.

He nodded. "Mac told us you'd be bringing a new female to the nest."

"So the *Saahaal* is in celebration," Aleeks deduced.

Evan smiled widely. "Would *Gran-seir* offer any less for a female?"

Miri swallowed hard at that. If the elder didn't approve of her, he would be even angrier at the waste of the precious spice.

Evan bowed his head to her. "You are most welcome, sister."

Miri started to stutter out her name, and Aleeks shook his head in warning.

"*Gran-seir* must meet you first. Otherwise, we offend him."

Evan's eyes narrowed, and his muscles tensed.

Aleeks motioned for patience. "A long story, but..."

"I understand. *Gran-seir* must hear it first," Evan replied. With that, he waved them further into the caves.

Aleeks drew Miri with him, offering Evan their unprotected backs. It was an incredible sign of trust. Miri glanced back, watching Evan follow them on silent feet. She'd never had someone she could trust at her back until Aleeks.

The center nest was a room large enough for dozens of people. Miri looked around at the women, noting that they all wore formal *S'suuhhea*. At once, she felt underdressed. If she was more human, she felt certain she'd be blushing furiously.

An errant voice in her mind reminded her that she'd never been invited or encouraged to wear the *S'suuhhea*. Her doubts reared up, frightening thoughts that she wasn't worthy of the traditional Xxanian dress, even with Aleeks's family.

No. Aleeks wouldn't treat me that way. No matter what his family thinks of me.

Evan moved to the youngest female, his hand stroking at her full and heavy womb. A small hand reached from behind his mate and fisted on Evan's jeans. Evan lifted a boy with human eyes but wearing the *S'suumea*.

An older Dominant, hairless but human in every way but his eyes and *S'suumea*, wrapped his arms around a female with stunning green human eyes and blood-red curls.

Until he leaned forward on his chair, Miri didn't see the elder. Bathed in shadow, his smooth, dark scales blended into the water-wall behind him. His mate was even further in shadow, at his back until her mate evaluated any threat to her.

Miri stopped short, trying again to escape Aleeks's hold, her breathing going ragged as the elder came to his full height and stared down at her. His ridge plates extended in show. That stopped her retreat, though her knees shook. Every instinct screamed at her to sink to the submissive. As if Aleeks could scent the thought, he gripped her arm to keep her standing.

The elder's forked tongue peeked past his barred teeth and took her scent. His eye slits narrowed. "I scent an old ally in this one...Uuumaal."

Miri's knees threatened to fold. *An old ally? Seir-God lives! When he learns I've killed that ally—*

Aleeks saved her the attempt to explain herself. "I fear your old ally has not treated his daughter honorably, *Gran-seir*."

Daahn's head cocked to one side, and his nose slits widened, then narrowed again. "Daughter? Uuumaal took another mate in his waning years?"

"No. Neither did he gift Miri his name."

Daahn's ridge plates came out to their full extension, the frill spikes of a *Grea* Elder warning that his anger was fierce and uncompromising. His growling sent Miri under Aleeks's arm and to his back. He didn't stop her, which frightened Miri even more.

"Tell me," the elder demanded.

Aleeks reached his hand back and covered one of hers with it. "They created Miri in their labs. She was starved, beaten, uncared for... And when Miri balked at Uuumaal's duplicity and deception to his own blood, he ordered her killed."

Miri chanced a look around Aleeks's body at a rush of movement. Her mouth went dry at the sight of Daahn holding the ancient weapons of a Xxanian warrior at the ready. The *zuahhhbeahhh* and s'*saahhta* were sharp enough to skin an enemy, she was certain.

She dropped to her knees, making herself as inconspicuous as possible, waiting for Aleeks's signal to hide herself while he fought. That signal didn't come, and the room went so silent that her breathing and clamoring heart were the loudest noises, drowning out even the babbling of water.

A clatter of metal sent her closer to her mate's legs, shivering. The hands reaching for her weren't Aleeks's. Miri held tight to her mate for a moment, then reasoned that Aleeks was letting the elder draw her out. She released his jeans and let Daahn lift her gently to her feet between the two males.

Aleeks cupped her shoulders in his hands. "*Gran-seir*...I present my mate, Miri Daahn, formerly Miri Johns, daughter of Marianne Johns and the criminal Uuumaal."

The elder's tongue extended again, scenting her in earnest. His head swiveled back and forth, undulating in a ritual dance she didn't recognize but knew she should. Her eyes slipped shut, and her head fell back. Her muscles unknotted, and her trembling eased.

Daahn's tongue was rough against her throat, and her breathing hitched at the touch. He was a hunter; he could rip her throat out, but he caressed her, imprinting her *Zhigaaal* mixed *Zhigaaah* on his scent memory.

His hand covered the soft meat of her belly, and his claws raked at her tunic. Miri's shaking legs abandoned her, and Aleeks lifted her in his arms, whispering her name. Her head spun, and the next few moments passed in a blur of hisses and trills that made little sense to her.

Aleeks shifted her, settling her into Daahn's arms. Her confusion and upset at the move emerged as little more than a whimper, and the elder rumbled something soothing in response. Daahn carried her further into the center nest.

The warm water soaking her clothing forced a squeak of surprise from her, and Miri turned, intent on escape. Aleeks's chest appeared, and she held tight to him.

Daahn released her. "Peace, young daughter. You need never hide in the nest."

Aleeks guided her further into the pool...to her hips, then drew her to kneeling so the water reached her shoulders. Little details made it through the fog of her mind, including the fact that Aleeks was nude. Swirls of water announced Daahn joining them. Miri dared not look around at him, certain that he'd be equally unclothed.

She sought out Aleeks's eyes, pleading for an explanation.

Her mate nodded. "You have never been bathed by your elder."

She was certain Aleeks said it more for Daahn than for herself. Miri knew what she had and had not done in her life, after all.

The elder's hands worked her tunic up. Miri let him, reasoning that he couldn't see her body in the water. It had been planned that way, she was sure. Aleeks pulled her trousers away, and she nestled further onto his lap.

The nip of oil against the sensitive skin of her shoulder preceded the smell of *Saahaal*. Miri snapped a look of shock at Aleeks. Daahn was wasting the spice on her? Why would he?

Aleeks rubbed the oil into her neck and down her chest. "You are a female, coming to the center nest for the first time. It is an honor for the elder that you have come to us, that one of his descendants was strong enough to bind a mate to him and to our nest. He shows you honor in the only way he can."

"The young one was never bathed?" Daahn asked.

"Never by the Xxan," Aleeks corrected. "Though I had no *Saahaal* to bathe her properly, as mate, I have done so."

There was a moment of silence, during which Daahn made a single swipe of the oil over her mating stripe and moved on to a massage of her opposite shoulder. To Miri's surprise, she felt no arousal when the elder touched her. She sighed in relief.

"You will bathe your mate daily with the *Saahaal*, Aleeks. Daily for a moon turn, in apology for neglecting her so long."

Miri opened her mouth to protest that Aleeks had never neglected her. He'd been diligent in her care and in more carnal matters.

Aleeks captured her mouth, silencing her and heating her blood for him. He broke away slowly. "Daily for a moon turn," he repeated. His *Zhigaaal* was pungent in the mist, a sure sign that the baths he'd gift her would be much more intimate affairs.

Her mate massaged the oil into her breasts, while Daahn moved down her back. His hand stopped, and both men tensed. Miri didn't have to question what the elder took exception to.

Daahn's voice was rough, a sure sign that his ridge plates and frill spikes were extended. "I will kill the one responsible for this. I vow it, little daughter."

Aleeks smiled weakly. "Miri has already killed several of them. I killed the last."

"You allowed—"

"Pardon my sloppy telling, *Gran-seir*. I met my mate in the midst of battle, a battle in which she killed three of the *Grea* Elders responsible for her abuse, as well as nearly two dozen Dominants, and a hand or two of Subdominants. She did so to protect the lie of peace her *seir* had promised...to protect the human Council, my men...all who had been promised safe passage and negotiation."

Daahn's hand moved on, spreading the oil diligently. Miri's heart pounded in fear of what he'd say next.

"Two moon turns, Aleeks. Such a female is a rare prize," he murmured. "This nest is blessed with such a female."

Aleeks came erect at that pronouncement. "Two moon turns."

"Which were responsible?"

Her mate didn't hesitate to share the news. "Uuumaal, S'Suuleahhn, S'sie, and Haauulen. I killed Haauulen myself."

Daahn made no reply to that. Miri suspected that the elder knew them all. Was he saddened to hear that they were lost to the vacuum? Angry that she'd killed them? Did he feel it justified? Did he wish he'd pulled the trigger himself?

He went to work on her arms, pausing again at the scar Haauulen had left her with. Daahn didn't ask for an explanation. "Your mate has had medical care for their abuses, I assume."

Miri shuddered at the bite in his tone, an edge of near-violence that said even telling Daahn that

Aleeks had delayed a day after meeting her would see him punished for it.

"She has." His eyes proclaimed that he still blamed himself for the delay.

"Aleeks has pampered me," she attested. "He has cared for me, insisting on treatment, even before I realized I was in need."

"Then he should do so now. Food is waiting."

Daahn tucked her head beneath his chin for a moment, closing Miri into the space between the two Dominant males. Then he moved away, leaving them alone in the pool.

Aleeks continued bathing her, stroking the stinging oil into every millimeter of skin, sensitizing her. His touch became more personal, more arousing, and Miri bit back a moan.

"We shouldn't," she breathed. "It's the center nest." Though she'd never been welcomed in a center nest before, she was certain it was only appropriate for an elder to mate in such a place.

Aleeks turned her, positioning Miri over the head of his primary. "It is expected that we'll mix our scent into the family space. Later, we will scent our rooms." There was something unsaid there.

"And?" she prompted him.

He thrust inside her, wrenching a mew of delight from her. Miri clenched her jaw shut, well aware that his family hadn't gone far. Surely, they could hear whatever sounds of pleasure she made.

"Don't," he ordered in a whisper. "If you don't vent your sounds, *Gran-seir* will think I'm being negligent in my care."

Miri didn't question that. She pushed further onto his cock, moaning.

Aleeks growled out his possession of her, his body pistoning in fierce hip thrusts not unlike the night he'd sated her quickening. Their sounds melded and rose to a crescendo at their climax.

In the aftermath, Aleeks rubbed his body against hers, scenting her heavily. His lips caressed her ear. "In our rooms, I'll be anointing you with my *Zhigaaal.*"

Her breathing hitched, and aftershocks wracked her body. His cock bucked inside her, and Miri screamed in pleasure.

Aleeks lifted her, carrying Miri from the pool and into the now-deserted center nest. He balanced her on her feet next to the elder's chair, lifted a beautiful red *S'suuhhea,* and dressed her in it. To her shock, he settled Miri in the elder's chair while he donned his *S'suumea* and then cradled her to his chest and carried her through a doorway and into a room with stacks of cushions and platters of food.

By appearances, no one had touched their food, not even Daahn himself. Miri tried to put that into perspective, but she couldn't. Elders waited for no one's pleasure to eat, and since there was food enough for all on the platters, he wouldn't concern himself with the new female in their midst having enough to eat, as Aleeks assured her a true Dominant would, when hunting was lean.

Aleeks settled her on the cushions and folded into them next to her, preparing to feed her. His head came up at Daahn's move.

Miri watched, amazed, as the elder crossed the room, the platter intended for himself and his mate in hand. He knelt before her and pushed a portion of his own food onto her platter. Aleeks's *seir* did the same. From their place, Evan and Zondra offered bows of their heads but not their food, though their platter held more than double the food of any other.

Of course. They are feeding the youngling and the babe Zondra carries. Miri offered a bow in response. She looked to Aleeks, her smile faltering at his seeming confusion.

"*Gran-seir?*" he prompted, a sure sign that this wasn't part of the typical welcome of a new female to the nest.

Daahn lifted a cube of meat from his own platter and brought it to Miri's lips. He didn't speak until she'd accepted it.

"Your mate carries, Aleeks."

"I know it." He sounded offended at that, as if the elder had accused Aleeks of negligence in his attention to her needs. Aleeks had increased Miri's food intake by a quarter again and insisted on baths and rest for her, immediately upon determining that she carried. "But Zondra—"

Daahn shot him a quelling look. "You were present when I determined your sister carried a young Dominant. You were away when I determined she carried a young female." There was something tender in that. "And you were too young to remember when I determined your *Hauaa* carried Zondra."

Miri swallowed, her heart skittering in understanding. Her hand crept to the flat plane of her womb.

Daahn's covered it. "You bless this nest with not one female but two, Aleeks." With that, he bowed his head and returned to his mate with the platter, offering her first pick of the remaining food as a sign of his love and protection.

Aleeks stroked his hand over her womb, his mouth closing on hers in a slow, solemn kiss that left her gasping for breath. Then he slipped a cube of meat into his mouth, chewing it for her. Morsel after morsel passed from his mouth to hers, until Miri felt she'd pass out from sheer pleasure.

She let her gaze drift to Evan and Zondra, watching the human Dominant mouth feeding his mate and poking cubes of meat into his son's mouth between. When feeding gave way to deep kisses and wandering hands, the boy pushed to his feet and made his way to Zondra's *seir*. He pulled at the Dominant's *S'suumea*. The big male didn't hesitate to pull the child into his lap, feeding the youngling with one hand while he fed his mate with the other.

Aleeks pressed Miri back into the cushions, and the feeding went on, each bite of food taking longer and involving more passion and less sustenance. His primary nestled into her thigh through their clothing.

Finally, her body rebelled. "I can't," she gasped. "I can't eat more." Miri intended no offense, and wasting of food surely was, especially food the elders had gifted her.

The elder Dominants rumbled their approval, and Aleeks smiled, letting her know that was what they'd been waiting to hear.

Across the room, Zondra begged Evan to take her to their rooms. Her mate scooped her up with a growl and strode away, leaving their son in the care of the elders.

Aleeks nipped at her ear. "Beg for me," he breathed. "My secondary is already rising for you."

"Please, Aleeks. I can't wait any longer for you."

He was in motion that quickly, out of the lounging room and up into darkened areas of the nest, past the sounds and scents of Evan anointing his mate behind a curtained partition.

"Once Sammy retires to his bed, every Dominant in the house will be anointing his mate." There was a note of self-satisfaction in that.

Aleeks pushed a curtain aside and strode into a room that carried his scent heavily. Miri closed her eyes, drowning in it, instantly at ease.

He lowered her to his bed, stripped her clothing away, then his own. She looked up at him, licking her lips at the sight of his secondary, already a quarter of the way risen and glistening with *Zhigaaal.*

Aleeks knelt to the bed, very methodically painting her lips with the beads. He pushed the crown into her mouth, and her senses exploded in the overload of pheromone. Miri suckled at him, raising him further, drawing out more of his *Zhigaaal.*

He backed away, then returned, bringing both heads to her lips. She engulfed him with a muffled curse, moaning at the two cocks filling her mouth nearly to discomfort. Aleeks had only done this with her a few times, though she wasn't certain why that was. He always came quickly this way, and they both enjoyed it.

Miri guided him in and out, careful not to catch either cock on her serrated hunting teeth. His groans turned to growls, and his secondary rose further, exploring her mouth then playing at her throat. She swallowed reflexively, and Aleeks climaxed, jetting both cum and *Zhigaaal* into her throat.

Her body went hot and lax, and Aleeks slid free of her mouth, massaging *Zhigaaal* up. Her breathing hitched, and her body wept *Zhigaaah* onto his bed.

That's what he wants. My scent is marking the room, reinforcing his claim.

His *Zhigaaal*-coated cock slid deep inside her, bringing her hips off the bed. Aleeks pinned both of her hands above her head in one of his, and she bucked against him, prompting growls of claim from his lips in response.

"Please, Aleeks." When he didn't react to it, she screamed out his name, begging him mindlessly for more of his musk.

His free hand massaged the base of his secondary, causing the *Zhigaaal* to fill her...then overfill her and run the length of her seam to her anus.

"Yes, more...please, more."

"Promise me everything," he demanded.

"Everything," she gasped. "Every way."

He left her body, and she cried out in dismay...just in time for his secondary to spread her rear entrance. He didn't thrust inside, as she expected he would. Instead, he climaxed, his cum splashing against her seam, cooling the *Zhigaaal* burn. The full load of his *Zhigaaal* coursed into her ass, soaking in quickly, making her boneless in anticipation, drunk on his fluids and needing his cocks.

She licked her lips, gasping at the slick of *Zhigaaal* he'd painted there. Aleeks smiled widely and massaged up more *Zhigaaal*. He painted her lips again. It was a taunt, a promise.

Then he reached down and turned Miri to her stomach. She pushed her slit up, whispering pleas for what she now knew he intended.

Aleeks played the *Zhigaaal*-covered secondary at her slit, and she thrust against him, her voice rising until she was begging him at the top of her lungs to take her again. Then, and only then, he pushed deeper, working his primary through the lubricated ring of muscle he'd prepared for it then pounding hard into her with both cocks.

"I'm going to eat our mixed fluids, Miri."

"Yes! Oh, yes, Aleeks!"

"I'm going to bathe you with the *Saahaal*."

Just the thought of the stinging oil mixing with the *Zhigaaal* sent flutters of pre-climax through her. "Oh, yes!"

On some level, Miri knew Aleeks was pushing her to this as a Dominant show. I'll make him a legend in his nest, she vowed. I'll scream for him all morning long.

His climax was long and hard, as if rewarding her decision.

Aleeks's hand covered her womb, caressing her.

The End

About the Author

Brenna Lyons wears many hats, sometimes all on the same day: former president of EPIC, author of more than 100 published works, owner of Fireborn Publishing, columnist, special needs teacher, wife, mother...and member in good standing of more than 60 writing advocacy groups.

In her first ten years published in novel-length, she's won 3 EPIC e-Book Awards (out of 15 finalists) and finaled for 3 PEARLS (including one Honorable Mention, second to NY Times Bestseller Angela Knight), 2 CAPAS, and a Dream Realm Award. She's also taken Spinetingler's Book of the Year for 2007.

Brenna writes in 26 established worlds plus stand-alones, poetry, articles and essays. She's a bestseller in indie/e fantasy and horror, straight genre and cross-genres thereof. Brenna has been termed "one of the most deviant erotic minds in the publishing world...not for the weak." (Rachelle for Fallen Angels Reviews) Milieu-heavy dark work is practically Brenna's calling card, with or without the erotic content.

She teaches classes in everything from POV studies to advanced editing, networking to marketing. Brenna enjoys hearing from people who read her work and can be reached by e-mail.

Website: http://www.brennalyons.com/

Facebook:
http://www.facebook.com/brenna.lyons

Email: brennalyons4168@live.com

Also by this Author

Available from **Fireborn Publishing**

KEIF'S DEN AND PACK
Keif's Pack
Mother of the Keif
Keif's Den (Coming Soon)

PROPHECY
Prophecy: Revelations
Prophecy: Rapture
The Prophet's Mate
Prophecy: Rampage - Meet Gavin
Prophecy: Rampage (Coming Soon)

RENEGADES SERIES
TYGERS
Renegade's Run
Max Sec

THE FANTASY CLUB
The Consort

INSTINCT SERIES
Animal Instincts

KEGIN SERIES
Earth-Born Lord
Graham: Training the Earth-Born Lord

NIGHT WARRIORS
Claiming a Lady
Stone Lord
Mother's Son
Night Warriors
Will of the Stone

Time Currents
Cubed

STAR MAGES
Written in the Stars
The Master's Lover

DAN AIDAN FAIRIES
Fairy Dreams
Monsters of Myth Anthology

XXAN WAR
Daahan Rising
Raashh Decisions

MYTHOS SERIES
The Punishment of Phoebus Apollo
Black Sail

IT'S ALL GREEK TO ME...
All's Fair...

SANCTUM
Dream Walk

GRELLAN WAR
With Great Power

BLOOD MAGES
Enslaved

CARSON COUSINS
All I Want for Christmas is You

FATES WAR
Fates Magic

Beyond the Veil

Mine for the Night
Once in a Blue Moon
Overtime Pay
Stay With Me
The Fire God's Woman
Nevermore
Bride Ball
Undead in Blue
Mama's Tales
Unexpected Daddy
We Shall Live Again
May the Best Man Win
Marked
And It Was Good
Monsters of Myth Anthology

Available from **Under The Moon**

Evil Overlords Union Issue #1 Anthology
Undead Embrace
"Playing Games" in *Forbidden Love: Bad Boys*
"Marked" in *Forbidden Love: Wicked Women*
"The Master's Lover" in *Forbidden Love: Sacred Bands*

Available from **Logical Lust**

"Mine for the Night" in *The Cougar Book Anthology*

Available from **Coming Together Charity Anthologies**

INSTINCT SERIES
"Foundling" in *Coming Together: Into the Light Anthology*

"Claim Mate" (available separately and as part

of the *Coming Together: Against the Odds*
Anthology)
"The Fire God's Woman" in *Coming Together:
Under Fire* Anthology

Available **self-published**

Snapshots from a Poet's Life

Award-Winning Books

EPPIE/EPIC eBOOK AWARDS WINNERS
Coming Together: Against the Odds- 2010
Time Currents- 2010
Coming Together: Into the Light- 2011

EPPIE/EPIC eBOOK AWARDS FINALISTS
Fion's Daughter- 2004
Collected Poems: Book One- 2005 (now titled
Snapshots of a Poet's Life)
Renegade's Run- 2005
Rites of Mating- 2006
All I Want for Christmas- 2006
Phaze in Verse- 2008
"The Fire God's Woman" in Coming Together:
Under Fire- 2009
Three Wishes- 2010
Matchmaker's Misery- 2010
The Cougar Book- 2011
The Master's Lover- 2011
Bride Ball- 2011

DREAM REALM AWARDS FINALIST
Last Chance for Love- 2003

PEARL HONORABLE MENTION
Night Warriors- 2004

PEARL FINALISTS
Schente Night- 2003 (now included in *The Last
of Fion's Daughters*)
König Cursebreakers- 2004 (now titled *Will of
the Stone*)

JOYFULLY REVIEWED BEST BOOKS OF
2010

Written in the Stars- 2010

SPINETINGLER'S BOOK OF THE YEAR 2007
NOBODY: An Anthology of Dark Fiction- 2007
(Brenna's pieces of the anthology can be
found in *Beyond the Veil*)

TRS's CAPA FINALISTS
Ultimate Warriors- 2004 (Brenna's portion is
now available as *With Great Power*)
Written in the Stars

LOVE ROMANCE AND MORE CAFÉ BOOK OF
THE YEAR RUNNER UP
Last Chance for Love- 2008

ROAD TO ROMANCE REVIEWERS' CHOICE
AWARD
Prophecy: Revelations- 2004

LOVE ROMANCES REVIEWERS' CHOICE
AWARD
Black Sail- 2003

ROMANCE JUNKIES BOOK CLUB STAFF
PICK
TYGERS- 2003

FALLEN ANGELS ROMANCE
RECOMMENDED READ
Devon's Price-2005 (now available in *Bearing
Armen*)

JOYFULLY RECOMMENDED READ
Fairy Dreams- 2008
The Last of Fion's Daughters- 2009

TREBLE HEART FINALIST
Prophecy: Revelations- 2003

www.ingramcontent.com/pod-product-compliance
Lightning Source LLC
Chambersburg PA
CBHW020253200626
46816CB00001BA/264